Freedom

Freedom

Book Four
The Tyke McGrath Series

by

William Woodall

Jeremiah Press · *Antoine, Arkansas*

Jeremiah Press
PO Box 3
Antoine, AR 71922

First published by Jeremiah Press on 12/10/2013.

Printed in the United States of America.

This book is printed on acid-free paper.

ISBN: 978-0-9833298-6-2

For Elisabeth,

Who asked for this book.

Behold, I am the Lord, the God of all mankind.
Is there anything too hard for me?
-Jeremiah 32:27

Thoughts of a Lost Boy
By Tycho Nicholas McGrath

"It's altogether possible for the heart of a man to die long before his mind or his body follow, but when it does then he's no longer fully human even though he may still look and sound like it."

"It seemed to be perpetually midmorning, as if time were frozen, which gave the whole place a strange, timeless quality that's hard to explain. It reminded me of what all the hymns say about Heaven; perfect, beautiful, unchanging and eternal."

"Even the brave and the good don't always find a happy ending."

"It was people just like that who created the Orion Strain, and even though the motive may have been different the reasoning and the attitude were exactly the same; that life is cheap, and individuals don't matter, and it's worth inflicting terrible harm in the name of some greater good. That kind of thinking is nothing but pure evil."

"The world is full of more wonders than I ever dreamed, back in the days when I thought I knew it all."

"Love is easy, for those who do it."

"My heart was still bitter from thinking we'd found a friend and then finding out she was no such thing. Treachery stings, even when you know full well that you should have seen it coming."

"They say God watches over kids, drunks, and fools, and I guess at the time we had all three bases covered pretty securely."

"Sometimes it's amazing what you can get away with as long as you don't look nervous about it."

"I was much more comfortable with scientific matters which could be tested, and God can't be. Asking for a miracle is like asking your father for a dollar. The choice is up to him, and whether he'll do it or not isn't a question that science can answer."

"Natural laws are just a pattern to which events have to conform. If God is real then it would be silly to think He couldn't do things if He liked, just the way we can."

Contents

Chapter One
Saturday, June 17, 2157

"Something just happened," Jesse said.

"What are you talking about?" I asked absently, not especially curious. We were right in the middle of our weekly Saturday night survivor search, but that had long since turned into a more or less perfunctory and dutiful kind of chore after so much time with no results.

"There was an energy surge just now, out over the Gulf of Mexico," Jesse said.

"Lightning, you think?" I asked.

"No, it's definitely not lightning. I'm not sure what it was, but it sent out a blast of neutrinos like you wouldn't believe," Jesse said.

"Really?" I asked, my interest piqued for the first time.

"Yeah, really. And it can't be a solar flare, either; the sun's been quiet for days, and besides it was much too localized for that," Jesse said.

"What do you think it could be, then?" I asked.

"I don't have the slightest idea," Jesse confessed.

"Where exactly did it happen?" I asked, rolling my chair over beside him to look at his computer screen.

"About thirty miles offshore from the mouth of Tampa Bay, actually," he said, pointing out the location on his screen.

"Really?" I asked again, even more interested. Anything that close to my old stomping grounds always held an extra bit of significance.

"Yeah. The burst started at exactly 1:48:32 a.m. local time and ended less than a second later," Jesse said.

"Dang, is it already that late over there?" I asked. It wasn't even quite nine o'clock yet in Hawaii, and in Florida it was already well into the wee hours of Sunday morning. It made me sleepy even to think about it.

"Yup, 'fraid so," Jesse said.

"You're sure it wasn't just a glitch in the instruments?" I asked.

"No, I already thought of that. Everything checks out fine. Something weird definitely happened," Jesse said.

"Did you check it out with the visual satellite?" I asked.

"Yeah, clear skies and calm seas, nothing to see. Or at least nothing I could see in the dark," he amended.

"What about the infrared?" I asked.

"Well. . . that's pretty useless in the Gulf, you know, unless it's something really big and either really hot or really cold. Ocean temperatures are warm as bath water this time of year and that makes it hard for anything to stick out. That said, I *think* there might be two very small points of heat out there, but I can't tell for sure," he said.

"People, you think?" I asked

"Couldn't be. There was no ship, no plane, nothing like that within miles. There's no way people could have dropped into the ocean from nowhere, is there?" he asked.

"Well, no," I admitted.

"I'm not sure if those heat signatures are even real, much less what they could be. They're so small and so close to water temperature, they might only be a false return," he said.

"Yeah, but still. Maybe we should go check it out tomorrow, you think?" I asked.

"Yeah, I guess we better. Just in case," he agreed.

"So how do you think we should work this? Fly to Tampa and then take a boat out to those coordinates?" I asked.

"Yeah, we'll take some instruments with us, see if there's any residual radiation from that neutrino blast. Or anything else for that matter. Who knows, Tyke. Maybe it's an alien spaceship that crashed in the ocean and they'll give us a million dollars apiece for saving them," Jesse said.

"What would we do with it even if they did?" I pointed out.

"Oh, don't be a spoilsport. We could at least dump it all out on the middle of the floor, and then roll around in it like a pile of leaves and pretend we're the richest dudes in the world," he said, and I laughed.

"You're crazy, boy," I said.

"Well, hey, if we can't spend it then we might as well enjoy it some way or other," he said.

"You do know that money has more germs per square centimeter than a toilet seat, don't you?" I asked conversationally, and he wrinkled his nose. I didn't strictly know if that were true or not, but it sounded pretty convincing. When Jesse's in one of his silly moods all you can really do is mess with him in return.

"Oh, forget it, then. I'll just tell them to write me a check," he said.

"No other interesting little tidbits tonight?" I asked, getting back to business.

"Nope. Nary a blip," Jesse said.

We usually would have called it a night by nine o'clock, but we stayed till ten that time for fear we might miss something important. But nothing else happened, so we finally gave up the ghost and went home, leaving some of the equipment running just in case there were a radio signal or anything else to be detected. Then we left the university and walked through the silent streets of Kailua Kona till we made it back to the little strip of beach homes where we all lived.

The town looked reasonably lived-in nowadays; Philip and Chris and several of the others made it a point to keep all the yards mowed and the streets swept and those kinds of things, or at least as much as they could manage. It would have been a full-time job even if they hadn't had anything else whatsoever to do, but it made all of us feel a lot more at home than we ever could have felt if weeds and grass had been allowed to overrun everything. Which, believe me, doesn't take all that long to happen when you live in a place like Hawaii.

Philip and Chris had their hands full with lots of things besides mowing the grass, though. They had to maintain the electricity and the water system, fix the vehicles, and all those sorts of things, too. Even with help from Jesse and Hunter and sometimes the rest of us, I still didn't see how they kept up with it all. Not to mention the fact that Philip is also our preacher, dispute-settler, and general all-around leader.

We all had to wear several different hats, actually, with as few of us as there were. We were the last twenty human beings left alive, after a man-made plague known as the Orion Strain wiped out every warm-blooded species on earth only three years ago. We few had survived by escaping to the Moon for a little while, and then finally we'd been able to come home again after I discovered a workable vaccine.

Ever since then, we'd lived in the little town of Kailua Kona on the big island of Hawaii, trying to maintain a working society as best we could. One of the ways we did that was by teaching the younger ones whatever we knew. We'd started using the old Kailua Kona High School a few months earlier since that was another thing which helped to maintain a sense of normalcy. Emily and Leah looked after the really little ones and the babies, and Aunt Joan taught the older ones except when she had to put on her doctor's hat and take care of somebody. Jesse taught advanced math and coached athletics when nobody needed him to pilot a plane or help with maintenance, and he also spent as much time as he could spare trying to teach Hunter how to fly so we'd have a backup airman if we needed one. Johnny taught music when he wasn't practicing or doing performances for us. Other than me, he was the only person in our whole group who got to spend almost all his time doing the thing he was actually trained for, and that's only because we all agreed music is an important skill which we didn't want to lose.

As for me, I was almost always busy with genetic engineering, so usually the only other thing I had to do was teach a science class twice a week and help Jesse with the survivor search on Saturday nights. Danielle was the chief cook and bottle washer, so to speak. She made sure we all got fed and that our clothes were clean, and she took care of the cows and chickens and weeded and watered the vegetable garden, and even helped me in the genetics lab now and then when she could spare the time. We were all busy as bees in the springtime, and occasionally that meant we had to pitch in and take over somebody else's job for a while, whether that involved changing a baby or changing the oil in a car. None of us could afford to be a slacker.

Everybody was sitting around a bonfire on the beach when we got home that night; another Saturday evening tradition. We were late, of course; that's what we got for poring over the instruments for an extra hour. But nevertheless everybody was still eating and socializing, so we didn't miss *too* much.

I grabbed a plate of chicken stir-fry and sat down next to Danielle on a palm log, hungry enough to eat the plate right along with the food. I attacked it with gusto, and she watched me with a half smile on her face.

"I take it you like the chicken?" she asked.

"It's delicious," I said with my mouth full, paying close attention to business. She laughed a little.

"Then slow down and enjoy it. I promise there's more if you want some; you don't have to inhale it," she said.

"But I'm *starving*," I said, taking another bite.

"You must be. Did you not eat lunch today?" she asked.

"No, I was too busy," I admitted.

"Well, see, there you go. If you wouldn't skip meals then you wouldn't need to wolf it down like a python," she said. I made an effort to slow down just a bit, if only to please her.

"We found something interesting tonight," I said, as much to change the subject as anything else.

"Really? Survivors?" she asked.

"Well, possibly, I guess. It was a powerful energy surge that was over in less than a second, but we can't think of any good explanation for it. It happened about thirty miles from Tampa Bay, out in the Gulf," I said.

"That's strange," she said.

"Yeah, it is. If it had been on land I might have thought it was some kind of explosion, but what is there to explode in the middle of the ocean?" I said.

"A drifting ship, maybe?" she asked.

"No, we would've seen anything like that with the satellite, even in the dark. I don't have a clue what it was. But there were two possible point-sources of heat floating in the Gulf afterward, if they weren't just false returns. Jesse couldn't tell for sure," I said.

"That's interesting," she said.

"Maybe. It might all be a bunch of nothing, actually. But I think we might pay a visit tomorrow, just to make sure. Want to come? We'll only be gone for a day or so," I said. She and Jesse had both decided to accept the offer to become Avengers, leaving us with only a single empty slot remaining. Both of them had sworn the same oath as me, to fight evil with all their strength and to do good whenever possible. The expedition to Tampa might or might not involve anything related to that, *per se,* but you never could tell. That meant Danielle was the top choice for going along on such a mission, if she was up to it.

"I think I'll pass, this time at least. I'm still not quite back to normal yet," she admitted. That was undoubtedly true, even though she rarely mentioned it. Having a baby is hard work, no doubt about it.

"I'm sorry, beautiful," I said, and she shrugged a little.

"Eh, it is what it is. They always say the first one is the hardest," she said.

"I'm glad you can be so philosophical about it," I said.

"Maybe Joan is rubbing off on me. She talks like that all the time," she said, with a little laugh.

"Yeah, I guess she does. Where's Josie?" I asked.

"She's with Emily for a little bit, probably asleep," she said.

Just as I once thought, Kona was starting to feel like a nursery school. There had been three babies born that month, and that's a lot to handle at one time. Chris and Emily had a second daughter, Andrea, to join her sister Virginia. Danielle and I also had a girl, who we named Josefina because coincidentally we both had a great-grandmother by that name. Jesse and Leah had the only boy that time around. They named him David, though sometimes I think Goliath might have been more appropriate. He weighed nearly ten pounds when he was born and hadn't slowed down growing ever since. I think he practically killed his mother, being the small, petite little thing that she is.

But in any case, even though there was never a dull moment on the home front, I did sometimes find myself thinking it would be nice to get away from it all for a few days or so. We rarely did, mind you, but the trip to Tampa was a nice change of pace to look forward to.

The *Tyler James* had been officially retired from service as soon as we got back from the Moon, without the slightest regret. That meant our flight would take longer than it would have otherwise, since a regular plane can't match a trans-atmospheric vehicle when it comes to speedy arrival. One of our first projects when we got home from the Titan expedition was to hop over to Honolulu and fetch one of the corporate jets from the airport. The one we took had belonged to a pineapple company back in the day, and it had an incredibly realistic picture of several luscious, mouthwatering-looking slices of fruit painted all down the side. Every time I saw it I got hungry. But it had been the newest and the best jet we could find, and Jesse and I both agreed that the pineapple motif definitely had a certain kind of retro coolness. We christened it the *Pineapple Express*, since it didn't have any other name when we found it.

It was pretty luxurious inside, first-class all the way, and if we'd only had some pretty flight attendants to serve us chilled pineapple chunks in crystal fruit cups then it would have been perfect. But alas, we had to make do without.

We headed out early the next morning, but what with the long distance and losing five hours flying east, we didn't arrive in Tampa till almost nine o'clock that night, much too late to even think about mounting an expedition out on the Gulf.

"How's Hunter doing with his lessons?" I asked as we came in for a landing.

"Oh, pretty good. He's still a little green, but he works hard on the simulator and he's got in about sixty hours worth of flight time with me on the *Pineapple Express*. I might even be ready to let him take her out solo here before long," Jesse said, laughing a little.

"Good deal. Then *he* can fly us around sometimes," I said.

"Dang straight. I'm tired of being on call twenty-four seven. You ought to learn how yourself, Tyke," Jesse said.

"Not me, buddy boy. I hate heights," I reminded him.

"Got to overcome your fears sometime, you know," Jesse said philosophically.

"Easy for you to say," I said.

"Well. . . just think about it, okay? But anyway, what do you say we spend the night at the Academy tonight? We'll need some good computers tomorrow morning if we want to try to locate those heat signatures again," Jesse suggested.

"Sounds good to me," I said, even though if I were to be completely honest, I didn't much look forward to the idea. We hadn't been back to Tampa for over a year and I'd somehow managed to forget how oppressively quiet and empty it is. Spooky, even, in spite of the fact that I knew there was nothing that could hurt us other than maybe a snake or a spider.

The Academy was in better shape than most spots, of course, since we'd lived there as recently as eighteen months ago and also made sure the place was shut down properly when we left. So at least we had working lights and hot food for supper and all those kinds of things. Better than we could've had most anywhere else in the city.

We slept indecently late the next morning, with our bodies still set on Hawaiian time as they were. We didn't get up till almost noon, and then we had to spend at least another hour fiddling with the computer system to get it back online and reconnected to the satellite grid. However careful you think you've been about shutting things down properly, time still takes its toll.

But we did eventually get it working, and the first thing we did at that point was to take a quick look at the area by visible satellite, to see if there were anything obvious by daylight that we might have overlooked in the dark. There didn't seem to be, so then we switched over to infrared to see if we could spot those two little tell-tale heat signatures.

We still didn't find anything worth noting out in the ocean, and I chewed my lip thoughtfully.

"If those heat signatures after the explosion were really people then I'm sure they would've tried to swim for shore. Don't you think?" Jesse asked, and I nodded.

"Well, let's assume for a minute that's what they were. Could a person swim thirty miles across the ocean? And how long would it take if they did?" I asked.

"I'm sure they could. People have swum farther than that before. There's no way of knowing how long it would take without knowing what the currents were like and that kind of thing, but my best guess would be about eighteen to twenty hours," Jesse said.

"All right, let's make a sweep along the coast and see if we find anything that way," I said.

"Look there," Jesse said a few minutes later, at the exact same second that I saw it myself. There were two moving heat signatures on one of the islands at the mouth of the Bay, and I quickly switched back to visual to zoom in on that area.

Sure enough, there were two people walking on the beach. The resolution wasn't good enough to tell us much about them other than the fact that they were human beings, but that didn't matter. We'd find out who they were soon enough.

"Come on, let's go," I said decisively, and Jesse followed me without a word. We immediately drove to the closest marina and boarded a seaworthy boat to head out to Edgmont Key.

"Who could they be, do you think?" Jesse asked when we were well underway.

"Your guess is as good as mine, buddy boy. We'll find out soon enough," I said.

We landed at the old naval station on the southern tip of the island, and I tried not to pay attention to the skeletons. We didn't often see them in Tampa proper since most of the ones inside the city itself seemed to be hidden away inside homes or buildings, but here there were a lot of them scattered everywhere, still dressed in tattered slate-blue Defense Forces uniforms. But the station was set up in such a way that we had no choice but to pass through the building to reach the island, and that was rattling.

"I really hate places like this," Jesse commented as we crossed the main courtyard.

"Not real fond of them myself," I admitted, glancing at the skeletons again. It looked like they'd been on duty till the last possible moment and then died with their boots on, so to speak. Poor devils.

But finally we made our way to the northern wall and opened the gate, letting us out onto a breezy white-sand beach which was a welcome sight after the inside of the station. I kind of wondered why they bothered to build a wall around the place to start with, but I don't pretend to know the answer.

"So where do we go from here?" Jesse asked.

"Let's try the northern tip of the island. We might as well start where we saw them last," I said.

"Sounds good to me," Jesse said.

So with no more ado we set off along the beach at the best pace we could muster without wearing ourselves out. Walking in sand is hard work, believe it or not. It's all fine and well as long as you're going for a leisurely stroll, but it makes life difficult when you're trying for speed.

We found footprints of bare feet before we ever saw anyone, but finally we spotted the castaways far off down the shore. Jesse pulled out his ancient 45-caliber pistol and fired a round up into the sky to get their attention, not bothering to warn me first. Most people would have had a laser weapon, of course, but Jesse has always enjoyed the way that old gun kicks and smokes. It's also loud enough to wake the dead at such close range, and I clapped my hands over both ears.

"Dang, Jesse James, you could've said something first," I said.

"Sorry," he said, shrugging.

But it had the desired effect. Both people turned their heads to look, and before long we were both headed rapidly towards each other.

Then I stopped, suddenly uneasy for some reason.

"They look awfully familiar for some reason," I said doubtfully. They were still too far away to tell for sure, but I was almost certain I'd seen them somewhere before.

"Yeah, they do," Jesse said, scrutinizing them himself.

But even though we stopped, the other people didn't, and soon they were close enough to remove all doubt.

"It's impossible," I muttered under my breath. I always used to think it was just a tired old cliché when people talked about not being able to believe their own eyes, but I promise you it's not. Wait till it happens to you one of these days and then you'll see.

Because what I was seeing was literally impossible. I wanted to pinch myself but I *still* don't think I would have believed it. Standing right there on the beach in front of me, looking exactly the same as the last time I'd seen them fifteen years ago, were the very last people on earth I ever would have expected to meet.

We'd found my parents.

Chapter Two

I was too tongue-tied for words, and they seemed to be as well. But then Jesse broke the silence.

"Uncle Mikey?" he asked uncertainly, like he thought he might be dreaming.

"Jesse?" my father asked, and that was enough to break the logjam. Before I knew it I took a step forward, and then I was enveloped in arms and covered in tears, some of them mine I think. But when things had had time to subside after a little while, I still found that I didn't know how even to begin to ask all the questions that burned in my mind. Ever since I was four years old I'd thought my parents were dead, drowned in the Bay, and as far as I knew so had everyone else. Now here they were, looking barely older than I was myself.

I thought immediately of the story Uncle Philip had told us on the way back from Titan, about time travel and all the rest of it. Could that have been what happened? It would explain a lot of things, after all; maybe even that strange energy surge we'd seen on Saturday night. I couldn't keep my mind from chewing on the problem and analyzing every possible facet, but in the meantime Jesse had no compunctions about talking.

"But how can this be? We always thought y'all drowned in the Bay when me and Tyke were four years old. That's what the letter we got from the Defense Forces said; I've even seen it myself," Jesse said.

"We almost did drown. But we had the tachometer so we were able to escape by jumping fifteen years ahead. It's a long story, but we'll tell you everything as soon as we get a chance. But in the meantime where's everybody else? Who all is left?" my father asked.

"We're living in a little town named Kailua Kona, on the big island of Hawaii. There are twenty of us now, mostly family and friends. Mom and Dad, Chris, me, Veronica, Tycho; several others too, but I'm not sure which ones you'd know and which ones you wouldn't," Jesse said.

"We probably know several of them, actually. Is Katrina still with you? What about Amos, and Luther and Jenine, and the Bartows?" he asked.

"I'm afraid they've all passed away," Jesse said, in that uncomfortable way that people use when they have to regretfully inform someone that a friend has died.

"Oh, I see," my father said awkwardly.

"Well, I guess I should say Lucia is still with us. That's Amos and Katrina's daughter. And then Tommy and Amie Anderson are still alive, and Leah and Hunter Bartow. I'm married to Leah now, actually; we've got a little boy who was born just a couple weeks ago," Jesse said.

All this talk about death reminded me of something important, and I spoke up for the first time.

"I don't know if you know it or not, but there was a deadly plague that came through here just a couple years ago. It wiped out every warm-blooded life form on the planet, and there are still lots of spores in the ground. It kills within thirty-six hours after exposure, and I don't doubt you've both been exposed by now. So we better get you back into town and get you vaccinated, or this might turn out to be a pretty short reunion," I said.

"Yeah, Tyke's right about that. We better go while there's still time. We can talk on the way," Jesse agreed.

So that's what we did, and I found out quite a lot of things that day that I'd never known before; some of it stuff I wasn't quite sure I *wanted* to know. It turned out the boating accident had been no accident, for one thing; the Defense Forces had tried to murder all three of us that night. I never used to remember anything about the incident myself, but when my mother told that story it brought back vague memories of dark stormy waves and salty water stinging my eyes and nose, and fear and terror and other highly unpleasant things which I'd just as soon had stayed buried. I didn't want to think about that kind of stuff, not now and not ever, and when I heard that Hunter and Leah's father had been the commander of that mission it only compounded the issue.

But I kept my thoughts to myself till we got back to the Academy and at that point I gratefully refocused my attention on what needed to be done to prepare some anti-Orion serum. I knew exactly what needed to be done this time, but at least it occupied my mind and kept me from thinking about all that other stuff.

"So you're a great biologist now, is that it?" my mother asked, watching me work.

"Molecular geneticist," I admitted, kind of shyly.

"We always knew you'd do something wonderful like that," she said, and it was good to hear it even though it puzzled me.

"I always thought you wanted me to be a physicist or an astronomer. Isn't that why you named me after Tycho Brahe?" I asked.

"No, not exactly. Tycho Brahe was your daddy's hero back when he was in college, that's all. He wanted you to have somebody to look up to," my mother said, and I laughed a little bit.

"I think having you two around is going to end up destroying a lot of preconceived notions I've always had," I finally said dryly.

"No doubt, but it's never a good thing to let your mind get stale and fossilized, now is it?" she asked, and I laughed again.

"Well, no. No, it's not," I agreed.

The serum was finished, and as soon as I gave our two newest survivors their doses we were ready to leave. I cleaned up the lab while Jesse shut down the computers and the power supply, and then we all rode out to the airport to board the *Pineapple Express* and head home. It's a strange thing, but when you're headed west in a plane the sun barely seems to move in the sky at all. We gained five hours by the time we landed in Kona, and even though it had been almost sunset when we left Tampa, it was still early in the evening when we landed.

So then there were twenty-two of us in our little island paradise, and I have to say that my parents blended in pretty quickly. They were already thick as thieves with Uncle Philip and Aunt Joan, of course, but out of the younger folks only Chris and Jesse and I could remember them at all, even though they'd known almost everybody's parents at least socially back in the old days.

They found a house on the same strip of beach where we all lived, and we were always within walking distance if we liked. It was really hard at first, getting used to them being there, but before long things settled back into the old familiar pattern. They ended up taking over most of the teaching duties at the school since that was after all what they'd mostly always done before. It freed up Joan to help with the farming and Jesse to help with maintenance, so that at least was good.

My parents told me all kinds of interesting things over the next few months, actually, but one of the most thought-provoking tidbits they ever let slip was the simple fact that my father had warned the Defense Forces about the Orion Strain twelve years ahead of time, after he saw it coming with the tachometer. Not to mention Philip and Joan as well.

I could understand why Philip and Joan had never said anything; knowing the future is not nearly such a good thing as people sometimes think. It puts a burden on the knower, a straitjacket that he has to wear from then onwards. They carefully made arrangements so the XR planes would be ready at the right time, and I'm sure they did some behind-the-scenes negotiating with Dr. Weiss and various things like that, but they never let out a single peep that they knew anything. I didn't blame them for that, though; I knew they did it with everybody's welfare and happiness in mind.

No, what really interested me was what might have happened to the information Daddy had given to the Defense Forces. Philip and Joan didn't know the answer to *that,* and I couldn't help thinking it might turn out to be awfully important.

"I can't believe the Defense Forces wouldn't do something about a threat like that, if they knew it was coming," I said to Jesse one Saturday night.

"It's hard to believe they wouldn't, unless they thought he was lying," Jesse said.

"Well, true, but putting aside that possibility for a second, what would you have done if you were in their place?" I said, and Jesse thought about it for a few seconds.

"I think if I knew all that twelve years ahead of time then I'd start making some contingency plans, just like Mom and Dad did. There'd be no way of knowing what kind of germ they'd have to face or exactly what the circumstances might be, so first of all I'd try to assemble a team of the best microbiologists to be ready at a moment's notice to start analyzing the bug as soon as it appeared, hopefully to find a cure or a vaccination. And then just in case that didn't work, I'd either make sure I had an airtight facility to take refuge in for a while, or else I'd start building spaceships and considering where I might go to start over if the Earth turned out to be permanently unlivable or some such thing," Jesse said.

"Yeah, that's pretty much what I thought," I agreed.

"So then considering the fact that they would have already known the Moon is about to die before long and can't be salvaged, where do you think they'd decide to go instead?" Jesse said.

"I think I still would have gone to the Moon under those circumstances. Anywhere else they went they'd have to build airtight shelters to live in, and if you've got to do that anyway then why go far when you don't have to? Why even leave Earth for that matter?" I asked.

"I can think of a reason," Jesse said.

"Do tell," I said.

"If they wanted to start completely over, and I mean *completely* over, like permanently so, then they wouldn't build shelters on Earth and they wouldn't go to the Moon, either. They'd know it can't hold an atmosphere for very long. But there are other places that can. Mars and Venus come to mind, for example. Maybe they decided to work on terraforming one of those places. The technology exists, even if they might've had to do some hard digging to find it," Jesse said.

"I don't know about all that, Jesse," I said doubtfully. It sounded awfully far-fetched, even for a cold-eyed Defense Forces bureaucrat to sign off on. But then again, people have been known to do some pretty hare-brained things at times.

"It makes sense to me, at least. Think about it; if they devoted a lot of money and resources to the project, I bet they could have developed a workable space vehicle in five years or less," Jesse said.

"Maybe," I admitted.

"And then if they introduced a breeder gas into the atmosphere in one of those places, it'd grow exponentially and have the whole atmosphere converted in six months' time, tops. Ready for them to move in and comfortably start working on the rest of the process at that point. Once you could breathe and go without a space suit, things wouldn't be all that bad. No worse than living in a really harsh desert," Jesse said.

"Possibly," I said, still not sure whether I believed it or not.

"It's what I'd do," Jesse said, and I laughed then.

"This is *you* we're talking about, Jesse. But just for the sake of argument, even if you happened to be right, which one would you pick? Mars or Venus?" I asked.

"There are pros and cons to both of them, but on the whole I think I'd go with Venus," Jesse said.

"Why is that?" I asked.

"Because Mars is so much smaller, for one thing. It leaks atmosphere a lot slower than the Moon does, true, but it *will* leak it away. Venus never would; it's almost as big as Earth is," Jesse said.

"Hmm," I said, thinking it over.

"It'd be easy enough to find out," Jesse said brightly.

"How's that?" I asked.

"All we'd have to do is run a spectroscopic analysis of the atmosphere on both planets, to see what the composition might be. Then we'd know if anybody had altered them," Jesse said.

"I guess so," I admitted.

"We'd have to go up to the observatory for that," Jesse said.

"Let's go, then. You've got me curious now," I said.

It was almost nine o'clock, so we decided to call it a day when it came to the survivor search. Jesse shut down the computers, and then we drove up to the observatory on Mauna Kea after calling to let everybody know what we were doing. Philip recently got the telephone system working again, which is an awfully nice feature.

It took nearly an hour to reach the observatory, and Jesse parked on the gravel right outside the building. It was freezing cold up there, especially considering the fact that we were both in shorts and t-shirts.

"Hurry up, dude; it's freezing out here," Jesse said, clapping his hands against his sides while I fumbled with the door lock in the dark.

As soon as we got inside I switched on the lights and the heater, and grabbed a couple of blankets off the table which I'd brought up there for just such emergencies.

"Here, wrap up in this till the heater gets going," I said, handing one of them to Jesse and putting the other one around my own shoulders. It helped a lot, but I was still shivering while I set up the spectroscope. Being able to see your breath in the air while you work is not a good feeling, especially when you're not used to it.

"Is it working?" Jesse asked.

"Yeah, hold on just a minute," I said, adjusting the controls.

"Let's check Mars first, just in case. That'll be easier," Jesse said, and I shrugged.

"Whatever you say," I said, consulting the computer to find out where in the sky Mars ought to be at the time.

"Slight problem, buddy boy," I said after a while.

"What's that?" Jesse asked.

"Looks like Mars is behind the sun right now. There's no way to look at it for at least a month or two," I said.

"Well. . . try Venus, then," Jesse said, and I shrugged. It took several minutes to get the spectroscope set up and working properly, and then several more while it actually ran the analysis. Venus was low on the horizon by that time, just barely within range, but we were high enough on the mountain that I could manage. Eventually it was done.

"Now *that's* interesting," I murmured, staring at the readout.

"What's interesting?" Jesse asked.

"There's more oxygen in the atmosphere than there ought to be. About twelve percent, it looks like, and the rest of it mostly nitrogen. It's *supposed* to be ninety-six percent carbon dioxide," I said.

"Told you so," Jesse said, sounding satisfied.

"You really think they've got some kind of secret hide-out over there?" I asked.

The thought worried me, honestly. Much as I might have liked to think the world was safe at that point, it very well might *not* be if some of *those* folks ever decided to come back home. My parents' horror stories were still fresh and vivid in my mind, and the kinds of people who would do things like that are not at all the kinds of people you want to share a world with.

True, it was only by the sheerest of miracles that I'd ever been able to locate a cure for the Orion Strain, and without *that* the Earth was untouchable as poison. So we were probably safe at the moment, but that didn't mean somebody else might not come across the same cure sooner or later.

"I don't know what else it could mean. See if you can hack into the computer system at Southern Command and figure out what they were up to, right before the plague came," Jesse said.

It was a logical place to start since that was the military command zone in which Florida had been included, and if they'd taken note of my father's information at all then that would have been the commander who dealt with it. But hacking military computers is never easy, and the North American Defense Forces (aka the NADF) were by far the toughest nut on the tree when it came to security.

"That might not be so easy," I said doubtfully.

"I have complete faith in you," Jesse said, clapping his hand on my shoulder.

"Yeah, I bet you do," I muttered, but nevertheless I got started. Quite a few of the computers in the world were defunct by then, but the mainframe at Southern Command in Atlanta was still functioning, surprisingly. It was every bit as hard to crack as I thought it would be, but then of course I didn't have to worry about anybody noticing or caring, either.

Once I broke inside, I was able to access quite a lot of highly interesting and educational material. It turned out the Defense Forces had built six large colony ships at the personal direction of Colonel James Burns, who was the head of Southern Command. Each of them carried a thousand people, and his plan had been to send three of them to Venus and three of them to Mars, just in case one or the other expedition failed. There were tons of facts about the colonies and the planets themselves, all of it incidentally fascinating if you had a taste for things like that. For a science junkie such as myself it was like the heady aroma of meat and potatoes to a man who hasn't eaten in days, and I found myself getting lost in the data almost before I realized what I was doing.

"I guess there was no reason for us to hide out on the Moon, then," I finally said, with a wry shake of my head.

"Sure there was, if we wanted to survive. Do you really think they would've taken any of *us* along on those expeditions?" Jesse asked.

"Well. . . no," I admitted. Those colony ships had probably been reserved for high-ranking members of the government and the Defense Forces, along with whatever scientists and engineers they thought they needed in order to make a new life for themselves. A bunch of kids from a math and science school probably wouldn't have qualified, and neither would a motley crew of their parents, friends, and associates. We would have been left behind and forgotten beyond a shadow of a doubt, along with everybody else on Earth.

But that wasn't really important anymore at this point. We *had* survived, with no help from them, and for the moment at least we ruled the world. But twenty-two people couldn't stand against six thousand, if they ever found a way to come home. They'd barge in, shove us aside, and immediately take over and start running things however they saw fit. And judging from what my parents had said and some of the information I read in those files, none of us would like the way they wanted to run things very much.

But what could we do about it? We couldn't exactly wage war against our fellow survivors, and we wouldn't have wanted to do that even if we could have. Nor could we hope to hide from them forever. Refusing to give them the anti-Orion vaccine might keep them away for a while, perhaps, but they might still find it on their own someday. That was only putting off the problem, not solving it. Sooner or later we'd have to deal with those people, one way or another.

I only hoped it didn't turn out even worse than I feared.

Chapter Three

"I think we need to start looking for another space vehicle, just in case," Jesse declared one day not long afterward.

"Just in case of what?" I asked.

"Mostly just in case those NADF honchos show up on our doorstep unexpectedly. It might be nice to have a fast getaway vehicle that could take us anywhere we needed to go," Jesse said.

"That's true," I admitted.

"But even if they never bother us, it'd still be useful, you know. Think how nice it would've been to have one when we had to go to Tampa back in June. We could've gotten there in only two hours or so, instead of having to make an all-day red-eye flight like that. Wouldn't it be nice to be able to get back home sooner when we have to go places?" Jesse asked.

"Well, yeah, you're right about that, too," I agreed.

"So then it'd be worth looking for one, don't you think?" he asked.

"I guess so, but where would we start?" I finally asked.

"I'm not sure about that part. Mrs. Weiss didn't have any other ships, did she?" Jesse asked.

"Not that I know of. I think she only had the *Cabral* and the *Balboa*," I said.

"I don't think the Defense Forces would've left anything behind, either," Jesse said, frowning.

"They never built anything small like what you're talking about in the first place. All they ever built were those six humongous colony ships," I pointed out.

"Hmm. . . do you think we could build one of our own? We might find enough technical information and parts and suchlike, if we looked around for a while," Jesse said.

"Are you sure about that? Considering how the *Tyler James* turned out?" I asked skeptically.

"Yeah, but that time we had to work with scrounged-up parts from wrecks. We'd be working with brand new stuff this time, just putting it together like puzzle pieces," Jesse said.

"Maybe," I said.

"Aw, come on, Tyke. You know I wouldn't suggest doing something stupid and hare-brained, don't you?" he asked.

I was about to tell him I knew no such thing, but I refrained.

"There's one other possibility, though," he finally said.

"And what might that be?" I asked.

"As a matter of fact, it was the *Tyler James* that reminded me of it," Jesse said.

"Great. So what is it?" I asked again.

"Well, you know how the terraformers on the Moon basically abandoned everything when the Project was over, right?" he asked.

"Yeah, like they did with the *Tyler James*," I agreed.

"Okay, so they had to have a launch facility on Earth somewhere, too. We might get lucky and find an old XR down *here*," Jesse said.

"Yeah. A decrepit old wreck," I said.

"I don't think so. Earth is not the Moon, buddy boy. No hard radiation down here to mess up the circuit boards, no vampire roaches to fight off, nothing like that. If we found one, then it ought to be in a lot better shape than the ones at Desolation Island ever were," Jesse said.

I grudgingly decided he might have a point about that. Earth is unquestionably a much nicer place to live than the Moon, even for electronics.

"I don't guess you have any idea where the Lunar Consortium's launch facility was located, do you?" I finally asked.

"Not a clue," Jesse agreed.

"Then don't you think it might be kind of hard to find, seeing as how it was abandoned fifty some-odd years ago? There are not too many records left from back then," I pointed out.

"Don't worry, we'll find it. Might take us a while, but we'll find it," he said confidently.

"Whatever you say," I said, shaking my head.

And you know, he *did* find the place, surprisingly enough. The Lunar Consortium had been headquartered in Geneva, luckily, a city which had somehow managed to elude bombing and cyber-war. All the records were intact, and from there it was no great feat to locate the Consortium's private spaceport on the island of Socotra off the coast of Yemen in Arabia. I don't know why they picked that particular spot, other than the fact that it's close to the equator and it was an uninhabited place where they could do as they pleased with no interference.

So Jesse and I went to explore the place, taking Hunter with us so he could get in some real-world flight time. I couldn't help thinking the *Pineapple Express* looked glaringly out of place after we landed on that dusty runway in the desert. It was the kind of spot that made you think there'd probably never been a succulent slice of fruit within a thousand miles of the place ever since the dawn of time. It reminded me uncomfortably of Desolation Island, actually, and I found myself wanting to glance around for vampire roaches. I think it was the style of architecture mostly, but then I'm sure the same engineers had designed and built both places, so maybe it wasn't all that strange that they should resemble each other in certain respects.

The *landscape* certainly didn't look like anything on the Moon, or even on Earth for that matter. Socotra is one of those unearthly-looking places which has several types of endemic vegetation that grow nowhere else, and if you didn't know better you'd seriously think you were on an alien planet after walking around out there for a little bit. There's one particular type of plant called a Dragon's Blood Tree which is downright spooky.

But the desert climate definitely seemed to have helped preserve everything. We found no less than *five* working XR planes which needed either minor repairs or none at all; just a reload with fuel. I couldn't get over it.

"I can't believe these have been sitting here this whole time and nobody stole them," I said, marveling.

"What good would it have done to steal them? There was no use for them anymore, and no fuel being produced, and Socotra is pretty far from most places. Not worth such a long trip just for salvage," Jesse said.

"So how do we get them home then?" Hunter asked, and that was indeed a good question. Jesse looked at him thoughtfully.

"I might let *you* help me fly them back, if you think you can handle a solo," he said at length.

"I can handle it," Hunter said eagerly.

"We'll see about that. You better be careful, though, or it'll turn out to be the last flight you ever make. Not because I won't let you anymore but because you'll end up as a pile of roasted hamburger meat out there in the middle of the desert somewhere after you crash and burn," Jesse warned.

"I know," Hunter said, in a more subdued tone of voice. I guess the thought of getting turned into roasted hamburger meat must have knocked the edge off his enthusiasm. Not that I could blame him; I didn't like the image myself and I wasn't even the one at the controls.

But Hunter *was* careful, and over the space of the next few days he and Jesse gradually ferried all five of those old ships back home to Hawaii. There wasn't enough room to park that many planes at the airstrip in Kona, so they had to leave all but one of them at the international airport on the other side of the island at Hilo instead. You'd think it was the proudest accomplishment of their lives, from the way they both grinned.

Unfortunately, trouble was brewing that we didn't realize at the time, or Hunter might not have been quite so happy about getting his solo stripes.

It all started with that worrisome military colony on Venus, just as we feared it might. I'm not sure what it was that caused them to notice us after so long, but I highly suspect they must have detected that same surge of neutrinos over the Gulf that first alerted us to my parents' arrival. Neutrinos can pass right through a thousand miles of lead as if it weren't even there, and ten million miles of empty space is nothing to them. That surge would have been just as glaringly obvious on Venus as it was in Hawaii.

Anyway, *something* must have aroused their curiosity, and they must have been watching Earth pretty closely in the days and months following that event, and slowly but surely drawing up their plans.

Thus it was that toward the end of November, they sprung the trap.

It was Veronica's birthday when it happened, and Hunter's too as a matter of fact. We were having a party for both of them on the beach that night, with music and dancing and lots of good food and good times. Veronica had grown up to be a beautiful girl, tall and blonde like her brothers, and when she danced barefoot on the sand we all clapped and cheered. She's always loved to dance, ever since she used to do ballet when she was little. I don't know what name you'd use for the style she does now; I suppose it's her own personal invention. All I know is that she does it beautifully, in a way that makes it hard not to watch, and I don't often say things like that.

She was dancing with Hunter that night, actually, even though he's not very good at those kinds of things. Every once in a while he'd fumble a move, and then Veronica would gracefully cover for him in a way that made even the fumbles look beautiful. I honestly don't know how she does it.

I took note of the fact that she put a red lei around his neck and hugged him quite a bit longer than strictly necessary after the dance was finished, and he wasn't shy about returning the favor, either.

"Did you know Hunter and Veronica are going out?" I asked Danielle, watching them curiously while we sat together on our usual log.

"Of course. I've known about that for weeks," she said.

"Really?" I asked, and she laughed.

"Babe, you stay holed up in that lab too much. If you'd get out and socialize a little more then you wouldn't be so surprised by things like that," she said.

"Seems like it'd be strange, you know, with Jesse and Leah already married," I said, ignoring the comment about spending too much time in the lab.

"Why should it be strange? It's not like they're actually related or anything," she pointed out.

"Well. . . no," I admitted.

"Then don't worry about it. If it lasts then great, and if not then that's also fine. They're both still young," she said.

Veronica started in on her next dance routine, something a little more classical this time. She had Johnny Weiss play the ninth movement from Vivaldi's *The Four Seasons,* the one corresponding to the month of November. One of her favorite pieces of music, naturally, and it made for a slow and lovely dance which reminded me a little bit of a waltz. We've all become quite the connoisseurs of classical music thanks to hanging out with Johnny for so long. Veronica danced with Hunter again since she needed a partner for that piece, but I soon had much more urgent things to worry about than whether those two were sweet on each other or not.

All eyes were focused on the performance when we suddenly found ourselves surrounded by a hundred soldiers with laser assault rifles, dressed head to toe in biohazard gear. That put a sharp and sudden end to our evening's festivities, as you might well believe. Veronica's arms slowly went down to her sides, and she clasped Hunter's hand tightly as the last notes of *November* faded into silence. Some of the little ones started to cry, but the rest of us just sat there in numb shock.

Then one of the suited figures stepped forward.

"Who's the leader here?" he asked.

There was no point in fighting that many armed enemies when we had nothing more dangerous than a stick or a pocketknife among the whole lot of us, a fact which Philip must have recognized.

"That's me," Philip said, slowly standing up, and from then on the commander addressed no one but him.

"Do you have any more people elsewhere?" the commander asked.

"No, sir. We're all here for my daughter's birthday," Philip said, but if the subtle play for sympathy had any effect then it sure didn't show. The commander looked like some kind of sinister alien life form in his silvery-white biogear, and maybe at heart that's exactly what he was.

Philip preached a sermon once about how it's altogether possible for the heart of a man to die long before his mind or his body follow, but when it does then he's no longer fully human even though he may still look and sound like it. He was talking about the triune nature of man as a reflection of the Trinity, and I suppose it's always stuck in my mind ever since then. But whether the commander was fully human in that sense or not wasn't really important, I don't guess. He was every bit as dangerous either way.

"Get everybody lined up," he ordered curtly, and Philip nodded at us. I'm not sure why the man didn't just tell us to line up himself instead of asking Philip to have us do it, unless he was such a slave to protocol that he instinctively went through proper channels even when dealing with prisoners. Either that, or he might have thought we'd be more likely to listen to one of our own. Whatever the reason might have been, we did as he said.

Several of the soldiers came forward with white plastic leg irons to chain us all together, and then we were forced to walk halfway across town to a parking lot where everyone boarded buses. I was chained up between Jesse and Johnny, with Danielle far ahead of me.

"Who are these people, and where are they taking us do you think?" I whispered to Jesse after we got on the bus. Nobody had actually said we couldn't talk, but it seemed like one of those situations when you ought not to push your luck too far.

"I bet they're from that military colony on Venus, from the way they're dressed and the way they act. And if I had to guess, I imagine they're taking us to Hilo because that's probably where they landed. After that, your guess is as good as mine," Jesse whispered back.

That made sense, and when the bus left town on the mountain highway that ran through the pass between Kilauea and Mauna Loa there was no more doubt of the matter; we were definitely headed for Hilo. There are only a certain limited number of places where it's possible to drive on an island, and none of them are very far away.

They herded us into the cargo bay of a transport plane at the airport and chained us to the wall, where our only choices were either to stand up or to sit on the floor. I felt it when we took off, but since there were no windows it was impossible to see where we might be going.

"What do you think they want with us?" I asked Jesse, and he shrugged.

"It's only a guess, but if you were them, what would *you* want with us? They probably want to study us and figure out what it is that makes us immune to the Orion Strain, hopefully so they can copy it and come back to live here themselves," Jesse said.

"They'll never find it. It's a thousand wonders I ever did," I said.

"I wouldn't be so sure about that. Left to themselves I doubt they'd ever find it, true enough. But it changes the odds a little bit now that they've got us to poke and prod and run experiments on for as long as they feel like it," Jesse said.

"So maybe I should go ahead and tell them what they want to know; you think? It might be worth it if they'd turn us loose and leave us alone," I said.

"Yeah, but I'm not sure they ever would, Tyke. People like that don't think that way; they usually want to control *everything*. Do you really believe they'd ever leave us alone, if we were the only thing that stood between them and ruling the whole world? I don't think so. We'd be like a rock in their shoe all the time," Jesse said.

"Yeah, you're probably right," I admitted.

"In the meantime, I think they're taking us somewhere else on Earth. This plane isn't the kind which is made for space travel, and besides that if we were leaving the planet then our weight would have started to drop by now," Jesse said.

"Yeah, but where?" I asked gloomily.

"Couldn't tell you that, buddy. The world is an awfully big place," Jesse said.

"So it is," I agreed, letting my breath out in a long sigh. My heart was heavy and I didn't have a clue what might happen when we reached whatever destination our captors had in mind. I couldn't reach Danielle or even talk to her, and that only added to my misery.

Things were about to get worse.

Chapter Four

We ended up landing in Atlanta early the next morning, a city I'd never visited before and wouldn't have recognized at all if it weren't for the road signs we passed. I suspected they took us there at least partly because it was the headquarters for the Southern Command, and if Jesse were right about them wanting to use us for experiments then they'd need some pretty serious biohazard labs to work with. Nor would they want to take us back to Venus and risk contaminating the colony there. This was probably something along the lines of a high-risk mission for a few specially chosen elite troops and scientists.

My guesses turned out to be more or less correct when we pulled into the parking lot at the command compound. It was gray and overcast, and we were led inside shivering in our light beach clothes. Even Georgia is cold sometimes, at the end of November.

It was blessedly warm inside the building, and they took us through a maze of corridors and stairwells till I was hopelessly lost in that huge complex. Eventually we reached a fork of ways on the third floor, and that's when they separated us. All the men and teenage boys were taken down one hall, and the women and the little kids down another. We didn't even get a chance to say goodbye.

I'm sure they did it to discourage any kind of escape attempt, and I have to admit it was pretty darned effective in that respect, too. They also took our clothes away and dressed us instead in dark gray suits made of paper, which rattled and crinkled every time we took a step. The texture reminded me of the stuff they used to make dollar bills out of a long time ago, kind of tough and silky. Even our shoes were made of paper.

The seven of us who were in the adult male group eventually got turned out into a cavernous room which reminded me of a dormitory. There were rows of beds, and here and there a few couches and other amenities like that, plus thick glass walls on one side which looked out across the North Georgia hills. They finally took off our leg irons at that point, but the place was still a prison; there was only one door made of heavy steel, and there was no chance of getting it open unless you had an access code from outside. We were well and thoroughly trapped.

Philip immediately gathered everybody together as soon as they left us alone.

"Needless to say, nobody should tell these people anything at this point, at least not till we understand the situation better. They've probably brought us here for testing and experimentation, and if that's true then we're most likely safe for the time being. Don't give up hope, though; we've been through tougher things than this and lived to laugh about it later. We'll be all right, no matter what," he said, and then concluded with a prayer as we all stood there holding hands in a circle.

They brought us food not long after we arrived, which was good since none of us had eaten anything since the night before at the party. It wasn't much; various and sundry canned goods of one kind or another, but we were too hungry by then to care about the menu.

I tried not to think about Danielle and Josie, but then of course you know how that is. If you try not to think of a pink elephant, then that's exactly what you'll end up thinking about. Not that I'm comparing Danielle to a pink elephant by any means, but the principle is the same no matter what it is you're trying not to think of.

They kept the television going the whole time, full of moving and pseudo-patriotic propaganda videos. Under different circumstances I might have thought they were funny, sort of like the stories in the supermarket tabloids. But when you're locked up under armed guard and the only choice you've got is either to watch the crummy vids or to sit and stare at the walls, then it's not so amusing anymore.

Later that same evening, our bio-suited jailers came back.

"Which one of you is Hunter Bartow?" one of them asked. I don't know how they figured out our names unless maybe the girls told them, but they didn't seem to have any doubt about it. Hunter slowly stood up from his place on the couch.

"That's me," he said, raising his hand a bit.

"Come with us," the man said, and then turned on his heel and left. Hunter glanced at the rest of us, but there was nothing for him to do except to follow the man.

"What do you think they wanted with Hunter?" I asked aloud to nobody in particular after the door was shut and locked again.

"Who knows? Maybe they need a lab rat," Jesse said.

"Any of us would've done for that. It sounded to me like they wanted Hunter in particular for some reason," I said.

"I'm sure he'll tell us whenever he gets back," Philip said.

But Hunter never came back, and as the days passed we started to wonder if he was even still alive and what they'd done with him.

We didn't learn much else in the meantime, either. Oh, they poked and prodded us and took blood samples and tissue samples and hair samples and pretty much every other kind of sample you can think of, and put us through all kinds of tests and procedures and injected us with who-knows-what on several occasions. But they never bothered to explain what they were doing or why, so we could only speculate that it was part of the effort to find out what made us immune to the Orion Strain.

I do know that one of the injections made me sick as a dog for days, to the point that I had a raging fever and couldn't eat a bite or even sleep despite the fact that I was exhausted. No one else got as sick as I did, but Chris and Johnny both looked pretty bad for a while.

"I wonder what they're doing to us," Jesse said, when I was well enough to get up out of bed again.

"Tyke's the biologist. What do you think, son?" my father asked, and I took a deep breath. I was still weak and felt like crud, but this was important.

"There's no telling. If we're right about them trying to figure out a vaccine for the Orion Strain then it's probably got something to do with that. They might be giving us some other kind of germ to see how it affects us," I said. That was only a wild guess, but it was all I had to go on.

"They might end up killing us, if they give us anything much worse than that last one," Jesse said.

"It sure does feel that way," I agreed. I'd never felt *that* bad even when I had radiation poisoning on the Moon.

"I think we should try to break out of here," Philip said abruptly, and just as you might expect, all eyes were fixed on him at once.

"I'm not sure that's possible," my father said, and I held a similar opinion myself even though I didn't want to say so.

"I'm not sure it is, either. I only said we should try, before they end up killing us," Philip said.

"But how?" Jesse asked.

"Well, I've been thinking about that. The way I see it, there are only three ways out of this room. There's either the door, the window, or the air conditioning vent," Philip said.

"None of which we can get out of. The door is locked. The windows are made of unbreakable glass which doesn't open, and it's way too high to jump down from here even if we *did* break one of them. The air conditioning vent is screwed on tight and we don't have a screwdriver or even a penny to get it undone, besides the fact that it's too high to reach anyway," Jesse said.

That was a depressing list, but unfortunately he was completely correct. I couldn't think of any possible way to get out of that room short of a bomb or a gun, and we had neither. Even the metal furniture was bolted to the floor, and there's not much you can accomplish with a pillow or a couch cushion.

"Maybe we could rip up the sheets and braid a rope to climb down to the ground," Chris said.

"We could do that if we had a way to break open the windows in the first place. But since we don't then that wouldn't be very useful," Jesse reminded him.

"It wouldn't help even if we did. We can't leave the girls behind," I said, and for a little while gloom settled over the group again.

"What about if we stood on each others' shoulders to reach the vent cover? We could balance against that column the TV is bolted onto," my father suggested after a while, and we all glanced up at the vent.

"Maybe. But we still wouldn't have anything to unscrew it with," Jesse said.

"I bet we would. We could tear the power cord loose from the TV and use one of the prongs. It's metal, and it's even the right shape," my father said.

"That might actually work, Mikey. Let's give it a try," Philip said hopefully.

The cord on the TV was only about four inches long and therefore hard to get a grip on, but Chris was the strongest of us and I'm sure he tried his best. He got a tight hold and then gave it a hard yank, only to fall flat on his back as his feet flew out from under him. Paper shoes on a tile floor don't give much traction.

None of us laughed.

"Try it barefoot, son," Philip said. Chris got up slowly, kicking his paper shoes aside, and then gave it another go. This time he had better luck. The cord broke loose from the TV, and even though he fell down again we had our makeshift screwdriver.

"Cool," Chris said, nodding with satisfaction from where he sat on the floor.

Reaching the vent cover turned out to be a little harder. We soon found out it was impossible to stand one atop the other, even with the column to help balance against. What finally worked was something Philip remembered seeing at Veronica's cheerleading practices, when the girls had to form a pyramid. Philip, Jesse, and Chris stood shoulder to shoulder on the bottom, and my father and Johnny stood barefoot on their shoulders, and then I was chosen for the honor of climbing up to the very top to stand at the apex since I'm the smallest.

I think I've mentioned before how much I hate heights, especially when I'm standing on top of a shaky pyramid of human flesh which feels like it might collapse in a tangled heap underneath me at any second. But I forced myself to ignore that possibility, and by stretching just a little bit I soon found that I was able to reach the vent cover. I kept my balance with one hand braced against the ceiling, and then with the other one I attacked the screws.

A power cord prong makes a lousy screwdriver, just in case you wondered. Not to mention the fact that I don't think those screws had been taken loose ever since they first built the place. But I made progress, and eventually I managed to get all but two of them out. Those two ended up getting rounded off by the power prong to the point that I doubt even a real screwdriver could have gotten them loose. Still, I was able to get my fingers up under the edges of the vent cover to pull on it, even though it made our little pyramid sway dangerously. I finally took a chance and yanked hard, tearing it completely free in my hands.

But that was enough to overbalance the pyramid, too. All six of us crashed to the floor, and I hit my head on the back of the couch hard enough to see stars. For a little while all I could do was sit there on the floor, half dazed.

"Well, that was fun," Jesse said, rubbing his hands together.

"You bet, but now let's braid that rope we talked about earlier and get the heck out of here," Philip said.

I let the others work on that while I rubbed my forehead and slowly came back to my senses, and by the time I was able to stand up without staggering they were finished.

Good thing, too, because it turned out I was the one who had to climb back up the pyramid for a second time and crawl inside the vent with the end of the rope held in my teeth to find somewhere to tie it off.

I didn't think I'd make it at first, dangling from the edge of the vent and scrambling with both hands to keep from falling. There wasn't much to grab hold of and my paper shirt didn't help matters, but finally my dad gave me a hard shove from below at just the right time, pushing me up into the duct itself and incidentally causing the rest of them to hit the floor again. I lay there in the duct for a few seconds, sweating and breathing hard from the exertion, then tore off my shirt so I could get some traction to pull myself forward.

It was cold in there, especially bare-chested and covered in sweat, and before long I was shivering. The ductwork was smooth as silk for a long time, but eventually I did find a place where there was a fan built into a side duct. The blades weren't moving at the time and it seemed fairly steady, so I quickly tied the end of the sheet to the motor, making sure it was tight. Then I jerked the rope a few times to let the others know it was ready for them to climb up.

A few minutes later we were all inside the ductwork.

All we could do was to move along in single file for a long time, but eventually we reached a place where several ducts met and radiated from a single point, and above them was an access door with a catch that I could turn even with my frozen fingers. A few seconds later we were all crouched on a metal catwalk in a narrow space which seemed to be a maintenance area, full of wires and ductwork and insulation.

The others had all ripped off at least the sleeves of their paper shirts so as to get enough traction to be able to crawl, and Jesse and Chris had torn theirs off completely, just like I had.

"So what do we do now?" Jesse asked.

"We've got to find the girls," Philip said immediately.

"Yeah, I know that. But how?" Jesse asked.

"Let's see if we can ask somebody," Philip said.

"Are you serious?" Chris asked, and Philip nodded.

"I'm completely serious. Let's find one of these yahoos alone somewhere and then we'll catch him by surprise and threaten to rip his suit open unless he tells us what we want to know. But we'll have to get down out of this crawlspace before we can do that," he said.

That part didn't turn out to be all that difficult, actually. All we had to do was follow the catwalk about a hundred yards to where a set of metal stairs came up from below, and at the bottom of those we found a wooden door that opened into a dimly lit hallway which reminded me of a hospital. All six of us quickly slipped out into the hall, and then followed Philip to the left. I don't think he knew which way he was going, but that was more or less back toward the area where our dormitory had been.

We were silent as cats in our bare feet, and as long as we moved slowly the paper suits didn't rattle very much. Maybe that's why we were able to catch the man by surprise.

He was sitting at a table right in front of our cell, and I think he was probably supposed to be guarding it. But he was dozing when we spotted him, leaned up against the wall with his head cocked over to one side. I don't guess he'd ever had any real need to be alert before now, but that was all to the good.

"Come on, boys. Let's get him," Philip whispered.

We tackled the dude, and he never stood a chance against six of us. We had him pinned down on the floor in seconds, and when he saw Philip's hand poised to rip his mask off he lay there frozen.

"One wrong move and you'll be breathing spores. Understand?" Philip asked conversationally. I could dimly see the dude's face through his mask, young and scared. He swallowed and nodded.

"Good. Can you open the door where the girls are locked up?" Philip asked.

"Yes," he said.

"Yes, *sir,*" Philip corrected him.

"Yes, sir," the guard said.

"Do you know where they are?" Philip asked.

"Yes, sir," the guard said, and Philip nodded.

"Good boy. Take us there and let them out, and if you don't cause us any problems then we'll let you go. Understand?" Philip asked.

"Yes, sir," the guard said.

They let him up, with Jesse and Chris keeping a tight grip on each arm and Philip carrying the man's electronic stunner while he walked a step or two behind. I was a little bit disappointed that the guard hadn't had a laser pistol instead, but a stunner is considerably better than nothing at all.

The guard led us through so many corridors that I couldn't have remembered them all to save my life, and eventually brought us to the place where the girls were being kept. The guard in front of their door wasn't sleeping, but we did catch her by surprise. Philip stepped around the corner and had her covered with the stunner before she had time to realize what was happening. Then my father slipped forward and took her own stunner from her.

"Open the door," Philip ordered, and under the circumstances the girl didn't have much choice but to obey. She punched in an access code on a keypad beside the door, and seconds later the door swung open.

"Go tell them to get out here, Tyke," Philip said, and I went inside to do that very thing.

I don't think they were expecting to see me, at least not judging from the scattered gasps of shocked surprise I heard, but there was no time to explain things.

"Come on, let's go. We've got to get out of here *now*," I said, jerking my head back toward the door. Aunt Joan briskly took over at that point.

"You heard him, girls. Let's go. Don't even stop to grab anything," she ordered, and within thirty seconds we were all outside in the hall. I would have dearly loved to talk to Danielle for a few minutes, but there was no time even for that. It would have to wait till we got somewhere safe. Then Jesse said something that brought all of us to a standstill.

"Where's Leah?" he asked.

"The guards came to get her the first day we were here, along with Davy," Aunt Joan said.

"Yeah, they came to get Hunter the first day too. But where are they?" Jesse asked.

"Do you know where they are?" Philip demanded, directing his question at the guards. They both shook their heads, and then for a few seconds there was a long pause.

"Come on. Take us to the front doors," Philip finally said decisively.

"Dad, we can't-" Jesse began, but Philip cut him off.

"Not now, Jesse. We'll come back for them as soon as we get these others somewhere safe. If we try to find them right now dragging twenty people through the halls then we'll get caught for sure," he said. I could see the desperate unhappiness on Jesse's face and knew exactly how he must have felt, but he knows good sense when he hears it.

The guards took us on another long excursion through the halls till we reached the front doors, and there we stunned both of them before leaving the building as quickly as we could, running across the grounds toward the parking lot and the expressway beyond it. If we made it past that, we could lose ourselves in the urban jungle of homes and businesses where they'd probably never find us.

The north wind felt like a blast of ice water against my bare chest, and those paper pants didn't do all that much for the rest of me, either. Within minutes I was numb and blue, but we soon had worse problems to worry about than the cold.

Someone must have seen us from the windows, because before we knew it there was the fire of blue lightning all around us from high-power stunner fire. One beam burned a smoking hole in the grass six inches wide, barely missing my left foot. We must have been almost out of range at that point, and I started to hope we might actually make it.

Then one of the stunners must have caught me in the back, and for a split second I saw the grass rushing up to meet my face at a much faster rate of speed than I would have liked. But my brain was already knocked senseless long before I had time to feel the impact, and for a while that was the last I knew.

Chapter Five

It wasn't actually very long before I started to come back to some vague version of reality; maybe fifteen minutes or so. By then they'd already carried me back inside the building and locked me up again, although they hardly needed to. I hurt too much at that point to walk away even if they'd left the doors standing wide open. I could feel a nasty burn several inches wide right between my shoulder blades from where the stunner beam hit me, which was scary even in hindsight. A direct head shot from one of those little boogers can sometimes cause permanent brain damage, ranging anywhere from mild to severe. You're not supposed to aim that high.

But they hadn't quite nailed my skull after all, even though I had a pounding migraine the likes of which I don't think you could possibly imagine. I knew it wouldn't last all that long, but it sure did make up in strength what it lacked in duration. I actually don't even remember the last time I cried from physical pain, but that headache was enough to push me over the edge. All I could do was curl up in a ball on the concrete floor and suffer, with tears running down to wet the cement. It was really that bad.

But gradually I did recover somewhat, at least to the point that I could sit up and wipe off my eyes and nose with my grubby hands and feel like I might live, after all. They had me in a ten by twelve foot cell, completely bare except for a metal bench bolted to the wall on one side and painted olive green. But it was warm at least, and that was good since even my pants were pretty ragged by then. Even the toughest paper in the world won't hold up very long under the kind of abuse I'd put it through lately.

As the migraine eased and I was actually able to think again, I sat there glumly and wondered if Philip and the others would ever be able to bust me out. I knew they'd try, of course, but I couldn't delude myself into thinking the odds were in my favor.

I didn't have time to ponder my sad situation for long, though. It couldn't have been more than an hour after the battle when the guards opened my cell again and shoved Hunter and Leah inside. Leah had Davy with her, but there was no sign of anyone else.

I hardly noticed *that,* though. For some reason, every inch of Hunter's skin that I could see had turned lemon yellow. His formerly brownish-blond hair had completely fallen out, leaving him bald as a cue ball, and even his eyebrows and lashes were missing. They were both wearing a set of paper clothes just like mine, only theirs were in much better condition.

"What happened to *you?*" I asked Hunter, staring at him.

"They doused me with nitric acid to kill off whatever spores I might have had on my body," Hunter said, his face reddening a little bit. Well, actually that bright yellow skin caused him to turn orange instead of red, but I knew what was happening.

"Did it hurt?" I asked.

"No, just stung my eyes a little," he said.

I didn't have time to ask him anything else, because just then the guards came back to fetch me for my own nitric acid bath. It stung like the devil on my scrapes and burns, and they took me back to the cell looking every bit as yellow and hairless as Hunter had been, dressed in a brand new set of paper clothes. Then Leah and Davy had their own treatment.

It wasn't quite so bad for Hunter and me, but I couldn't help feeling sorry for Leah; her hair had been down past shoulder-length, and that takes a long time to grow back. She sat on the green bench hugging Davy and crying after she got back, but there was nothing we could do to comfort her.

Oh, I knew we wouldn't look like bananas forever, of course. The yellow stain would fade away in a few weeks or so, and our hair and lashes would grow back in roughly the same amount of time. Soon enough you'd never be able to tell anything happened. But in the meantime we looked pretty ridiculous.

"Where have you two *been* all this time since we got here?" I asked him.

"They were pretty nice to us, actually. We had to have a bunch of blood tests done and who knows what else, but until today at least they let us have normal clothes and they kept us locked up in a pretty nice apartment together. We couldn't get out, but we could have pretty much anything we asked for," Hunter said.

"That's weird," I said, wondering what it was that made those three so special. It wasn't that I grudged them the upscale treatment, but I couldn't help being curious what the reason for it might be. The Defense Forces never do anything without a purpose.

"Very weird, but they never would tell us much," Hunter said.

"That seems to be standard operating procedure around this place," I agreed.

"Anyway they came and got us from the apartment about an hour ago and sprayed me down head to toe with acid before they brought us here, and you know the rest of it," Hunter said.

"I wonder what's going on," I said, and Hunter could only shrug.

Before long we figured out exactly what was going on. Shortly after Leah came back from her shower, they hustled us outside to the rear of the building to where a massive spaceship sat waiting in the back parking lot.

"I don't like the looks of that," Hunter muttered under his breath, but we never got a chance to break free or run. Soldiers had us enclosed on all sides, and we were only outside for less than five minutes before they herded us into the ship.

As soon as they got us inside they stripped us completely naked and hosed us and the entire room down with nitric acid again for at least ten minutes. They mercifully put Leah in a different room for that humiliating debacle, but at least afterward they sprayed us clean with water and gave us towels and real clothes for a change, instead of the paper suits we'd had to wear before. They were only slate-blue Defense Forces combat fatigues, to be sure, but that was good enough for me.

We felt it when the ship took off, though we still didn't know where it was going. But when I felt the gravity fade away, I started to get some inkling of an idea.

"Do you feel that?" I asked aloud.

"Yeah, we're out in space. I wonder where they're taking us," Hunter said.

"My best guess would be Venus," I said.

"But why now? And why at all?" Leah asked, and I could only shrug in reply. Who knew?

"I think they only give out information on a need-to-know basis around here," I said, and for a while we all sat there in glum silence. There wasn't a prayer that Philip would be able to rescue us from another planet, so unless we figured out something for ourselves then we were most likely up the creek.

"I wonder what it's like on Venus," Hunter said after a while, and I was glad for the opportunity to turn my attention to something else besides contemplating our hopeless situation. I knew quite a bit about Venus, actually; the files in the NADF mainframe had been chock full of information about the colony there.

Back in the old days, Venus had been the hottest place in the solar system at over 800 degrees Fahrenheit, and the air pressure had been unbelievably high, almost 93 times what it was on Earth. The atmosphere was made up of 96 percent carbon dioxide and 3 percent nitrogen, not to mention a sizable amount of sulfuric acid. So if you wanted to live in a place where it's hot enough to melt lead and it rains battery acid, Venus would have been your place to pick.

The breeder gases had changed all that in a hurry.

They can't change one kind of atom into another, but they can break chemical bonds and rearrange them in any way necessary. They work as catalysts, facilitating reactions which wouldn't normally take place without them while remaining unchanged themselves. Thus they can break down carbon dioxide into free oxygen and solid graphite. They can break down sulfuric acid into water, oxygen, and free sulphur, and they can bind excess oxygen into surface rock. All that suddenly-solid carbon and sulphur precipitated out onto the lowlands, where it still causes dust storms sometimes. There are technical limits, of course, just as there are with anything; they couldn't make the atmosphere of Venus an exact copy of Earth's. There's simply too much mass of gas there, for one thing. But when all was said and done, they did manage to accomplish a very thick and heavy atmosphere about three and a half times as dense as Earth's, about 88 percent nitrogen and 12 percent oxygen.

That might sound like it wouldn't be enough to keep a flea alive, especially if you knew that Earth's atmosphere is something like 21 percent oxygen. But actually, after taking that heavy air pressure into account, you're far more likely to suffer from getting too *much* oxygen on Venus than not enough. Oxygen at high pressures becomes deadly poisonous, and if you're fool enough to set foot unprotected on certain parts of the planet where the pressure is exceptionally high, then it's entirely possible you might never live to tell about it.

There's also darned little water on Venus. Nowhere near enough to make an ocean, or even a decent sized lake for that matter. Even after terraforming, almost the entire planet is a windy and blistering hot desert, dry as a bone. The average temperature has dropped several hundred degrees, true, but it's still something like 150 degrees Fahrenheit, which isn't something you can survive for very long at a time. There are no seasons to vary it up throughout the year, and the day and the night are each two whole months long. But unlike the Moon, where the air was thinner and thereby aggravates temperature swings, on Venus the very opposite is true. The dense atmosphere means there's hardly any temperature variation at all.

It sounds like an awful place, but as I've said before, all things have their unexpected beauties. Here and there you'll find a really tall mountain or even a range of them, just like you would on Earth, and that's where Venus really shines. Temperatures drop with elevation, just as air pressure does, and way up in the tall mountains the conditions are pretty balmy. For the same happy reason, such little water as actually exists on the planet gets preferentially deposited right on those same mountains as rain or sometimes even snow if you go up far enough. It's like a land of eternal spring, always sunny and mild. The gravity is close enough to Earth that you don't really notice any difference, and the air pressure at that elevation has dropped to only a little more than Earthly conditions. The sky is a deep and cloudless blue, and if it weren't for the fact that the sun rises in the west, you might actually be deluded into thinking you were somewhere on Earth. As it is, that one thing tends to spoil the illusion.

Someday, in a hundred years or so, there'll be time for trees and plants to grow tall and to spread throughout the little range that they have available to them, and when that day comes the place will feel even more Earthlike. It'll never amount to *much*, of course; all the various livable regions of Venus put together still only add up to an area roughly the size of Alaska. That's not much land, compared to the surface of an entire planet. Just scattered islands of life and beauty in the middle of a sea of harsh deadness, but at least it'll last for as long as the sun shines and the rivers flow. Venus is big enough not to have to worry about losing its air.

There are only five sizable highlands on the entire planet, plus a few scattered small ones. I guess the comparison to islands must have struck those first settlers, too, because they named all five of those places after Caribbean islands. Eleuthera, Bermuda, and Barbados are spaced thousands of miles apart, and then Saint Thomas and Saint John are very close together and sometimes even lumped as one. I never managed to remember all the names of the little ones except for Tortuga, and the only reason that one stuck in my mind was because it turned out to be important later on. The deep, dense atmosphere looks almost as blue and hazy as an ocean when you look out on it from one of those mountains, making them feel even more island-like. In fact it's called the Cytherean Sea, after an old word for things that pertain to Venus. It's only an ocean of air and not of water, alas, but it does look that way sometimes.

When I was younger I once read a story about Venus called *Perelandra*, which I remember that I always loved and which has always stuck in my mind as one of the greatest books I've ever read. In that story the whole planet is covered in oceans, with little floating islands here and there. The real Venus is certainly nothing like the land of Perelandra; far from it, but the airy ocean and the few scattered islands did somewhat remind me of it.

The Defense Forces planted their colony on the largest of the highlands, Eleuthera, which is up near the Arctic Circle but every bit as tropical as anywhere else on the planet. They built it right on the southern slopes of Mount Freedom, by far the highest peak on Venus at more than 36,000 feet; taller than Mount Everest and capped with everlasting snow.

The peak was originally named after James Clerk Maxwell the scientist, but I suppose the staffers at Southern Command must have thought Mount Freedom sounded so much more dramatic and inspirational. *Freedom* also happens to be the English translation of the word Eleuthera, actually, and I'm sure that wasn't accidental either. The Defense Forces have always liked to think of themselves as champions of liberty, even at times when they were anything but.

Poor old Dr. Maxwell didn't get completely forgotten, though. The first NADF colonists supposedly named their little settlement Jamestown in his honor, although I suspect that had every bit as much to do with sucking up to Colonel James Burns, the head of the Southern Command who ordered the project to be done in the first place. And yes, I'm sure no one overlooked the reference to that other Jamestown in Virginia, the first successful English colony in America. Maybe they hoped the name would bring them good luck.

Supposedly they had one of the most beautiful views on Venus from that spot, but I suspect having a reliable water source from the snowfields on top of Mount Freedom probably had more to do with why they chose to live there than anything else; water is always in very short supply on that world.

But whatever the reason might have been, there on the bluffs overlooking the Cytherean Sea was the residence of almost three thousand human beings, a city built of stone and brick in the most unlikely place you would ever have imagined.

And all things considered, I don't suppose they had such a bad situation for themselves. They had it better than we ever did at

Lakeside, actually. Had we known about it at the time, we might have tried to flee to Venus instead of to the Moon. I couldn't blame them for wanting to come home if they got the chance, but it still seemed like a pretty soft and easy life to me.

All that was ancient history, though, and when it came to the subject of what might have happened in the years since the plague or who might be in control of Jamestown nowadays, that was anyone's guess. No doubt we'd find out soon enough.

It took only six days in space before we reached the place, and we never got to catch a glimpse of the planet before we landed. Our cell had no windows, and the Defense Forces didn't seem to think we were on a tourist expedition.

In fact we didn't see anything at all till we landed, but when they finally led us out onto the concrete tarmac at Jamestown the first thing I saw was the snowcapped height of Mount Freedom glistening in the morning sun. It was a warm and breezy day, with a strong sun overhead, and when the wind blew in off the Cytherean Sea I could smell the dry, sulphurous odor of the lowland deserts. Thankfully it didn't often blow that way; usually it came down from the heights instead, and then you couldn't smell anything but the crisp scent of distant snow. The immediate area around the airport was covered in trees and grass, like any alpine meadow on Earth might have been.

I noticed all these things as we were taken to a car and driven five or six miles into town, but it didn't seem the time to comment on anything. The buildings were stone and brick; I suppose there hadn't been time for very much wood to grow, yet. The architecture was all built in a similar style, sort of like on an army base. We passed several dozen people in Defense Forces uniform who glanced at us curiously, but then I couldn't really blame them for that. A car full of lemon-skinned baldies is sure to attract attention almost anywhere. They might have thought we were aliens, for all I know. I was pretty curious about *them,* actually, considering they were the first fresh human faces I'd seen in almost four years. Somebody behind the mask of a biohazard suit doesn't count for much.

All of them were young, no more than thirtyish at the very most, but then I guess that might simply have been because they were soldiers. They were about evenly split between males and females, and I couldn't help noticing after a while that every single one of them was remarkably good-looking. The guys were all handsome and the girls were all pretty, without exception. That struck me as a little bit odd, since I couldn't fathom why it should be. But other than that one interesting little tidbit there didn't seem to be anything obviously unusual about them as a whole; just ordinary people you might have met almost anywhere.

After I thought about it for a while I decided maybe all those pretty faces might not be such an oddity, after all. No doubt Colonel Burns and his staff had been painstakingly selective about who they chose for a colonization mission like this, and naturally they had the time and the authority to be just as picky as they pleased. Therefore it stood to reason that every single one of these people was almost certainly the cream of the crop, so to speak; the smartest, strongest, healthiest, most attractive and capable individuals the Defense Forces had been able to lay hands on. Why bring stupid or ugly folks if they didn't have to? They were awfully hard-nosed and practical that way.

The driver took us to one of the larger buildings which seemed to be the town hall, and then we were quietly ushered into a perfectly modern-looking waiting room. It even had tables made of cherry wood and matching leather furniture, and I couldn't help idly wondering how much tax money it had cost to transport all that fancy stuff so far.

The guard left us alone in the waiting room, but then I don't suppose there was any reason why he shouldn't have. We were helpless as goldfish if we tried to escape, in a city full of elite soldiers on an unlivable planet millions of miles from home. They might as well use their resources for other things besides guarding people who had nowhere to run in the first place. Like I said before, they're awfully practical that way.

"I wonder who we're here to see," Hunter said after a while.

"There's no telling, but maybe at least we'll get some answers for a change," Leah said, and we all nodded agreement with that.

"This place is really awesome, though; I can't believe they accomplished so much in such a short amount of time," Hunter commented, and even though I privately had to agree, I was in no mood for giving credit to the Defense Forces for anything at the moment.

"Yeah, the leather sofa is such a nice touch," I said dryly.

But we didn't have any more time to discuss the issue, because just then a secretary emerged from the inner sanctum, beckoning us with her fingertips. We filed into the room one by one, to find a man with salt-and-pepper hair seated in a large leather office chair behind a mahogany desk. His back was turned to us, but as soon as the secretary left the room he turned around.

I immediately heard audible gasps of shock from Hunter and Leah. I'd never seen the man in my life, but apparently *they* had.

Things were turning out to be even more interesting than I thought.

Chapter Six

The man seemed to be enjoying their surprise, because he allowed it to go on for a few seconds before he spoke.

"Mr. McGrath, it's such a pleasure to see you again after all this time, though I doubt you remember me. I do apologize for the regrettable nature of our meeting, but I'm sure you understand that my hands were tied. I'd like to think we can move forward into a more positive relationship henceforth. My name is Colonel Luke Bartow, and I'm the commander of this facility, not to mention Hunter and Leah's father. Kids, I can only apologize for having to disappear as I did, but you see what I've been up to. This place was meant to be the salvation of mankind; I hope you can forgive me for accepting the order to build it," Colonel Bartow said.

I think the others were absolutely speechless, but I was quiet for a different reason. I still remembered enough of what my parents had said about this man not to trust his genial manner or even a single word he said. That little disappearing act he'd referred to didn't incline me to trust him, either. Marie Bartow had idolized the man, and when he supposedly went missing in action in Burma in 2146 she never really got over it. I'd overheard her talking to Aunt Joan about it occasionally over the years, and now to find out that he'd deliberately led her and his children to believe that he was either dead or a prisoner of war when in reality he was sitting safe and contented on Venus the whole time disgusted me. It was the kind of heartless cruelty which there's absolutely never any excuse for. I did my best to cover up the look of instant dislike that threatened to appear on my face, but I'm not entirely sure I succeeded.

"I'm sure it must be overwhelming at the moment, but do sit down and let's talk a little while. I'm sure all of you have questions, just as I do," Colonel Bartow said, gracefully ignoring our silence.

"Why did you bring us here?" I asked, since the others still seemed tongue-tied.

"Good question, Mr. McGrath. I suppose the answer should be obvious for Hunter and Leah; I thought they were dead until very recently, and now that I know otherwise I'd like to get reacquainted. As for you, I believe you and I might have business to discuss," Colonel Bartow said.

"Business?" I asked.

"That's right. My team tells me you've managed to find a vaccination against the Orion Strain. And even though Eleuthera is a beautiful place, I'm sure you understand that our people would like to go home if possible. Our scientists haven't yet been able to find a proven vaccine, even with blood and tissue samples from the survivors to study, so if you have one then that would be of great interest to us," Colonel Bartow said.

"I'm sure it would," I agreed noncommittally.

"I realize your father may have told you certain stories, so let's clear that up right away. I'm afraid I'll have to be very blunt for a moment. Fifteen years ago I was under explicit orders to eliminate your parents as security risks. I wasn't given any option to do otherwise, and if I hadn't carried out the order then someone else would have. I only did what I had to do; nothing more. As a matter of fact, you were supposed to be eliminated also, but I was able to spare *you*, at least," Colonel Bartow said.

"Aren't you still under orders?" I asked. Leah shot me a warning glance, but I chose to ignore it. I wanted to know.

"I think we can all agree that circumstances are different now, can we not?" Colonel Bartow asked.

"Yes, sir. But I want to know exactly *how* different they are," I said, and Colonel Bartow laughed.

"I like you, Mr. McGrath. You're honest. Very well then, I'll tell you exactly how different they are. I'm the high commander on this planet. My word is law in this place. I'm answerable to no one at this point except to Colonel Burns on Mars, who has no interest in this matter and has quite enough of his own issues to deal with. Besides which, there are no more security leaks or outside subversive elements to have to worry about anymore. Every human being on this planet is handpicked to be here, and so are those with Colonel Burns. What we hope for is to go back to being a free and normal people in a free and normal world, without any of the extraordinary security measures which have been necessary for the past few decades or so. If any good should come of the plague at all, then perhaps at least it will set us free of all that. We'd also love for your little group in Hawaii to join us and become a part of building this new society, if you're willing," Colonel Bartow said.

I hesitated, weighing his words carefully. They were noble sentiments, if he really believed them. *That* was the part that worried me; it's all too easy to tell pretty lies with a straight face, especially if you're good at it. The high-handed way he'd behaved since he had us dragged off the beach in chains ten days ago gave me serious doubts that anything had really changed. And even if they had, it's *also* easy to have sincerely good intentions and then scrap them the second they become inconvenient.

"Let me think about it for a day or two," I finally said, and Colonel Bartow never even blinked.

"Of course. I understand your feelings completely. Take as much time as you need; we'll assign you a residence and a car and whatever else you need in the meantime," he said graciously.

"Thanks," I said, and he nodded.

"Now, I do hope you'll accept my sincere and humble apologies for the way you've been treated in the past. If there's anything we can do to make it up to you, please consider me at your complete disposal," he said.

"I'll keep that in mind," I said, feeling a twinge of uncertainty almost in spite of myself. He was being impeccably nice, and I had to choke down my natural impulse to accept the apology and move on with things at face value. I was still mistrustful of the man, in spite of his seeming graciousness. Having somebody round you up at gunpoint tends to do that to a person.

So I sat there quietly while he chatted with Hunter and Leah for a while about various things, and got up to hold Davy for a few minutes and congratulate Leah on getting married and Hunter for earning his pilot's stripes and such similar subjects. I couldn't tell what *they* thought about this sudden reunion. I could sympathize a little bit from my own experience, but the circumstances were very different in my case and the reasons not at all the same. But eventually the interview came to a merciful end.

"Now, as I said, I've assigned a house and a car for the four of you while you're here. There'll be an aide on hand at all times if you should need anything. If you'll join me for dinner this evening we'll continue our talk. But at the moment I'm sure all of you are tired and would like to get settled in, so I won't keep you any longer," Luke Bartow said, rising from his chair.

We did likewise, and when Colonel Bartow pressed a button on the desk, his secretary returned and quietly ushered us back out to the waiting room. The same man who drove us to the town hall was waiting outside to take us to the guest house, which he did without a word.

It turned out to be more of a cabin than a house, built of dark brown stone and set high on a cliff top overlooking the Cytherean Sea to the southwest. It was my first good look at the Sea, and it was then that I noticed how very much like an ocean it really *did* look; the air was so thick and blue we couldn't possibly see all the way to the lowlands at the bottom. But then again it didn't look *quite* like a sea, because there was no clear horizon or any sharp dividing point between air and water. I've never seen anything quite like it on Earth, or anywhere else for that matter.

The cabin itself had a wide lawn of rich green grass that extended right up to the cliff's edge, speckled with hundreds of little reddish-pink blossoms that I didn't recognize.

I stopped for a few seconds to examine them and to gaze out across the Sea, taking note of the small but intriguing fact that even the morning sun held a faint tinge of blue from shining through that dense atmosphere. I suppose it wasn't really the time for idle curiosity, but sometimes I can't help myself.

"At least it'll be interesting here," I muttered under my breath, and then hurried to catch up with Hunter and Leah before they left me behind.

The cabin had a bedroom for each of us, complete with civilian street-clothes in our proper sizes already hanging on pegs in the closets. That was a particularly nice touch, I have to admit. Combat fatigues are all fine and well, but they're not very comfortable if that's not what you're used to wearing. I gratefully slipped on a pair of jeans as soon as I spotted them.

If I'd been the suspicious type (which I was, under the circumstances), I might have wondered if those sweet new threads had some ulterior purpose beyond simply putting us at ease. That might have been part of it, true, but I couldn't help thinking they'd also make us stick out like flies in a mayonnaise jar amongst all those camo-clad soldiers if we ever took a notion to run away. As if the mustard-yellow skin didn't already do a fine enough job of *that*.

But I wore the clothes anyway; it wasn't like we had a snowball's chance of escaping in the first place. Might as well be comfortable in the meantime.

Our assigned aide was waiting on the porch when we came back outside from changing. Her name was Olivia Deming, and she was originally from Dalton, Georgia. She was twenty-three years old, a systems tech, and an expert in Venusian surface conditions, a combination which was probably what earned her a spot in the colony, if I had to guess. She was also even prettier than most, with flawless skin that looked like she'd never used makeup a day in her life, nor ever needed any.

But Olivia didn't have much to say unless we specifically asked for something, and I didn't trust her any more than I trusted Colonel Bartow. In fact, as soon as we got settled in, I led all of us away from the cabin and into the birch woods behind it.

"I don't like this situation at all," I said in a low voice as soon as we were far out of earshot.

"I don't either, but why did we have to go out in the woods to talk about it?" Hunter asked.

"I'm afraid the cabin might be bugged. My father told me they used to do stuff like that back in Tampa all the time," I said.

"Really?" Hunter asked, fascinated. Everybody had tried to avoid badmouthing Luke Bartow in front of his children, so Hunter didn't know most of the stories I'd already heard.

"Yeah, they did. I don't know that it's the same now as it used to be, but we'd be stupid to trust them without verifying it first. Especially after the way they've acted so far," I said.

"That's true," Hunter said, frowning a little.

"But how can we verify *anything*? They're they ones with all the cards," Leah said, speaking up for the first time, and that indeed was a good question.

I'd like to say I came up with some masterful plan to take care of everything, but unfortunately I was stumped at the moment. And from the silence that greeted Leah's words, I'd have to say she and Hunter were pretty stumped, too.

"Never mind. Colonel Bartow did say it was all right if we took a few days to think about everything. Let's take him up on that, and in the meantime we'll pretend we're having a good time and we're willing to let bygones be bygones. It'll give us a while to figure out what to do," I said at length.

So that's what we did, trying our best not to worry about the others back home or anything else. We pretended to be enjoying ourselves in all the touristy ways we could think of, partly to make Colonel Bartow believe I was seriously contemplating joining him, and partly because I wanted to figure out the lay of the land just in case we ever needed to know. There might not be any way to escape at the moment, but that didn't mean I'd completely forgotten about the idea. If an opportunity arose, I wanted to be ready to take advantage of it.

Olivia took us wherever we felt like going, if we asked. We had her take us on a flight up to the summit of Mount Freedom, and it was surprisingly cold up there; around 20 degrees Fahrenheit, and the snowcap showed no signs of melting.

We also visited other places around Eleuthera, to watch the soldiers planting trees and such things as that, and she even took us on a guided hiking expedition downslope into the lowlands to get a taste of the desert. Or at least Hunter and I did; Leah isn't the type of person who enjoys athletic activities like that. Even we didn't make it all the way to the bottom, of course; once the temperature got up to 110 we decided to call it quits, and we were still at ten thousand feet elevation at that point. Olivia said that way down in the very hottest depths of the desert the temperature occasionally hit the 200-degree mark; *definitely* not a place you'd want to visit.

They'd done a lot of work there, I have to give them that. Jamestown is built at the 20,000 foot level, which is close to perfect if you like the outdoors. Always breezy and sun-kissed, with never a cloud in the sky.

But it's also low enough in elevation that it practically never rains, and that won't do at all for crops and grass and most of those other green things people like. So they'd fixed that problem by building several huge dams on the rivers that flowed down from Mount Freedom, along with aqueducts for irrigation. They also had paved roads, sewers and electricity, and a massive farm with row crops that stretched to the horizon. Olivia mentioned that they could only grow things which had a life cycle of less than 58 days, but since that includes most of the common food crops it wasn't such a big issue.

We ate supper with Colonel Bartow at his private home every evening, waited on by aides who served our food on gold-rimmed china with silver forks and Wexford crystal goblets. Whatever else you might say about the man, he definitely enjoyed the sweet life. His house was three stories high, bigger than any other place in town, and it was built of white stucco with four Greek columns across the front of his porch. Pretty fancy stuff.

He was unfailingly courteous and charming whenever we saw him, and after a while I started to wonder if I might have misjudged the man after all.

All these things took several earthly days, but the whole time the sun never moved an inch in the sky, or at least not noticeably. It seemed to be perpetually midmorning, as if time were frozen. The Moon had been like that to a certain extent, but at least there you could very gradually notice the passage of time. Three or four days did produce some definite movement in the sun's position, at least. Here it didn't. The sun seemed to be in the exact same position as when we arrived, which gave the whole place a strange, timeless quality that's hard to explain. It reminded me of what all the hymns say about Heaven; perfect, beautiful, unchanging and eternal. I hope it's not too much to say that, but it's really what it reminded me of. No place else I've ever been has ever struck me quite that way.

But all the while I kept thinking about everything Colonel Bartow had said, about freedom and peace and all those things. I still couldn't quite bring myself to trust him entirely, but the only way I could think of to test the issue was to flatly refuse to give him the vaccine and then see what he did about it. That would be tantamount to calling him a liar and untrustworthy, of course, and if all this seeming niceness really *were* just a pretense then the consequences for not doing what he wanted could be severe. On the other hand, if I were judging him unfairly then I might be passing up a golden opportunity to achieve something wonderful. It was an awfully knotty problem, but try as I might, I couldn't think of any possible way to test the man without refusing to cooperate.

"I'm going to have to tell him no," I finally said one day.

"Why?" Hunter asked.

"Because that's the only way I'll know if he's telling the truth or not. If he accepts my decision and lets us go back home, then I can always change my mind and let them have the vaccine. If he tries to twist my arm and force it out of me then I'll know he can't be trusted," I said.

"He's never been anything less than kind and generous ever since we got here. It'll make us look like ungrateful snots if we say no," Hunter pointed out.

"I realize that, but like I said, I can't think of any other plan that might even remotely work. You know what they say; nothing ventured, nothing gained," I said, and Hunter shrugged.

"I'll do whatever you think is best," he said noncommittally.

"What do you think, Leah?" I asked, turning to her.

"I think he'll do the right thing and it'll all work out for the best for everybody. But you're the only one who can give him the vaccine, Tyke. So I guess it's like Hunter said; I'll go along with whatever you think we should do," she said.

"All right, then. Let's see what happens," I said.

Chapter Seven

Colonel Bartow agreed to see us immediately, just as I'd suspected he would, but I didn't look forward to the coming conversation, not one little bit. Olivia drove us to the town hall and the nameless secretary ushered us into his office after the obligatory ten-minute wait. The good Colonel seemed like his usual genial self, smiling and kissing Davy and all the usual things.

"So, have you decided to help us achieve our goal of a free and happy society?" he asked, looking at me expectantly.

"No, sir, I'm afraid I can't do that. I think everybody here is better off where you are, and so are we," I said firmly.

"I see. And can you explain the reasoning behind this decision?" Colonel Bartow asked.

"No, sir. But that's my decision and I have to ask you to respect it. Please let us go home," I said. Colonel Bartow looked at each of us long and hard, and then finally cleared his throat.

"I suppose the two of you would also like to go back to Earth?" he asked, directing the question to Hunter and Leah.

"That's where my husband is," Leah said, lifting Davy up just a bit, and Hunter only nodded.

"Well, then. I suppose there's really nothing else to be discussed, is there?" Colonel Bartow said briskly, pressing the button to call his secretary. For a second I actually thought I might *have* misjudged the man.

"Thank you, sir," I said, but Colonel Bartow seemed not to notice. Instead he began rummaging around in one of his desk drawers until he found a transmitter about the size of a candy bar.

"If you change your mind, make sure you press the button and let me know, and I'll have someone come and fetch you. But I wouldn't wait too long if I were you; it's awfully hot out there," he said calmly, and alarm bells started to ring in my mind right away.

"What do you mean?" I asked.

"I mean I had hoped we could do this the nice way, but since we obviously can't, then other methods will need to be used. The three of you will be dropped into the lowlands, and if Mr. McGrath changes his mind about giving me the vaccine then all of you will be rescued. If he doesn't then you can die in the desert together," Colonel Bartow said.

"But. . . " Hunter said, wide-eyed. If he was about to try to make some kind of claim on fatherly love, then Colonel Bartow dismissed it out of hand with a weary wave.

"Don't act so shocked and heartbroken, boy. You and your sister have both made it abundantly clear where your loyalties lie. So stay where your hearts are; I have no use for a faithless child," he said.

There are times when there's simply nothing to be said, I suppose, and that was one of them even for me. I remember thinking it all had to be some kind of huge bluff, some elaborate game of brinksmanship; that no one could possibly be so cold and cruel as to condemn his own children to death if he didn't get what he wanted. Of course I knew intellectually that there had been fathers and mothers throughout history who did exactly the same kinds of things, but somehow I'd always thought we lived in a kinder and more enlightened era nowadays.

I guess we don't.

But it still didn't really start to sink in until a pair of aides forcibly took Davy away from Leah and we found ourselves locked inside a military police helicopter with shatter-proof glass separating the pilot's compartment from the prisoners' area, while Olivia flew us out across the Cytherean Sea. If Colonel Bartow was bluffing, then it was a bluff which he had every intention of fulfilling. Leah was crying uncontrollably and Hunter was staring silently out the window; what either one of them might have been thinking at that moment I hardly wanted to imagine.

I thought once again about giving in and telling Colonel Bartow he could have the vaccine. To face a slow and cruel death by heat exhaustion is bad enough when it's only yourself you have to think of, but I was condemning Hunter and Leah to the same fate. They didn't deserve that.

But no. . . that was only fear whispering. I touched my Avenger's ring, and remembered what I'd promised, to fight evil no matter how high the cost. Philip would have told me to be faithful and true, I'm quite sure of it. And if he'd been the one in my shoes, then I knew already what choice *he* would have made, beyond a shadow of a doubt. I couldn't give in to treachery, nor could I willingly hand over the world to a cruel man who believed that the ends justified the means. He might end up getting it anyway, but he'd have to do it without any help from me.

But while I thought thus, Olivia spoke up for the first time.

"Are y'all gonna change your minds about helping Colonel Bartow?" she asked abruptly.

"No," I said firmly, before anyone else could speak.

"That's what I thought. He's really serious about leaving you in the desert to die, you know," she said.

"I know, but if you're trying to change my mind it won't work. I can't help a man like that rule the world, no matter what," I said.

"I'm not trying to change your mind, Mr. McGrath. But I think maybe there's something I could do to help you," she said, and at that I suddenly quit feeling like Bowie at the Alamo and started wondering if there might be a way to survive this thing after all.

"What did you have in mind?" I asked neutrally.

"Let me tell you what I can and cannot do. Colonel Bartow ordered me to leave you somewhere on a seamount in the high desert, where it's not too hot to kill you immediately but where it's too far to make it back to Eleuthera and you'll have to give in before long. I can't countermand a direct order. But he didn't specify which seamount it had to be. I can't be gone too long or it'll create suspicion, but I think there's time to make it as far as Tortuga. That's the closest highland to Eleuthera. If I leave you on a seamount really close to there at the ten thousand foot mark then that's still obeying orders, but you can pretty easily cross over to Tortuga and climb the rest of the way up to survive," Olivia said.

"I don't know how to thank you," I said.

"You just did. But don't thank me too much. We've been working on all the islands, but Tortuga is only partly finished. There's water to drink, and the rivers and creeks have been seeded with algae and fish and whatnot, but no one's worked with the trees or the grass much other than to scatter some seeds and some nitrogen-fixing fungi and bacteria into the soil. It'll be pretty barren, I'm afraid. There are probably a few workmen's sheds and such, but it won't amount to much," she said.

"It's more than we dared hope for," I said.

So that's what we did, and Olivia really did right by us; she left us just below the twelve thousand foot mark instead of at the ten, and she found us a seamount barely a mile from the main slope of Tortuga, and connected to it by a saddle not much lower than the place where she dropped us off. Even better, there was a little creek to follow upstream as soon as we reached the mainland, so we could stay cool and not get lost. It was still 100 degrees in the shade even at that elevation, and we definitely needed the water.

She pushed a button to release the locks and let us out when the helicopter landed, and the first thing I noticed was the sizzling heat starting to pour in as soon as the first crack appeared in the door. But there was no time to waste if we wanted to survive, so we jumped out and immediately headed for the saddle on foot while Olivia took off and headed back to Jamestown. No doubt to report to Colonel Bartow that her mission was accomplished, I thought bitterly.

It only took us about thirty minutes to reach the creek coming down the main slope, and from there we headed upwards as fast as we dared. The creek was no more than a trickle that far down, since most of it had already evaporated by then. That's how all the creeks and little rivers on the Venusian highlands are; they rise in rain and snowmelt on the high mountains, flow downhill for a little way, and then evaporate in the pitiless heat below a certain elevation. Then part at least of the water vapor rises right back up to fall as snow again on the very mountain it just came down from, and so the cycle begins once more.

Twelve thousand feet is almost the extreme limit of where you'll find anything living on Venus. Below that and it's just too hot for most things to survive. Temperatures above 105 degrees Fahrenheit will destroy enzymes in living cells, and if conditions don't cool off pretty soon then any organism exposed to those kinds of temperatures will die. There are certain kinds of bacteria and very specialized worms which can survive hotter environments in water, true, but when we're talking about ordinary living things like animals, plants, or human beings, then as soon as the mercury hits the 105 mark you better start saying your prayers.

That's why, on Venus at least, the lowermost limit of a highland area is by definition set at 12,000 feet, because that's the uttermost limit of where ordinary living things can reasonably be expected to survive for any length of time.

But we still had ten thousand feet of hard climbing to reach the place we were shooting for, and that's a tall order, pun definitely intended. Think of having to climb a medium-sized peak in the Rockies all the way from base to summit and you'll get a good idea of what a long hike we still had to face. That's a workout for anybody.

It took us two days to make it, mostly because we had to take it easy in the lower stretches because of the heat. But that gradually slacked off as we got higher, till we finally reached an elevation where the conditions were roughly similar to Jamestown. That's where we stopped, and truth to tell there wasn't really much more mountain left above that point. Tortuga is a tiny spot on the map, only about the size of Key West; it was *nothing* compared to one of the massive highlands like Eleuthera or Saint Thomas.

But that also means it's a much dryer place than Eleuthera, since the one and only mountain is nowhere near as high as Mount Freedom. In fact it's not even tall enough to be snowcapped, and that means Tortuga is completely dependent on such scanty rainfall as there is, since there's no snowpack to serve as a storage device.

There are only a few little creeks on the whole island, and even those are not always entirely reliable.

I think the island used to be a volcano, actually; there are an awful lot of those on Venus. The reason I think so is because the mountaintop contained what looked like the remains of an old caldera, along with a small crater lake at the bottom. It was cool enough up there to need a windbreaker, and I suppose the low temperature probably helped prevent as much evaporation as there might have been otherwise. Considering the precarious nature of the island's water supply in general, that one little permanent lake was a good thing indeed. It was enough to feed and water us in a pinch, even if everything else dried up between showers.

In any case, the creek Olivia had left us to follow flowed right through the semi-abandoned base camp which the soldiers used from time to time when they came down to work on the island, so we moved into one of the cabins there and made ourselves as comfortable as we could. There was practically nothing to eat besides fish, and I thought to myself what rich irony it was that no matter where I traveled in the entire universe, I seemingly could never escape having to eat fish.

But I didn't grumble about it this time, much as I wanted to. I've learned to be a lot more philosophical about hardships than I used to be.

It was a little harder to be philosophical about the idea of spending the rest of my life barely clinging to survival in the backwoods of Venus, though I couldn't think of any way to get around it unless I decided to submit to Colonel Bartow's demands. Other than that, we could no more cross the desert on foot than we could have crossed the galaxy on a motorcycle.

Or so I thought, until we came across the thermal suits.

I suppose the workers had to use them now and again, when they had business that took them somewhere uncomfortably far downslope into hotter territory than they liked. Nothing very unusual about that, nor even about the fact that they'd leave a couple of them stored at the base camp. After all, what could happen to them? But those two suits immediately gave me an idea.

We could walk it.

I'd done something similar on Titan, after all, and Venus should be a cakewalk compared to *that*. True, the distance was a lot farther, but on the other hand we'd also be able to eat and drink along the way and rest when we needed to, and that makes a big difference. Then whenever we made it back to Jamestown, we could steal one of the colony ships and hightail it back home. Hunter would have to fly it, but supposedly Jesse had taught him all that stuff. Leah would have to stay behind on Tortuga since there were only two suits, but she shouldn't have any problem surviving till we could come back and scoop her up. She might die of boredom in the meantime, but at least that would be the worst problem she had to face.

"Here's what I think we should do," I said one night, and proceeded to tell them my whole plan for getting us out of there. We were sitting around a campfire by the creek eating roasted fish, and I judged the time was ripe.

"Do you think you can fly one of those big ships, Hunter?" I finally asked, turning to look at him. That was the linchpin of the whole plan, of course, and if Hunter wasn't up to it then we might as well forget about the idea and try to work out some other strategy.

"I can handle it," he agreed quickly.

"Even the part about flying us home? You've never been out in space before," Leah reminded him. She'd been coping better without Davy than I thought she would, but maybe it did her good to be making some concrete plans instead of living in agony without hope.

"No, but Jesse's been teaching me. I think I can do it. There's always got to be a first time for everything, you know," Hunter said. That wasn't the most reassuring way of putting things, but since the only other alternative was to live out our lives on Tortuga scrabbling for survival, I was inclined to risk it.

"How far is it to have to walk?" Leah asked.

"About eight hundred miles, maybe a little more," I said.

"Do you have any idea how long that would take?" she asked, sounding skeptical.

"If we managed to walk twenty miles a day, which is about normal, then it'd take us about forty days," I said.

"That's impossible," she said flatly.

"Not quite. Hard, yes, but not quite impossible," I said.

"You do realize it'll be after dark by then, don't you?" Hunter asked, and to be honest I hadn't thought of that. As I said before, you tend to forget about the passage of time on Venus after a while. But sure enough, in forty days it would be several days after sunset, and I already knew without needing to be told that the Venusian night would be black as pitch. The planet has no moon at all, and the atmosphere is so thick it scatters light far more than Earth's does. Think of the darkest night you can ever remember, and that's something like what the nights on Venus are *always* like. Not to mention the fact that the darkness would last for 58 earth-days just like the sunshine had.

But then again, twilight also lasts a long, long time, so it would take several days to get completely dark after sunset. If all went well, we ought to have just enough time.

"I think it'll be all right. We've still got twilight to back us up," I said, with more confidence than I really felt.

"We'll have to carry enough food and water to last us. That won't be easy," Hunter said.

"Food we can handle, even if it's only dried fish. Water we'll have to recycle, but that's okay; I see plenty of plastic bottles and tubes around here. It's not hard to build a distillation apparatus with stuff like that," I said. The thought of drinking recycled sweat and urine was mildly disgusting, I have to admit, but it's really no different than what happens in a spaceship on long voyages.

"What about Davy?" Leah finally asked, and that was a question I'd been dreading.

"I'm not sure. We'll have to see where he is, and if there's anything we can do to get him out. We won't abandon him, I promise," I said, hoping we'd be able to keep that promise.

It puzzled me at first why Colonel Bartow wanted to keep Davy like that, but I suppose even a man of such low caliber might still have his own obscure scruples. From what I hear, he supposedly fished me out of the Gulf fifteen years ago and even took the trouble of having me delivered to Philip and Joan's house. So maybe he didn't like to hurt little kids; God bless him for that much, at least. And then again Davy was his grandson, after all, and no doubt he probably thought a six month old baby was still young enough to mold and shape the way he wanted him to turn out. There was probably a certain amount of truth to that, sadly. And then he probably *also* thought it might cause Leah to put some extra pressure on me to give him what he wanted, out of fear for her baby. Whatever his precise reasons might be, I was sure as taxes that everything he'd done was calculated right down to the last jot and tittle for maximum manipulation value.

In fact, a dim suspicion had begun to grow in my mind that maybe even Olivia's apparent kindness might not have been quite what it seemed. Looking back, it was hard to believe that she would have bucked official orders like that, even though she'd tried to make it appear that way. But it was too easy to track where the helicopter had been, and it seemed unlikely that Colonel Bartow would have entrusted such an important mission to someone who was anything less that one hundred percent loyal; that seemed to be something he placed a huge premium on. And if that were the case, then he'd meant for us to end up on Tortuga from the very beginning.

That made sense, in a way; we wouldn't have survived very long on a hot seamount with no water, and Colonel Bartow wouldn't have given me that transmitter if he didn't still want the vaccine.

So maybe everything that had happened so far had all been just an elaborate game of chess, and Colonel Bartow was pulling our strings like any good manipulator, scaring us with how ruthless he was willing to be and then keeping us off balance by making us think we had a friend who wasn't all bad, while in reality condemning us to live on a barely-survivable mountaintop in the middle of nowhere until I cracked from the pressure and gave him what he wanted.

The more I thought about it the more certain I was that I had things figured out, and the more disgusted I felt with the man. All I ask is to be treated honorably, not maneuvered and stage-managed behind my back. If Colonel Bartow had simply come to Kona himself at the very beginning and explained his situation and asked for my help, then chances were I probably would have given him the vaccine just for the asking. There was never a need for *any* of this.

But then again, if Colonel Bartow had been the kind of man who dealt fairly and treated people with respect, then quite a few things would have turned out differently already. If he'd never tried to kill my parents then my life would've turned out radically different. If he hadn't left his family for his work then Hunter and Leah never would have gone to the Moon with us, and then Davy never would have been born. There was no telling what other things might have changed.

One of Philip's favorite things to say is that all things work together for good to those who love God; not just some things or most things, but really and truly *all* things. And when I considered it I guess I could see the truth of that in some cases. The jury was still out in others (like right then, for instance), but I sure did hope Philip was right.

That didn't mean I had to like or approve of Colonel Bartow or his actions, of course; it only meant he'd eventually go the way of every other wicked villain I'd ever read about whose plans fell to nothing in the end. And that was an amazingly encouraging thought, under the circumstances.

We immediately got to work on my escape plan once everything was decided, drying fish and building a portable plastic water distillery, which is one of those indispensable items you really should never leave home without. Then when all was said and done, and the food was packed along with as much water as we could carry, we put on our thermal suits and headed out.

Chapter Eight

I'm not sure what I expected things to be like, down there in the lowlands. I knew it would be hot, of course, and I wasn't disappointed in that respect. Thermal suits have built-in air conditioners for situations like that, but we didn't dare use them any more than absolutely necessary. AC units pull quite a bit of power, and even though the batteries on our suits were designed to recharge themselves automatically from solar cells, they couldn't keep up with a constant load like that. If we dragged them down faster than they could replenish themselves then soon enough they'd go dead, and then it wouldn't be too long before we ended up the same way.

So it was miserably hot and stayed that way, and sometimes the temptation to flip the switch on high and be truly cool for a while was almost unbearable. Only the knowledge that it would mean certain death kept me from doing it. I had sweat soaking my hair, sweat trickling down my back, sweat getting into my eyes and burning. Not to mention my boots were usually ankle-deep in sweat by the end of every day, which I then had to pour into the distillery and drink for breakfast. Nor did we dare let the dry salts go to waste, either. We had to eat those to keep up our electrolyte balance. Yummy thought, isn't it?

But the heat and the sweat I was in some measure prepared for. What I *wasn't* prepared for was the pressure. It grew and grew as we descended the mountain, and by the time we reached the lowlands it felt almost like we were walking along on the bottom of a swimming pool. It took extra work to breathe, and even though the wind was slow it was also heavy, like ocean waves. Anytime a little gust came along it was liable to knock us over or even pick us right up off our feet like a leaf in the breeze if it was just a bit stronger. Not only that, but sounds were incredibly magnified, to the point that it was almost painful sometimes even to listen to the tread of our own footsteps.

Our whole world was made up of burning hot sands of gritty black graphite, the waste products of terraforming the atmosphere. The black sand reminded me crazily of Titan, and the foul rotten-egg smell of sulphur hung heavily in our noses when it mixed with our sweat. My Avenger's ring turned black as coal with tarnish as the silver reacted enthusiastically with the sulphur in the air, to the point that I couldn't even read Barthélemy's name anymore. Here and there were slabs of dark basaltic rock we had to avoid, but for the most part it was nothing but eternal plains of hardpan desertscape, interspersed with multicolored dunes of black graphite or yellow sulfur or even whitish ones of real sand, with the horizon forever cloaked in bright and beautiful blue from that thick air. In fact it was an almost incredibly bright and beautiful blue, like the color of the ocean around some coral reef in the tropics.

I don't know if it was a curse or a blessing, but we also started to get intoxicated from the excess nitrogen pressure after a while, just like divers sometimes do when they go too deep or stay down for too long. The only difference being, of course, that we couldn't drown on Venus. We just got semi-drunk and stayed that way almost the whole time. That's an insanely unwise thing to do when you're in dangerous circumstances because then you can't think as clearly as you should, but I have to admit it kept us happy as clams while we crossed what ought to have been a terrifying landscape. We laughed when the wind tossed us around like scraps of paper, even when it hurt. We sang old songs and told stupid jokes and laughed without a care in the world, and slept like babies curled up on the burning sands.

But there was something down there even more dangerous than all the other perils put together, and that was the constant threat of oxygen poisoning. You need about 200 millibars of oxygen pressure to survive, and you can get along all right on less than half that. But anything over about 400 millibars is deadly. It takes a little while to kill you, of course; anywhere from a few hours to a few days, but it will most certainly get the job done sooner or later. The oxygen pressure in the Venusian lowlands varies anywhere from 300 to 500 millibars depending on exactly how deep you actually are, and we didn't have the instruments to tell us that information. All we could do was march blindly ahead and pray we didn't blunder into any dangerously low spots.

No sane person would have kept going under circumstances like that, so maybe it was a good thing after all that we stayed too drunk on nitrogen to think about it much. When I look back now I shudder, but at the time I honestly remember thinking it was the grandest adventure I'd ever had in my life. Such of it as I can remember, that is.

In fact, I can most humbly say that it's only by the grace of God we ever made it across at all. By all rights, our skeletons should still be lying there as relics for some future archaeologist to wonder over. But they say God watches over kids, drunks, and fools, and I guess at the time we had all three bases covered pretty securely.

But the narcotic effect of the nitrogen gradually started to fade as we climbed the steadily rising shelf that led up into the highlands of Eleuthera, and along with it went all our boozy good times. We started to remember that it was blistering hot, that our bodies hurt and our lungs ached, that we were hungry and unbelievably thirsty and that we hadn't had a bath in forty days.

Eventually we climbed high enough that the temperature dropped into the 80's outside, and at that point we gladly shed our thermal suits.

It was long after sunset by then, and we found ourselves crossing an almost table-like plain in the slowly gathering dusk. It was covered in tufts of short grass, and before we knew it we found ourselves splashing into a shallow lake of unbelievably foul-smelling sulphurous water.

We couldn't have cared less about that, since we were both pretty foul-smelling ourselves, I'm quite sure. We plunged into the bathtub-warm waters, washing away our sweat and grime and drinking huge mouthfuls of the stuff. At any normal time it would have tasted just as nasty as it smelled, but these were no ordinary times.

"Where are we, do you think?" Hunter asked when we'd had our fill of splashing and dragged ourselves to the rocky edge of the pool to keep soaking our aching muscles for a while longer.

"Somewhere in Eleuthera, that's all I know," I said.

"I don't see the mountain," he pointed out.

"No. . . we must have come up somewhere pretty far from Jamestown," I agreed.

"How do we find it, then?" he asked.

"Well, we've got to be somewhere on the southern coast, and so is the town, so that means it can only be one of two directions. Either west or east," I said.

"Yeah, but which one?" Hunter asked.

"That I don't know, buddy. We must have drifted off course along the way, but it's hard to say by how much. To tell you the truth, I was so drunk on nitrogen it's a wonder we ever made it here at all," I said, feeling a chill in the pit of my stomach at the thought. It's funny the way memories can scare you like that, isn't it? You'd think there'd be nothing in the world less scary than something you already know turned out all right, but that's not the way the human mind sees things, I don't guess.

"Yeah, me too. I don't even remember half the trip," Hunter admitted.

"Well, let's try to reason it out if we can; at least enough to make a guess. The wind probably blew us off course quite a bit, even if nothing else did," I said.

"Well. . . we had to be somewhere between 30 and 60 degrees north latitude. That's supposed to be in the westerly wind flow zone, so it seems like we'd end up too far eastward in that case," Hunter said.

I'd forgotten about wind flow zones, actually, although it didn't surprise me that Hunter knew; I'm sure it was something Jesse taught him as it related to piloting. But he was overlooking one thing: Venus rotates backwards, and that means the wind flow patterns are exactly opposite of what they'd be on any other planet.

"That's true, on Earth. But don't forget about the retrograde rotation here. That should invert all the wind flows," I said.

"So then the wind would have pushed us too far west?" he asked.

"That's my best guess. It's a miracle we ever survived out there," I said, glancing southward again.

"God must have something left for us to do, that's all," Hunter said, trying to make light of it.

"No doubt He does," I agreed.

"But anyway, what do we do for the night? We won't be able to travel in the dark, you know," Hunter said.

"You had to mention that, didn't you?" I said, shaking my head.

"It's kind of important, don't you think?" he asked.

"Yeah, I was just being ironic. I guess we might as well stay here by the lake. At least that way we'll have plenty of water, and maybe even some fish," I said, and Hunter nodded.

"I guess so," he agreed.

So that's what we did, and on the whole I can't really complain too much. It was dark as black velvet except for a billion stars strewn thickly across the sky, just barely enough light to keep from stumbling over our own feet. A cold breeze started wafting down from the mountains to the east as the night wore on, chilly enough that Hunter and I had to sleep with our backs up against each other to try to conserve some warmth, since we didn't have any blankets. We gathered up a bed of hay to make things a little more comfortable than sleeping on the bare ground, but there's really not much you can do by starlight except sit there and talk.

We did an awful lot of that over the next seven weeks, waiting for daylight to come. Hunter and I had never been particularly close before then; up till very recently he'd always been one of the little kids in my mind, one bean in a pod along with many others, someone I helped with algebra now and then or the boy who

stepped on a bug and nearly got all of us eaten alive at Desolation
Island on the Moon. But now I started to realize he was actually
beginning to grow up into an interesting person in his own right.
And what's more, I liked him. He was a refreshingly down to earth
kind of kid, low-key and easygoing.

"So what about you and Veronica?" I asked one day, mostly out
of curiosity.

"What about us?" he asked.

"Well, I guess you two are going out, right?" I asked.

"Yeah, since last spring. Jesse keeps ribbing me about going out
with older women 'cause she's two whole *hours* older than I am,"
Hunter said.

"Yeah, that sounds like something Jesse would say," I agreed.

"He tried to tell her she's a cradle robber but she told him it was
either me or Johnny and that kind of shut him up, I think," Hunter
said.

I could see how it would, at that. Johnny Weiss is an okay dude,
I guess, but he's not the kind of boy you'd want your little sister to
go out with. Or at least not the kind Jesse would want *his* sister to
go out with, I should say. Jesse is too much of a proud red-blooded
hayseed and Johnny is too refined and musical. Both of them are
good people in their own way, but put them together in the same
room and they clash painfully.

We talked about that and all kinds of other things during the long
night, and when I wasn't sleeping or talking to Hunter I was usually
thinking about Danielle and wondering what she was up to. In
reality she'd never been far from my mind, of course, except maybe
while I was crossing the desert and too drunk on nitrogen to
remember my own name half the time.

There was no telling what might have happened to her and the
others, though. I *hoped* they'd gotten away and gone back home to
Hawaii, or failing that I hoped Colonel Bartow still had them locked
up at Southern Command in Atlanta for his techs to run
experiments on. I didn't want to consider the other possibility, that
he might have eliminated all of them as being no more use to him.

"What do you think he's done with Davy?" Hunter asked on
another occasion.

"I think he probably means to keep him and raise him the way he thinks a kid ought to turn out. I don't figure he'll ever give him back willingly, if that's what you mean," I said.

"No, I didn't think so either. I think even if you pushed the buzzer and gave him the vaccine, then as soon as he got what he wanted he'd just drop us all three off somewhere else in the deep desert to laugh our heads off while we died from heat stroke," Hunter said bitterly.

"I'm sorry about what happened, buddy boy. That was uncalled for, the way your dad acted," I said.

"Well. . . it is what it is. If he doesn't want me then that's his own loss, not mine," Hunter said.

"If it's any consolation, the rest of us are awful glad to have you," I said, wanting to make him feel better. And he did smile a little.

"I know. Like I said, it's his own loss, not mine. He's got screwy ideas about what's important in life; he always has had. I was only five when he disappeared to take this assignment; he was willing to let me and Leah and Mama think he was dead because he felt like this was more important. And I'm not even necessarily saying it wasn't, you know; I understand that people have to make sacrifices sometimes for the greater good. It's just. . . I don't know, I wish it seemed like he *cared*, that's all, like he at least missed us a little. It's not nice to feel like you don't matter," Hunter said.

"No, it's not," I agreed.

"I doubt he knows we're back on Eleuthera, though; he wouldn't think it's possible to walk eight hundred miles across the deep desert with nothing but a thermal suit and a homemade plastic distillery," Hunter said, changing the subject.

"I don't know that I blame him. If I had it to do over again, knowing what I know now, there's no way I'd try to pull a stunt like that again. The nitrogen alone could have killed us, or there could have been a dust storm that buried us alive, or we could've died from electrolyte imbalance, or all kinds of things. I *still* can't believe we survived," I said, shaking my head.

"Me neither, but since we *did* survive then we should probably start making some plans about what to do from here on out, don't you think?" Hunter asked.

"Snatch a colony ship, pick up Leah, and then go home," I said.

"Well, yes, but these *are* Defense Forces soldiers we're talking about, even if they're mostly on agricultural duty nowadays. They've got some discipline and firepower, you know," Hunter said.

"That's true, but I bet they've gotten pretty careless about guarding things in a place like this, considering there's really nothing to guard against. They won't be expecting *us* to show up, as long as we don't tip them off," I said.

"Well, we're both about the right age to be soldiers," he said.

"I'm not sure we could just blend in, Hunter, if that's what you're thinking. Even if we managed to steal some NADF uniforms, these yellow fingernails would still give us away in a heartbeat," I said.

Our skin had worn back down to normal again while we crossed the desert, and our eyebrows and lashes had grown back too, along with enough burr-headed hair that we didn't look like egg-heads anymore. But fingernails and toenails take a lot longer to grow than skin does, and *those* at least were still yellow as lemons. There was no way they'd pass for normal if anybody got a good look at them.

"Not if we wore some gloves," Hunter pointed out.

"That's true, if we could find any. I don't remember seeing anything like that very often while we stayed at the cabin. It's never cold enough to need them," I said.

"Well. . . maybe by morning they'll have time to grow off and it won't matter anymore," Hunter finally said.

He did have a point when it came to that; dawn was still over a month away, and nails do grow off eventually. I couldn't remember offhand how long that was supposed to take, but when I thought about it I realized we would have spent nearly four months on Venus by the time the sun came up. Surely that was enough time to grow a fingernail.

"Maybe so," I agreed.

"Then I guess we'll wait and hope for the best. But either way I still think we should try to get hold of some uniforms. That way we can move around a little easier without getting caught," Hunter said.

"All right, good enough. But I still don't know what to do about Davy. Snatching one of those ships and getting away ourselves will be hard enough, but finding *him* and getting away might be a whole 'nother thing altogether," I said.

"Yeah, I know," Hunter admitted.

"Don't worry, though; we'll find him somehow. No man left behind, you know," I said wryly, quoting one of the Defense Forces' own most famous mottoes.

"Not to mention Jesse and Leah would never forgive us if we left him," Hunter said.

"No doubt," I agreed.

"I doubt he'll be with my dad, if that's any help. I'm sure the great and powerful Colonel Bartow is much too busy and important to have time to take care of a baby. He probably farmed him out to an aide," Hunter said.

"Probably so, but I imagine he takes a pretty personal interest, too. He'd probably keep him *fairly* close by, if not in the same house then at least next door," I said.

"Well, then, the first place to look would be at the Colonel's house," Hunter said.

"Yeah, but it'll need to be during the workday while he's not at home. That way there won't be near as many people around. We'll have to be careful about that," I said.

"All right then; that's what we'll do. But there's one other thing, though," Hunter said.

"What's that?" I asked.

"What do we do when all this is over? I mean yeah, we might all make it back home, but what then? There's nothing to stop them from mounting another stealth operation to capture us again, anytime they feel like it," Hunter pointed out.

"Yeah. . . that's true," I admitted.

"So what do we do about it, then? There aren't enough of us to man the planetary defense systems, not even by computer. We'd never know when they were coming, and even if we did there wouldn't be much we could do about it," he said.

"Let me think a minute," I said, waving my hand for him to stop. I hadn't thought that far ahead, truthfully, but he was absolutely right. Escaping now wouldn't mean a thing if they could come scoop us up again anytime they felt like it. We were completely at their dubious mercy, and somehow, some way, that had to change or we'd *never* be safe.

But what could we do?

I suppose we could've killed Colonel Bartow, much as I didn't like the idea. But that wouldn't do a whole lot of good unless we killed Colonel Burns too, and probably several of their chief underlings to boot.

Or I suppose we could have come back and spread some Orion spores on Venus and Mars and probably wiped out both colonies completely. But there was something in my heart that wouldn't let me even think about taking Dr. Weiss's path. That would have turned us into monsters; even worse ones than Colonel Bartow and his henchmen were. I may be a lot of things, but I don't have it in me to become a mass killer.

Then I thought of another possibility. We could always blow up the colony ships.

There were only six of them altogether, and it was highly doubtful the folks on Venus and Mars would ever be able to scrounge up the technical skill to build a new one. It takes an entire functioning technological society to be able to produce a complex piece of equipment like that, and a few thousand people living in a wilderness colony wouldn't even begin to have the resources and the know-how. They'd be stranded, with only the faintest of hopes that they'd ever make it back to Earth.

That plan definitely had possibilities.

"What do you think about blowing up their ships?" I finally asked, and Hunter was quiet for a minute while he considered it.

"You don't think they could fix them, or build new ones?" he asked.

"Not if we make sure to wreck them so badly they can't be fixed. They don't have mines or refineries here, nor circuit board factories or precision machining nor anything else they'd need to rebuild a ship. They'd be stuck here for decades at the very least before they could build up enough industry to rig a ship, and by that time they might not have the know-how anymore. For all practical purposes they'd be stuck here," I said, warming to my plan.

"Seems kind of cruel to leave them here like that, don't you think?" Hunter asked.

"Not so much. These people always believed they'd have to live here forever even before they first set foot on Eleuthera. We won't be taking anything from them that they weren't already prepared for," I said.

"What about the ones on Mars? Won't they come rescue them?" Hunter asked.

"They might. We'd have to make an expedition to go blow up their ships, too," I said.

"If you say so," Hunter said, sounding skeptical.

"I know it wouldn't be easy, but can you think of a better plan?" I asked tiredly.

"No, not really," he admitted.

"Then we better try it. There are missiles on board those big colony ships, aren't there?" I asked.

"There should be," Hunter agreed.

"Then let's do it," I said.

Chapter Nine

By the time the first golden rim of the sun inched its way above the horizon in the west, our yellow-stained nails had finished growing off and we were finally back to normal again from head to toe. We trudged eastward across a seemingly endless plain covered in tough grasses and pockmarked here and there with shallow sulphurous lakes, sometimes literally a mile wide and ankle deep. We found out later that most of western Eleuthera is like that; a vast plateau ringed by high mountains everywhere except on the south, which has the effect of trapping snowmelt in the center and creating those myriad little foul-smelling lakes and playas. It's a watery situation which exists nowhere else on Venus, and I guess it must have reminded somebody of home, because on the map at Jamestown it's labeled as the Minnesota Plain, and the mountains that surround it are called the Mesabi Range.

It turned out we were almost two hundred miles from Jamestown, when all was said and done. But it was hard to get lost on that flat and empty tableland, and then looking out from the eastern face of the Mesabi Range we were finally able to catch a glimpse of Mount Freedom, glistening white in the early morning sun. After that all we had to do was set our sights on the peak.

The closer we got to Jamestown the more cautiously we proceeded, wary of any teams who might be out working the land.

But we saw no one, and by the time we slipped into the vicinity of the airfield we were a little more confident. The place seemed to be completely deserted, which reinforced my theory that the Defense Forces had gotten lax and careless about guard duty on a planet where there was nothing to guard against. I didn't see the colony ships, but there were several planes and helicopters we probably could have slipped away with right then and there. There wouldn't have been a soul to stop us or even to notice.

"Awfully sure of themselves, aren't they?" I muttered, looking out across the airfield.

"Yeah, but why shouldn't they be? They're they only human beings on the planet, after all," Hunter pointed out.

"Except for us, you mean," I said.

"Yeah, except for us. But I'm sure that idea never crossed their minds. If they ever thought there was the slightest chance of us escaping from Tortuga they probably would've shot us first and asked questions later," Hunter said.

That was no doubt true, and as a matter of fact was probably *still* true; a thought which I didn't like to ponder too much.

"I wonder where the colony ships are," I said.

"Maybe they don't usually keep them here. This is awfully far north to build a spaceport, you know," Hunter said, and that was undeniably true, of course. Jamestown is located at sixty-two degrees north latitude, which is somewhat comparable to Anchorage, Alaska. *Not* a good place for a spaceport. Ships could *land* there, of course, and probably often did when they had cargo to unload. But for launches you really need to be as close to the equator as possible, and Eleuthera is just about as far from the equator as you can possibly get. Under those circumstances it was entirely possible and even likely that they might have built a launch facility somewhere else on the planet.

"Maybe," I said, not liking that idea. The plan would never work if we couldn't figure out where the ships were kept. It was probably common knowledge in Jamestown, of course, but for that very reason it would make us look odd for having to ask.

"There might be a map somewhere inside the airport," Hunter suggested, and that was actually a pretty good idea.

"Well, let's slip over there and see if we can find some uniforms, then," I finally said, nodding at the terminal building. There was no way to hide or be stealthy at that point, so our only choice was to walk as quickly as possible to the terminal and slip indoors, our hearts in our throats the whole time for fear that some half-sleeping guard might spot us and cry an alarm.

But that didn't happen, and once inside the terminal we found several dusty airmen's uniforms. It wasn't exactly what we'd been hoping for, but they were definitely better than the ragged and filthy street clothes we'd been wearing every single day for the past three months. We quickly changed, using the terminal's small restroom to clean up and brush our hair and try our pitiful best to make ourselves look snappy. NADF soldiers *never* went out in public looking slovenly and disheveled; it simply wasn't done. Showing up in Jamestown looking like we'd slept in our clothes and forgotten what a comb looked like would have been as sure a way to get busted as if we'd gone right up and knocked on Colonel Bartow's front door.

Then I found myself balked by a ridiculous thing. Hunter didn't have to shave yet but I certainly did, and that takes some doing when you've got a three month beard to get rid of. There was a pair of scissors in the restroom which I could cut it short with, but that wasn't good enough. Soldiers were always clean-shaven, without exception, and unfortunately there was no razor to be found anywhere in the building.

I managed it eventually by using the big blade of my pocketknife and a bar of soap, but dang it *hurt*. Try scraping your hair off with a knife sometime and see how it feels, no matter how sharp the blade may be. I left the restroom with my face stinging, and Hunter looked at me sympathetically.

"You're bleeding, you know," he finally said.

"Is it bad?" I asked. Going downtown with a wooly booger beard would have gotten us arrested, but it wouldn't be very much better to show up looking like a stuck pig, either.

"Bad enough. It looks like you tried to shave with a really dull razor and cut yourself several times, that's all," he said.

"That's pretty much what I *did* do," I said dryly.

"Well. . . maybe it'll stop in a minute. We can't go out on the streets with you looking like that," he said.

"Just wait; your time's coming soon enough," I said.

"I'm sure it is. But what's the plan? Where are we headed first?" Hunter asked.

"Colonel Bartow's house, I guess, to see if we can find Davy. It's 9:45 in the morning according to that clock in the restroom, so that's about the best time of day we could hope for," I said, and he nodded.

There was indeed a huge wall map of Venus inside the terminal, with all the highlands and seamounts above 12,000 feet colored green and everything else dark blue. All the principal features were named, and there were color-coded flight times between all major points. Exactly the kind of thing you might expect to see in an airport almost anywhere, I suppose. It turned out the spaceport was located on Barbados, about fifteen hundred miles to the southwest and only twenty degrees north of the equator; a much more favorable location for launches. According to the map there was an average flight time of exactly eight hours and eleven minutes to reach it.

"We can handle that, I think. We'll have to take a plane or a helicopter from here and then swing by to pick up Leah before we head over to Barbados to get the colony ship. Just a minor adjustment," I said, feeling relieved.

We had to wait nearly an hour for my face to stop oozing blood, but when I finally washed it off and dried my tender skin with a paper towel I looked at least semi-respectable again. Then we were ready to go out and face the world.

We didn't try to be stealthy anymore, since that would only arouse suspicion if anybody saw us. Two soldiers in airmen's uniforms walking down the road from the landing field wasn't anything particularly noteworthy, so we took the main drag into Jamestown just like we belonged there. It turned out to be a moot point since we never actually met anybody, but it never hurt to be careful.

There were only a few people in town who might have recognized us on sight; Colonel Bartow himself, of course, and then

Olivia and possibly one or two others. The rest of the soldiers only knew us as the yellow-skinned prisoners, if they'd ever seen us at all. It would have taken a severe case of bad luck to run into anybody who knew us, and thankfully we didn't. Everybody avoided eye contact and went about his or her own business, taking no interest at all in what ours might be.

We made it to Colonel Bartow's house with no incident, but there we met a problem. There was a single bored-looking guard standing on the porch. I'm sure his only purpose was to screen visitors and keep unwanted ones from disturbing the Colonel at home, but he might as well have been a brick wall when it came to keeping us out. We walked right on past the house without so much as a glance to the side, as if we'd never meant to stop there in the first place.

"So what do we do now?" Hunter asked in a low voice when we got about a half block past the house.

"Let's circle the block and come up the alley behind the house. Then we can try the back door," I said. It was a mildly risky thing to do, but if anyone questioned us then we could always say we were only using the alley for a shortcut.

So we turned into the alley just like it was the most ordinary thing in the world, and sometimes it's amazing what you can get away with as long as you don't look nervous about it. No one paid us the slightest attention.

And then we had one more bit of luck, or so it seemed at first. The back yard of Colonel Bartow's house was separated from the alley only by a chain link fence overgrown with morning glory vines, and there was no mistaking the sight of Davy playing on the grass beside a metal table in the center of the yard. That was the good luck. The bad luck was, there was a young woman sitting at the table beside him and reading a paperback novel. She was facing partly away from us, but I recognized her almost immediately as Olivia Deming. She hadn't noticed us yet, so I stepped back out of sight behind the edge of the neighboring fence, grabbing Hunter's jacket to pull him back with me.

"What is it?" he asked.

"Didn't you see? That was Olivia," I hissed.

"Do you think she recognized us?" Hunter asked, sounding alarmed.

"I don't think she even saw us. She was too wrapped up in that book she was reading," I said.

"Yeah, but she'll recognize us the minute she sees us, and then it's over. All she's got to do is scream and she'll bring the whole place down around our ears," Hunter said.

"Hold on and let me think a minute," I said, trying to do just that. Olivia's unexpected presence had suddenly thrown a monkey wrench into the whole plan and I couldn't yet figure out a way around it. There'd be no fooling *her;* no coming up with any half-baked ruse to get inside the house and then snatch Davy and run. She'd have us hauled off to jail before we had time to blink.

"Any ideas?" Hunter finally asked.

"No, not really," I admitted.

"What we really need is an ally, you know. Somebody who knows their way around here and can help us," Hunter said.

"Yeah, but who?" I asked.

"Well. . . have you noticed the way nobody will meet your eyes? People act like that when they're nervous or scared. Dad controls this place with an iron thumb. Seems to me there might be several people willing to help us, in exchange for a trip home," Hunter said.

"That's probably true, but those same people will be afraid to believe us, too. How would we know who to trust?" I asked.

"What about Olivia?" he suggested.

"Are you crazy, boy?" I asked.

"I don't think so," he said.

"You sound like it. She's obviously one of Colonel Bartow's most trusted aides," I said.

"Well. . . she *did* help us out in the desert," he said.

"I think that was just a ploy to keep us off balance," I said.

"Are you sure? If he wanted to exile us to a desert island then he could have done that from the get-go, or if he wanted to change his mind later then she could have told us that and it would've made him look merciful. I think it was her own idea to help us," Hunter said.

"I'm not so sure about that. You have to be really careful when you're playing chess with a grand master like your dad, you know. He's always got you pegged at least two or three moves ahead," I said.

"He's not all-knowing, Tyke. You can't get yourself so tied up in knots that you're afraid to take any risks," Hunter said.

"I didn't say we shouldn't. I just meant we need to think about it first, that's all," I said.

"What is there to think about? We'll never know anything more to base a decision on than what we already know. Do we take a risk and find out whether we can trust somebody, or do we not?" Hunter asked.

"And what happens if she screams for the guard?" I asked.

"Maybe only one of us should go talk to her first. That way if it turns out she's faithless then one of us will still be free and maybe can do something to bust the other one out of jail or whatever," Hunter said.

"Maybe. I'll go talk to her first. If she screams then I'll knock her out and grab Davy, and then I guess we'll have to make a run for it. Wait here, where she can't see you," I said, and Hunter nodded.

"I'll be praying for you, buddy," he said solemnly.

"You do that," I agreed, and then took a deep breath before heading back down the alley again.

Before long I was standing nervously by the fence, with my sweaty palms resting on the morning glories. Olivia was still reading her book, seemingly oblivious to my presence.

"Olivia!" I called, as loudly as I dared. She looked up reflexively, and she must have recognized me immediately because her eyes flew open in shocked surprise and her hand went up to cover her mouth as she gasped.

"Please don't scream, I just want to talk to you," I said quickly.

Maybe she felt like she had the situation in hand on her own, or maybe she was only curious, but whatever the reason might have been, she didn't scream. She calmed down almost at once and came over to stand across the fence from me.

"Well, Mr. McGrath, this is certainly an unexpected meeting. Do you mind if I ask how you got here?" she asked.

"We found some thermal suits at the base camp on Tortuga and walked," I said.

"That's impossible," she said flatly.

"No, just highly improbable," I said dryly.

"But what about food and water? What about the pressure and the nitrogen narcosis and the dust storms?" she asked.

"We carried some dried fish, we built a water distillery out of plastic bottles, we didn't run into any dust storms, and we stayed drunk as boiled hoot owls the whole time," I said.

"I can't believe it," she said, shaking her head.

"Me neither at times, but I promise you that's what happened," I said.

"You keep saying *we;* is there somebody else with you?" she asked, and I wanted to kick myself for letting it slip that easily. But that's what happens when you're nervous; it's hard to remember what to say and what not to.

"Can I trust you?" I asked, and her eyes narrowed.

"What do you mean?" she asked.

"Are you gonna call the guards? Will you help us?" I asked. It was blunt, but I didn't have time to dance around the edges of the issue. I had to know immediately.

"I won't call the guards, and I'll help you to the extent that I'm able, without cutting my own throat," she finally said.

"Fair enough," I agreed, and turned my head to where Hunter was still waiting just out of sight. I waved him over, and before long he was standing beside me.

"Master Bartow. I'm sure the Colonel would be amazed to hear that his son walked a thousand miles across the deep desert," Olivia said.

"It was only eight hundred, but yeah, I'm sure he'd be so proud," Hunter said sourly.

"Well, be that as it may, both of you come inside, quickly. We can't be seen talking here," Olivia said, opening the back gate. She scooped up Davy and then all four of us went inside the house. It was quiet inside, and she led us directly to one of the bedrooms on the third floor. I think it must have been Colonel Bartow's, because there was a big four-poster mahogany bed with a shiny crimson silk coverlet, and several other sumptuous-looking accoutrements like that. He seemed to enjoy the finer things in life every bit as much in his private space as he did elsewhere.

"I don't want Charlie to hear us talking in here. Supposedly I'm the only one in the house," she explained.

"Charlie's the guard?" I asked.

"Yeah. He won't bother us, but he might get curious if he heard voices inside," she said.

"All right. Well, let's get down to business, then. Leah is still down there on Tortuga. What we had in mind was to steal a plane, pick her up, take one of the colony ships from Barbados, and then hightail it back to Earth," I said, getting right to the point.

"You have to have a personal access code for that or the onboard computers won't let you start the engines on anything," she said. I hadn't known that little tidbit, but I was careful not to let it rattle me.

"We hoped you might be able to help us with that, if we took you back home with us. Tycho could give you the vaccine so you'd be immune to the plague," Hunter said, and Olivia was quiet for a long time.

"That's a lot to think about. What happens when Colonel Bartow comes after us later on? Because he would sooner or later, you know," she said at length.

"We thought about blowing up the other two ships before we left. I think it's safe to say he'd never be able to fix them, isn't it?" I asked.

"It's highly doubtful, if you damaged them badly enough. But there's always Colonel Burns on Mars," she said.

"We'd have to take them out, too," I said.

"You realize that would mean leaving thousands of people stranded on these other worlds forever, don't you?" she asked.

"Yeah, but that's nothing they didn't already expect when they first came here," I reminded her.

"No, they only expected to have to stay between twenty and thirty years; not forever. Just till the spores died out," Olivia corrected me.

"But don't they know the spores can survive for hundreds, maybe even thousands of years in places where it's cold?" I asked.

"They didn't tell us that, but it wouldn't make any difference even if they had. Most of Earth is not frozen," she said.

"No, but do you really think two or three hundred years from now somebody won't take a notion to go exploring one of those areas and then carry the germs right back into civilized areas and start the plague all over again?" I asked.

"I think they believe they'll find the vaccine before then," she said.

"They might, I guess," I admitted, shrugging. It seemed like an awfully big gamble to take, but then again people have done stupider things and lived to tell about it.

"That's a long time in the future, though. It's not the main reason why we don't want them back on Earth right now," Hunter said.

"Oh? And why do you not want them back right now?" Olivia asked.

"This culture and society they're building is. . . bad. It's like everybody is on lockdown all the time, where you've got to be afraid of what you say or who you trust. Philip says it used to be like that on Earth back in the bad old days before the plague. We don't want that same old situation to come back again. I want to be free to say and do what I like, without having to worry that I'll get banished to a desert island or killed if the higher-ups don't like it. I don't think that's too much to want," Hunter said.

"I couldn't have said it better myself," I agreed.

"There's some truth to that," Olivia said softly.

"So will you help us, then?" I asked.

"I'll help you under one condition," she said.

"Which is?" I asked.

"Every person here and on Mars was handpicked by Colonel Burns. Most of them have the same attitude about the way things should be that he does; they're born and bred to the Service, true believers and loyal to the core. That's one of the main criteria he used for selecting recruits. But not all of them are like that. There are a few who might have said something similar to what Hunter just now said, if given the chance. I'd like to bring as many of those along with us as we can. The others can stay here and build whatever kind of world they like," she said.

"How many people are we talking about?" I asked.

"No more than a few hundred at the most," she said.

I considered it, worried about the logistics of the thing. It would be awfully hard to slip that many people out of Jamestown without anybody else noticing. Not to mention the fact that it's almost impossible to form a conspiracy with that many people, especially in a place where suspicion and treachery reigned supreme. Somebody was bound to let something slip, or even worse to intentionally rat us out.

"You don't think we'd run a serious risk of getting found out?" I asked doubtfully.

"We would. That's why we can't tell anybody till the last minute. But in the meantime I can start feeling some people out, seeing who might be worth asking. Colonel Bartow already keeps a list of people he suspects of disloyalty, so I'll start with them," she said.

"So what do we do in the meantime?" Hunter asked.

"For now, you and Tycho can hide out at the cabin where you stayed to begin with. It's pretty secluded, and there's nobody living there right now. I don't think anybody would find you. Then when it's time to go, I'll come get you," she said.

"All right, sounds good to me," I agreed, and Hunter nodded.

"Okay, then. Let's get some regular uniforms for both of you instead of those airmen's outfits; then you'll blend in a lot better. You'll have to walk to the cabin, but I don't think anybody will pay attention. You do remember the way, don't you?" she asked.

"Yeah, I remember," I agreed.

"Good," she said, and then got up from her spot to fetch two pairs of slate-blue combat fatigues from the closet, the normal daily wear in Jamestown.

"The Colonel will never notice that these are missing, and if he does then I'll just tell him I sent them out to be laundered. He approves of clean clothes," she said, and I nodded. No doubt he did.

"What'll you do with these airmen's uniforms?" Hunter asked.

"Take them with you. The Colonel definitely doesn't need to find *those* here," she said. So we quickly changed in Colonel Bartow's fancy marble-tiled bathroom, and came out looking just like professional NADF soldiers.

"All right, we're done," I said, straightening my jacket.

"Good. It's probably best if you head on over to the cabin now, but I'll be in touch later on," Olivia said.

We left the house through the alley, both of us a little bit giddy that we actually seemed to be on the verge of getting away with a major conspiracy right under Colonel Bartow's nose. Hunter had been completely right about how valuable an ally could be.

Twenty minutes later we reached the cabin. The place seemed not to have changed at all since we'd last been inside, and there was even still food in the cabinets.

"Cool. Let's fix some *real* food for a change," Hunter said, pulling boxes and jars out of the cabinets.

"What, you mean you're not hankering after some dried fish and pond water?" I asked, joshing him.

"I never want to see another fish in my life," Hunter said with feeling, and I laughed.

"Me neither, buddy boy. I was way past that point even by the time we left the Moon," I said.

Before long we were sitting down to a heaping plate of scrambled eggs and artificial bacon, with biscuits and gravy on the side. It was the quickest hot meal we could cook, even though it was really closer to lunchtime than breakfast by then.

"Do you really think all this will turn out okay?" Hunter asked, shoveling a spoonful of eggs and gravy into his mouth at the same time.

"I hope so," I said. I was guardedly optimistic at that point, but I could also think of a million things that might go wrong.

Unfortunately, it wasn't meant to be. We were still in the middle of eating when a squad of soldiers kicked in the front door.

"Run!" I yelled at Hunter, throwing down my fork and scrambling for the back door.

They tackled us right on the back steps, and even though we fought hard, it really didn't take them all that long to beat us down. I ended up with a bloody nose and some kicks to the ribs before it was all over, and Hunter was no better off.

Olivia had betrayed us, of course; that was the only rational explanation. They never could have found us that fast unless somebody tipped them off, and she was the only other person in Jamestown who knew where we were.

"Come on, get up," the leader said curtly, jerking his rifle. We both struggled to our feet, and they chained us together with those same plastic leg irons I remembered so well from Kona. Then they marched us across town to the jailhouse and locked us up in a ten by twelve foot cell behind a steel door.

Chapter Ten

Sitting in jail is one of those things which isn't remotely like what you'd think if you've never been there before. The worst thing about it isn't really the lack of freedom, it's the sheer and absolute boredom. When you've got nothing whatsoever to do except sit and twiddle your thumbs for hours on end, it starts to drive you crazy after a while. There's nothing to do, nothing to look forward to except meals, and no prospect of anything changing.

"I can't believe she stabbed us in the back like that," Hunter said after a while. We were both sitting on the concrete ledge below the single window, with our ankles still chained together and our bodies still hurting from the scuffle.

"Oh, I can believe it. I told you she's one of your dad's main toadies; didn't I say that from the beginning?" I asked. I probably shouldn't have thrown it in his face that way, but my heart was still bitter from thinking we'd found a friend and then finding out she was no such thing. Treachery stings, even when you know full well that you should have seen it coming.

Even worse, she and Colonel Bartow now knew all our secret plans.

"Yeah, you were right. But we had to try, didn't we?" Hunter asked.

"Yeah, we had to try. But now it's hopeless; they know everything we meant to do and all our plans. We'll never surprise them at this point. I told you Colonel Bartow always thinks two or three moves ahead. I bet he had Olivia act like our friend when she dropped us off on Tortuga just so she'd be the one we came to for help *just in case* we ever managed to escape somehow. I bet that's exactly why she's the one who got assigned to take care of Davy, too; so we'd be sure to meet up with her. And we fell for it, Hunter; hook, line, and sinker," I said.

"Well. . . maybe. But I'm not ready to give up yet," Hunter said.

"I'm glad to hear it. Neither am I for that matter, but I can't think of a way out of here to save my life," I said

I didn't add that that was probably literally true. The best we could hope for was a one-way ticket back to Tortuga, only this time with no thermal suits left behind. We'd be well and truly stuck out there in the middle of the Cytherean Sea, with not a prayer of crossing the deep desert again. And that was the *best* option. I didn't even want to think about what the worst option might be, because it probably involved a game of laser tag with live rifles, with me and Hunter as the unarmed targets.

It was a hopeless situation, no matter how you looked at it.

When I was little my mother used to tell me stories sometimes about my grandpa Nicholas, the one I'm named after. He was a rebel soldier who was commended for exceptional bravery at the battle of Shiloh in Tennessee, and one of my earliest memories is of Mama telling me that story and then singing *The Yellow Rose of Texas* to put me to sleep at night. That song isn't the silly thing most people learn nowadays, with the words all changed to make it sweet and politically correct. It's a war song, about your feet being torn and bloody and your heart full of woe at being far from home in a strange land and missing your beloved. Mama is like that; she's never tried to hide the fact that the world is rough sometimes.

I remember wishing back then that I could be brave like that someday; courageous and unflinching, the kind of dude who laughs in the face of danger, so to speak. All I can say is that things like that sound really good when you're too young to know any better, but sometimes the price can be awfully high when it comes time to pay the bill. That's not whining, it's just the simple truth. Sitting there in that concrete cell, torn and bloody and heartsick myself, poor old Nick had more of my sympathy than my admiration at the moment.

It's also sad-but-true that even the brave and the good don't always find a happy ending in life, much as we might like to think so. Nicholas never did, after all; he ended up buried in a nameless grave somewhere far from home with a little white cross above his head and never got to see his wife or his daughters ever again. I could only hope I didn't end up the same way, with Danielle and Josie never even knowing what happened to me.

It was a depressing thought.

It's strange what you think about sometimes, when you've got nothing but time on your hands. I was veering dangerously close to feeling sorry for myself, actually, and that's never a helpful thing to do. All it does is make you feel rotten, when you ought to be focused on trying to think of some kind of solution to your problem.

"You know, Saint Paul got put in jail quite a few times when he didn't deserve it. God always made a way for *him* to get out," Hunter said after a while. I'm sure he was remembering his lessons from Aunt Joan like the good kid that he was, and I didn't have the heart to tell him that both of us put together were still nineteen decimal places from being on a par with Saint Paul. If it gave him comfort to believe we'd get some kind of miracle to bust us out of jail then I'd be the last person in the world to try to take that away from him.

Besides which, it might after all turn out to be true. Things like that do happen sometimes, even though I didn't expect to see one every time we got in a pinch.

"Maybe," I said noncommittally.

"Just wait and see," Hunter said with conviction.

"We'll see what happens," I agreed.

For several days, what happened was precisely nothing. We sat in our cell and talked about various things, or sometimes just stared at the walls. It was the same perpetual daylight as always, of course, which aggravated the situation because we soon lost track of what day it was and how much time had passed.

But things must have been happening out there in the wide world beyond the confines of our little prison cell. Maybe Colonel Bartow announced our wicked plan to the whole community so as to make an example of what happens to plotters and schemers, or maybe it was just the good old fashioned grapevine. However it happened, it soon turned out that practically everybody in Jamestown knew who we were and what we'd meant to do.

And that turned out to be a very good thing indeed.

I don't know how many days it might have been at that point, but after a certain period of time a soldier came to our window in the middle of the night. At least I judge it was the middle of the night by the fact that Hunter and I were sleeping; by the sun it was still the same bright and cloudless morning it had already been for a week or more at that point.

His name was Captain Brandon Stone, though I didn't know that till later, and he was from Piedmont, Alabama. Nothing particularly surprising about that; a sizable number of the colonists on Venus and Mars had come from within a two-hour radius of Atlanta, no doubt for the very simple and practical reason that Colonel Burns had his office there and it was easier to look for recruits close by whenever possible.

But all I knew that night was that somebody was tapping on the bars of our window with a rock. I was only half asleep, so I shook myself awake and stood up to see what was going on. Outside was a soldier in the same slate-blue camo they all wore, young and athletic as they all were, with the gold pins on his left shoulder which identified him as an officer of some kind, although I wasn't familiar enough with NADF insignias to be able to tell exactly what his rank might be. He had deep blue eyes that reminded me of Uncle Philip's, and hair which was almost fire-engine red. I'd never seen him before.

"Is it true you've got the vaccine against the Orion Strain?" he asked in a low voice, and under the circumstances I didn't see any point in denying it.

"Yeah, it's true," I agreed.

"Are you still interested in going back to Earth?" he asked, and you better believe *that* got my attention.

"What did you have in mind?" I asked.

"There's a little group of us here, we don't like the way things are turning out. We expected to have more freedom after there was no one left on the planet but us. But it hasn't turned out that way, so we've been looking at other options. We're willing to give you the access codes for one of the colony ships and help you destroy the other ones, if you'll give us the vaccine against the plague after we get back to Earth," he said.

"How many of you are there?" I asked.

"About two hundred," he said.

"I'll do it if you can rescue my cousin's wife from Tortuga, and if you can get Davy Parker away from Colonel Bartow," I said.

"We'll find a way. The young lady on Tortuga isn't such a problem. Colonel Bartow's grandson might be, but we'll see what we can do. It may be a few days, but be ready," he said. I thought about saying something about how I'd make sure to clear my calendar, but then I decided it probably wasn't the time for a smart mouth.

"We'll be ready," I said, and that was that. Captain Stone disappeared from our windowsill, leaving us every bit as much alone as we'd ever been. The jail in Jamestown was rarely used; it had only three cells, and as far as I know we never had company.

But I got to thinking about what Hunter said about Saint Paul and decided maybe I should have had more trust, after all. I offered a silent prayer of apology and thanks, and resolved to do better in the future.

"Do you think that dude will really come back?" Hunter asked after a while.

"I don't see why he wouldn't, if he doesn't get caught," I said.

"Yeah, but I was thinking about that, you know. You remember what Olivia said about that list of potentially disloyal soldiers, don't you? It sounds like they might be on to this little group, from the way *she* talked. They might even be dangling you and me as bait to try to catch those others. That might be why they haven't killed us yet," Hunter said.

"You have the most deceitful ideas, for a kid your age," I said dryly, and Hunter laughed.

"Maybe it runs in my blood," he said.

"No, never think like that," I said quickly.

"Oh, I don't; I was just joking, honest," Hunter said.

"Okay, then," I said.

"But I hope they don't get caught, anyway," he added.

"Yeah, me too," I agreed.

It was several days later when the door rattled and an NADF soldier pushed it open. It was a girl this time, and she shook her head and put her finger to her lips to tell us to be quiet. She quickly undid our leg irons and left them on the floor, and then we had to help her drag an unconscious guard in from outside and lock him in the cell.

I couldn't help wondering how the rebels had managed to work out all the tactical issues of transporting over two hundred soldiers to Barbados in a single airlift. All the copters and planes at Jamestown put together were barely enough to hold that many people at once, and we didn't dare make more than one trip.

Not only that, but the eight-hour flight time would give Colonel Bartow plenty of time to discover the theft and warn the garrison at the spaceport that we were coming. I didn't look forward to a laser battle as soon as we got there. But the girl didn't see fit to share any plans, so all we could do was follow her quietly and trust that our new friends knew what they were doing.

And you know, at first I thought we might actually slip out of town with no problems. Everything was calm till we reached the airfield, and sure enough there were something like two hundred rebels gathered quietly together on the tarmac in their slate-blue fatigues. A few of them were already starting to board the planes.

That's when we were attacked.

I'm sure the ambush was laid with military precision, at just the right place and time. Maybe Hunter was right about his father using us for bait to draw out what he considered the disloyal element in his little society; I'm not sure. All I know is, we suddenly found ourselves locked into a desperate battle against a force almost ten times as large as ours.

Laser rifles are silent and deadly things, just in case you didn't know. They don't make the slightest bit of noise, only pulses of ruby red light, and battles of that kind aren't bloody, either. Laser beams may put a hole straight through a person, but they also instantly cauterize the wound so it never bleeds a drop. What people die from are burns, not blood loss. A laser battle is a soundless and almost beautiful thing to watch, like a kaleidoscopic light show.

If it weren't for the screams, that is.

No one trusted me or Hunter with a rifle, but even I knew the odds were hopeless in a situation like that. There are reflective mirror-suits you can wear for at least partial protection during a laser fight, and most of Colonel Bartow's soldiers were wearing them, as a matter of fact, silvery-bright and shiny as a brand-new dime in the noonday sun. But none of the rebels had one, and that meant we were getting slaughtered without mercy.

The best we could do under those circumstances was to man the aircraft and try to save as many as we could. Hunter and I were hustled on board a helicopter, which took off along with every other craft on the place. That added to our firepower, but at the same time I watched several of them get shot down in fiery crashes. I couldn't tell how many got away.

But ours did, crammed so full of people that we were piled on top of each other. Several of them were badly burned from laser hits and groaning in pain, but there was nothing we could do to help. Two of them didn't make it, actually, and riding for eight hours in a cramped helicopter with a couple of freshly dead comrades is not an experience I would wish on anybody. But the only other alternative was to throw them out to land in the desert far below us, and nobody even suggested *that* idea.

But eventually we did reach Barbados, and the rebels must have had a prearranged meeting point just in case trouble occurred. We all came together on the east side of the island, to lick our wounds and take stock of what needed to be done next.

There were only eighty-seven of us left. Well over half had been killed in the battle at Jamestown or died later on during the flight, and of the ones who did survive there weren't many who escaped with no injury. We had six helicopters and four planes left, and that was just about it.

We buried the dead in an alpine meadow full of golden yellow wildflowers, each of them marked with a stone cross laser-cut from the black Venusian basalt. Twenty-three of them in all, not counting the ones we left behind in Jamestown. So we prayed and sang hymns, and then left them at peace in that high place which is as much like Heaven as anywhere I've ever seen.

We didn't dare wait too long to let Colonel Bartow regroup; we might have taken most of his aircraft, but that didn't mean he might not have others stowed away somewhere. They almost surely had a few at the spaceport, if nowhere else, and as soon as he figured out where we were then we'd have another battle on our hands. One which we might not survive next time. But Captain Stone was nothing if not a man of his word, so as soon as the funeral was done he came to me.

"Y'all go get your friend while there's still time," he said, handing me a slip of paper with a sixteen-digit access code scrawled across it. He looked weary and sad, but then I guess I couldn't blame him for that. There was one question I had to ask while I still could, though; there hadn't been time at the airport, but I couldn't face Leah without knowing the answer.

"What about Davy?" I asked.

"I think the Colonel knew our plans. The squad I sent to pick him up never showed, so I figure they were either killed or captured. I'm sure the Colonel made sure to keep his grandson safe, but I'm equally sure he's still somewhere back in Jamestown. There's nothing that can be done about it now," Captain Stone said.

"Well. . . thanks for doing what you could. We'll be right back as soon as we can. And thanks again," I said, handing the paper to Hunter.

Captain Stone nodded and waved us off, already involved with something else, and Hunter and I scrambled into the nearest helicopter and buckled in. He quickly punched in the access code on the computer, unlocking the command screen and letting us start the engine. Then we took off.

"Are we really gonna leave Davy behind?" Hunter asked after we were in the air.

"No way. But I couldn't tell Captain Stone that," I said.

"But what'll we do?" Hunter asked.

"I don't know yet, kid. Let me think," I said, sighing.

I had plenty of time for thought, since Barbados is darned near as far from Tortuga as it is from Eleuthera. It took us six hours to make the trip, and Hunter mostly left me alone to think the whole time.

He finally landed us right across the creek from the base camp, and Leah came outside as soon as she heard the rotors, looking ragged and dirty. The joy on her face when she recognized us was something to treasure forever, but when the hugs and kisses were over, there were some serious questions.

"Where's Davy?" she asked immediately.

"He's still in Jamestown with your dad, but we're fixing to go get him," I explained quickly, and then went on to give her a short rundown on everything that had happened since we left.

"But how can we get him?" Leah asked.

"Um. . . I'll have to show you," I said, temporizing. I actually did have a half-formed plan in mind, but I still hadn't worked out all the details.

"Then let's go while we've still got time. Things are happening pretty fast right now," Hunter said.

So that's what we did, and instead of heading for Jamestown itself I told Hunter to set a course for Mount Freedom.

"What are we doing up there?" he asked.

"Wait and see," I said, with a lot more confidence than I felt.

Chapter Eleven

I believe I've said before that Mount Freedom is by far the highest peak on Venus, but it's also the widest and the biggest. With a summit of over thirty-six thousand feet, it contains a snowfield over a hundred miles wide and nearly two hundred miles long. That's twenty thousand square miles of snow and ice locked up in that one spot, an area roughly the size of West Virginia which contains more than eighty percent of the usable water on the whole planet.

All that water had given me an idea.

You see, cities have to have water. For drinking and washing and irrigation and all sorts of things, and Jamestown was no exception. But you can't drink snow, and you can't irrigate crops with ice. So as I mentioned earlier, the Defense Forces had built dams across all three of the big rivers that flowed down from the heights, to store the snowmelt in reservoirs and use it later for all those various things.

I was betting on the dams.

No, I didn't want to blow one of them up and create a complete disaster area by destroying the colony and drowning half the people who lived there. That was uncalled for. What I wanted was to throw open the gates and create a *small* flood; just enough to cause chaos and hopefully let us slip into town unnoticed and snatch Davy before anybody had time to realize what was going on.

"Which dam should it be, though? The one on the James river?" Hunter asked after I explained my plan. That was the river which ran right through the middle of Jamestown, naturally enough.

"Yeah, it'll have to be that one," I agreed.

"You know, there might actually be people *working* at those dams. What if we run into somebody? They won't just stand by and let us open the floodgates," Hunter pointed out.

"We'll have to cross that bridge whenever it gets here. Hopefully there won't be anybody there; it looked like everybody in Jamestown was at the airport earlier," I said.

"I'm not so sure about that, but we'll see," Hunter said.

I had Hunter land us at the edge of the snowfield where the James River began, flowing down as an ice-cold rivulet over the stone.

"Dang, Tyke, it's *cold* up here; couldn't we have landed somewhere lower down?" Hunter complained when we got out. And indeed it was. The temperature was right at the freezing point, and that's no fun at all when you're wearing nothing but a set of light combat fatigues and no jacket.

"That's exactly why we landed here. Nobody else ever comes up this way because they don't like the cold, either. Not to mention we can follow the river down to the dam, which is important since there are no roads up here and I don't especially feel like getting lost in the woods today. We'll just have to deal with it," I said.

There was a single laser rifle which somebody had left behind in the copter, so we took that with us and headed downhill beside the river. Walking helped, but it was still unbelievably frigid up there and the wind certainly didn't help matters. After spending so much time down there in the deep desert it was hard to believe any such place as that could exist on such an otherwise blistering planet, but I promise you it does. The freezing line is right about at 32,000 feet, but we felt the cold wind at our backs for a long time after that.

Jamestown itself has a mostly dry and sunny kind of climate, but it isn't like that on the upper slopes of Mount Freedom. Even after you drop below the freezing zone, you start getting into a region where it's almost always rainy and the thick woods are shrouded in cold white mist. It's what's called a cloud forest, and there are a few of them even on Earth, in places where there are really tall mountains towering above really hot areas. But I'd never had a chance to visit one before, and in spite of the cold and the wet I couldn't help being fascinated by this one. I stopped now and then to examine the plants and the insects, amazed at how well they'd adapted to Venusian conditions.

"Snap out of it, Tyke; you're slowing us down," Leah said, and I realized guiltily that I probably had been. This was no leisurely field trip to study comparative biology; it was a desperate rescue attempt which couldn't be put off just to satisfy my curiosity.

"Sorry," I said, my cheeks reddening.

At least there was no more wind in the cloud forest, even though it was still chilly. Jamestown is only about twenty miles from the snowline, but that's still a long walk, and a steep one too. Thankfully the dam was only about half that far, and by the time we reached it we were footsore and tired. The temperatures had climbed back up to almost sixty by then and the cloud forest had disappeared, but we were walking through an open park-like forest of oak and hickory trees instead.

"There's the dam," Hunter said in a low voice, stopping in his tracks when he spotted it and pointing through the trees. Sure enough, there it was, and there were three cars parked in the lot, too.

"Looks like there are people there, too," I said, disappointed.

"So what do we do?" Leah asked, and that was indeed a good question.

"I've got an idea," Hunter said.

"What is it?" I asked.

"See there where the floodgate lets the water through, down at the bottom? Let's take two of the hydrocells from the cars and stick them up inside there and blow the gate open with the rifle. That way they won't be able to close anything off till the whole lake drains out, plus we won't have to deal with anybody inside the building and it'll also leave us with the only car," Hunter said.

"That sounds like a great idea," Leah agreed.

"You don't think they'll see us fooling around with the cars and the gate like that?" I asked doubtfully.

"You're forgetting this place isn't all beefed up on security like it used to be on Earth. I bet we could walk right in there and never be noticed at all because they won't be expecting us, especially not after they practically wiped out the rebels this morning. If they do notice then we'll have to fight, but hopefully they won't," Hunter said.

"I'll go set the hydrocells, then," I said firmly.

"No, I'll do it," Hunter said, and from that point there began the strangest argument you could imagine, with Hunter and me fighting over who got to put himself in danger. Leah was too small and petite to have the strength to carry even one hydrocell, much less two, so all she could do was stand aside and watch uncomfortably.

"Y'all are wasting time. Let's draw straws, for pity's sake," she finally said.

"What do you mean draw straws? You can't do it anyway," Hunter said.

"No, but you and Tycho can. I'll hold the straws," she said.

"Actually I've got an even better idea," I said.

"What's that?" Leah asked.

"Those hydrocells are pretty heavy when they're full, which I hope they are. If both of us carry one then maybe we'll get done faster," I said.

"All right, fine. Leah can man the getaway car and be the lookout in the meantime," Hunter said.

With that agreed, we all three slipped down to the gravel parking lot and immediately lifted the fuel door on the first one.

"Dang it, only half full," Hunter said, shaking his head.

"Never mind, it'll just be lighter to carry, that's all," I said.

We unscrewed the plastic twist-locks that held the hydrocell in place, and Hunter yanked it out. They're made to be easily interchanged like that, since lots of the older and smaller hydrogen stations don't have the capacity to refill tanks on the spot and so you have to switch out the whole cell instead. One of the filling stations in North Carolina where we used to go on vacation was like that, and I can remember Philip griping about it every time we had to stop there. To be fair, Chris and Jesse and I did our own fair share of muttering about it ourselves at the time, but in hindsight I was glad we had to learn how.

Of the others, it turned out one of them had about a third of a tank and the other one was almost full, but we left the one-third full tank alone as our getaway car. We wouldn't need much fuel to make it down to Jamestown and back, and we needed as much oomph as possible to blow that floodgate. Someone had left a laser pistol in one of the cars, too, and we gladly added that to the rifle.

Hunter and I each carried one of the hydrocells down into the rocky bed of the river and thence upstream till we reached the foot of the dam. I let him carry the lighter one since he was younger and not quite as strong as me, but those things are heavy no matter how you slice it. A full one weighs close to eighty pounds, and that gets wearisome after a while. We balanced them on the backs of our shoulders and held them in place with both hands, which meant we had to pick our way carefully so as not to lose our balance on all those wet rocks.

Finally we made it inside the tunnel where the floodgate was located, and it was downright spooky in there if you want to know the truth. Our footsteps echoed hollowly against the metal tube, and I kept imagining millions of gallons of ice-cold water gushing right over the place where our feet were walking. There'd be no warning at all if they decided to open the gates for some reason, and even worse, no time to make it back outside before we drowned.

But it didn't do any good at all to think about *that*, and I firmly put it out of my mind. We finally came to the area where the turbines and gate assembly were located, and since Hunter was smaller he actually crawled up between those huge metal blades and wedged the hydrocells as deep inside the machinery as possible. I don't know that I would have had the courage to go that far, even if I could have fit.

Then we hit a snag.

"Uh. . . now how do we set them off?" Hunter asked, staring at the nearest cell. It was visible, but barely so. There'd be no way we could shoot the laser at them from outside and make it work; it was much too far to get a good enough aim. But the only other option I could think of was for one of us to stand there and fire at them from point-blank range, thereby killing himself when they exploded. I wasn't ready to go *that* far yet.

Then I thought of something else.

"Don't worry about it. We can just short circuit the power pack from the laser and let it overheat. If we put it next to one of the hydrocells, it'll explode when it gets too hot," I said.

"You know how to do that?" Hunter asked.

"Yeah, it's easy," I said.

"How long do you think it'll take to blow up?" Hunter asked.

"As soon as it melts through the casing of the hydrocell, which shouldn't take long. No more than a few minutes at the most. It'll be white-hot within five minutes after I short circuit it," I said.

"That won't give us much time to get out," Hunter said.

"No, but I think it'll be enough if we run," I said.

So we broke down the rifle to pull out the power pack, and I quickly rearranged the wires to short circuit it. Then Hunter had to take it back inside the floodgate and set it down next to the fullest hydrocell. It must have been getting awfully warm already, because I could hear him juggling it around like a hot potato until he was able to set it down. Then he crawled back out and we ran like a band of demons and half the Devil's lawyers were hot on our heels.

We didn't quite make it. We were still about ten feet short of the tunnel mouth when the first explosion went off far behind us, followed quickly by another one. You wouldn't think it would be all that powerful from so far away, but I guess the tunnel must have focused the blast. Anyway, it picked us up and threw us outside into the rocky riverbed, and landing on rocks even from a short height is a pretty excruciating experience. But we didn't have time to curl up and get over the pain even for a minute or two. The floodgate was shattered, and within seconds we were about to find ourselves in deep water.

I got up and hobbled to the bank as fast as I could with Hunter right behind me, but the water was rising fast and we could barely keep ahead of it. Actually it was gaining on us in spite of all our efforts, and by the time we made it to the car we were sloshing through freezing water that was already knee-deep. Leah drove as fast as she could, but there's only so much speed you can make in water that deep. It was also pouring into the car itself around the bottoms and sides of the doors, and I think if the road hadn't gone uphill a bit as it left the parking lot we never would have made it out at all.

"That was a close one," Hunter said as we got back onto dry ground again. The car was still full of river water several inches deep in the floorboard, even after we cracked the doors to let most of it out.

"Too close," I agreed.

"How long do you think it'll take for the water to make it down to Jamestown?" Leah asked.

"Maybe fifteen minutes or so. Right about the same time we do, actually. You better drive as fast you can, though, or we'll end up cut off somewhere with the road flooded in front of us and behind us, too. There are some pretty low spots through here," I said.

The warning turned out to be a good one, because the river was already up over the bridge barely a mile downstream. Only a few inches, to be sure; we could still see the pavement underneath since the water was clear, but we all held our breath till we got across. It doesn't take very much depth of flowing water at all to push a car off a bridge or a road.

But after that the road straightened out a little bit and I think we started gaining on the flood, because when we came into Jamestown ten minutes later there was no sign of it yet. People already seemed to know it was coming, though, because they were scrambling around like ants and heading for the hills, so to speak. I guess the folks at the dam must have called ahead to warn them. Nobody paid the slightest attention to us.

"Head for the Colonel's house," I said, and Leah tried her best. It was hard to get through the streets, clogged as they were with people and cars. She was kept busy laying on the horn and revving the engine, but in spite of the chaos we managed to make it to the alley behind Colonel Bartow's house just as the first trickles of muddy water were starting to fill the streets.

"Come on!" I yelled, opening my door and running for the back porch. The other two were hot on my heels, and I didn't hesitate to kick in the door without knocking. We ran all through the house looking for Olivia and Davy, but they were nowhere to be found.

"Where are they?" Leah yelled, when we all ended up together again in the upstairs hall. I was about to say I didn't know when I heard the unmistakable sound of a helicopter's rotors.

"Up on the roof!" I cried, and we ran up there just in time to see Olivia getting into the back seat of a black helicopter. If we'd been even a few seconds later she would have gotten away, and as it was only a well-placed shot that took out the tail rotor kept them from escaping even then. But as soon as she saw that the copter wasn't going anywhere, Olivia went on the offensive.

She was a darned good marksman, too, and we soon found ourselves pinned down under expert laser fire. Hunter wound up with a nasty-looking burn on his left forearm, and the rest of us didn't escape without injury, either. She grazed me right above my right ear, and that's too close for comfort to a head shot. I could still smell the singed hair.

"She's trying to hold us off till backup can get here," Hunter said, and I nodded.

"We can't let her do that. We've got to find some way to take her out," Leah said.

"Keep her busy; I've got an idea," I said, and without another word I ran back downstairs to grab the crimson silk bedspread off Colonel Bartow's four-poster. No, I didn't have a sudden attack of the chills or anything like that, but I happened to remember something. Olivia had a standard-issue Defense Forces laser, and that meant it was red. Crimson red, almost exactly the same color as that dadgummed comforter. And if you can't get a mirror-suit made of reflective fabric during a laser battle, then something the same color as your enemy's beam is the next best thing. Especially something which is a little bit shiny, like that pretty silk. It turned out there were matching satin sheets underneath, and I quickly grabbed those too.

I wrapped myself in the bedspread and went back up to the roof, where the others looked at me like I'd lost my mind.

"Okay, here's what we need to do. I'm fixing to run over there and tackle her. As soon as I knock her down, come after me and help. Wrap yourselves in the sheets so the pilot can't get you. It won't be complete protection but it'll help a lot," I said, passing out the bedding. Then I took a deep breath, pulled the bedspread over my face to keep Olivia from blowing a hole in my head, and ran across the rooftop directly toward the helicopter.

I don't know what Olivia thought when she saw me coming, but she didn't hesitate to fire at me. And like I said, red cloth is no sure and certain protection; it just *helps* somewhat. I coughed on the acrid scent of burning silk, and I felt an agonizingly painful wash of heat flare against my ribs on the left side. But there was no time to stop and think, and before I knew it I was at the copter, and then Olivia and I went down on the roof in a tangled mass of flaming silk. I could feel it burning me all over, but at least it was burning her too. I was able to knock the laser out of her hand and off the roof, and in the meantime Hunter attacked the pilot, wrapped in his red satin sheets like a bloody ghost.

And Leah. . . no one could have stopped *her*, I don't think, even if she hadn't had any protection at all. She ran directly to the helicopter and grabbed Davy while the rest of us were busy fighting, but that was all right; that was exactly what she needed to do.

"Get back downstairs with him!" I yelled when I saw what she was doing, and she nodded and did exactly that.

In the meantime the battle was winding down, and we had Olivia and the pilot disarmed and standing at gunpoint.

"You'll never get away," Olivia said calmly, like it was the most obvious thing in the world. She was burned and disheveled, just like we all were, but she didn't seem to be letting it bother her.

"We'll see about that as soon as we get to the airport. See you later, traitor," I said scornfully, firing the laser at her feet just to make her jump. Yeah, I know it was petty, but I couldn't help myself.

We locked them onto the roof, using the laser pistol to melt the doorknob shut. I knew it wouldn't keep them up there for long, but hopefully it would buy us at least a little time.

Then we ran.

The streets were thigh-deep in water by then; much too flooded to even think about driving the car. We headed west at first, which was the wrong way to go if we'd meant to go directly back to the helicopter up at the snowline, and Hunter noticed.

"What are we doing? This is the wrong way," he said.

"Hush. I told Olivia we were headed for the airport, and I want her to see us going that way so that's where they'll be looking for us. We'll turn around in a few blocks," I said.

"Playing chess, huh?" Hunter asked, with a half smile.

"I learned from the best," I said wryly.

We found a canvas bag floating in the middle of the street not long afterward, and I grabbed it and gave it to Leah.

"Here, put Davy in there and sling him over your shoulder like he's a bag of something you're trying to save. He makes us stick out too much," I said.

"He won't like that," she said.

"No, but he might have to put up with it for a little while anyway," I said.

She reluctantly did as I said, and even though Davy cried inside the bag there was too much other noise for anybody to hear him very well.

As soon as we got out of sight of Colonel Bartow's house we turned north and then east, which had the added advantage of causing us to move in the same direction as everybody else trying to outpace the flood. Nobody paid attention to three soldiers carrying a canvas bag, and we managed to make it out of town in the confusion with nothing worse than a wetting. After that it was only a matter of climbing the mountain again. We struck the Rainy River a few miles into the woods, and then started uphill as fast as our weary legs could take us.

We had to stop and rest for a few hours right below the cloud forest, and then we made a forced march the rest of the way. It was hard on all of us and especially Leah, but she was determined to get her baby away from Eleuthera even if it killed her. But at long last we reached the helicopter, and fell into our seats in utter frozen exhaustion while Hunter took us out across the endless blue of the Cytherean Sea.

Chapter Twelve

For the next eight hours we took turns sleeping on the way back to Barbados. Even Hunter got to rest for a little while, since there wasn't much to do except keep an eye on the controls and make sure nothing went wrong. But nothing did, and finally we landed right outside the same rebel camp we'd left behind four days ago. It seemed like an eternity had passed.

I think it seemed that way to Captain Stone, too, because he scowled at me when we first met.

"You were only supposed to go to Tortuga," he said as soon as he spied Davy.

"You wouldn't say that if you knew what all we just now did," I said, and proceeded to tell him the whole story. He laughed when he heard about the flaming bedspread, and then clapped me on the shoulder.

"You should go tell the others all that. It'll give them some heart," he said.

"I'd be glad to," I said.

"But you still should only have gone to Tortuga," he said, the frown returning to his face.

"Maybe, but all the same I won't say I'm sorry, Captain Stone. No man left behind, remember?" I said, sticking my chin out a little bit. He looked at first like he might say something harsh, but then all of a sudden he laughed again.

"I knew there was a reason I liked you, Mr. McGrath. You would have made a fine soldier, you know," he said.

"Not my cup of tea, but thank you, sir," I said.

"So what's happened since we've been gone?" Hunter asked, getting us back to practical business.

"Well, not much. I think the remaining injured will survive at this point, if they're allowed," Captain Stone said.

"Allowed?" I asked.

"We still have to fight the garrison at the spaceport, you know. They've got the ships on lockdown till we can break in and get access to the command computer. That's the only way to release the lock. There are only ten soldiers guarding the place, but that's still enough to hurt or kill several of our people before we can blast them out," Captain Stone said.

"You're sure there haven't been any reinforcements?" I asked.

"No, we've been patrolling the island with our own craft ever since we first got here. Nothing has landed or taken off since we arrived," Captain Stone said.

"At least there's that much," I said, letting out a long breath.

"It's not *too* much to get excited about. Those ten over at the spaceport have already had a chance to get dug in, and I'm perfectly certain Colonel Bartow has reported all this to Colonel Burns on Mars, and probably asked for reinforcements too. If he has, then it'll only be a few more days till they get here. Then we're finished," Captain Stone said.

"Then we've got to capture the spaceport immediately, no matter what," I said, and Captain Stone sighed.

"True enough, Mr. McGrath, but that's easier said than done. It'll cost a lot of lives, which are worth something to *me* at least. There's an old saying about how the man who saves one life saves the whole world. If more commanders remembered that fact then there'd be a lot fewer needless wars. I remember it every day when I look out across this camp. So should you, if you ever hope to be a leader of men," he said sadly.

I started to say that I'd never really thought about being a leader of men before, but then I shut up. You never know what the future may bring, and it would be foolish to say I'd never find myself in that position. So I took note of what he said, and stored it away in my heart.

But the stubborn fact remained that if we captured the spaceport then at least some of us *might* survive, while if we failed to capture it then all of us were *sure* to die. Captain Stone might weep for the necessity, and so did I for that matter, but there are times when it can't be avoided.

I tried to imagine what N'grumth would have said, with his brave heart and his finely-honed sense of honor. I think he would have agreed with me. I hadn't thought about my alien friend in quite some time, but if I were really a nobleman of A'rath then it behooved me to act like one. It behooved me to remember my Avenger's oath, as well.

Therefore I thought long and hard, and even while I was telling the story of our adventures to all those young men and women and listening to them cheer, my mind was far away. And when all was said and done, I had a plan in mind.

That night I went to see Hunter in his tent. He was lying on his bedroll reading when I got there, with his tent flaps pinned open to catch the breeze, but he smiled and sat up when he saw me.

"What's up, Tyke?" he asked, setting aside his book.

"There's something I need to talk to you about, buddy," I said.

"Sure, come on in. You want some tea or something? They gave me a whole cooler full earlier, left over from supper. It's real sweet," he offered, moving aside so I'd have room to sit down.

"Yeah, I'd love some actually," I said, and he poured me a glassful from the plastic cooler at the back of his tent.

"So what's on your mind?" he finally asked.

"We've got to capture that spaceport," I said.

"Yeah, I know. But the garrison has it pinned down, remember?" he said.

"Maybe not. I think I know another way to bust in there, but I'll need your help," I said.

"Yeah? What did you have in mind?" he asked.

"You're absolutely sure you can fly one of those big colony ships, right?" I asked.

"Yeah, I think so," he agreed.

"Could you do it by remote control?" I asked.

"Hmm. . . well, yeah, probably. It'd be more or less like using a simulator, and Jesse used to use one of those to teach me stuff now and then whenever we went over to Hilo for something," he said.

"Well, here's what I had in mind. If I can get close enough to one of those ships to link up with its computer, then maybe I can hack inside and take command. Then you could fly it by remote control somewhere far enough away from the spaceport so we could all get on board to do things the old-fashioned way from then on out," I said.

"No, that won't work, Tyke. All spaceports have an anti-interference shield to keep out hackers like that. It wouldn't matter how close you got. The only way to get access to the ship computers is directly from the spaceport computers, and the only way to get access to *them* is by direct line hardwire. That's what Captain Stone was talking about when he said they had the ships on lockdown. You're barking up the wrong tree," Hunter said.

"I was afraid of something like that. But what if we got to the spaceport itself and managed to hook into the system with a hard wire? I'm sure there are access ports at various places on the outside of the building," I said.

"I'm sure there are, but I wouldn't know where to find them. And besides that you'd get fried with a laser beam if they caught you sneaking up on the building like that," Hunter said.

"Maybe so, but it's either that or get everybody together and try to swarm the place in a direct frontal assault. We might win, but Captain Stone tells me a lot of people would die in the process. He doesn't want that to happen, and neither do I," I said, and Hunter considered that for a few minutes.

"So what are you saying, then? You want to go over there and try to make some kind of cyber-attack on the compound?" he asked.

"The thought had crossed my mind," I said, and finally Hunter smiled.

"I love it. When do you want to get started?" he asked.

"I expected you to be a lot harder to convince," I said skeptically.

"Well, you know me. Always the optimistic type. I actually believe we might pull it off without getting ourselves charred to ashes, but hey, that's just me," he said, laughing.

"Now that you put it that way it almost makes me want to change my mind again," I said dryly.

"Nah, it'll be all right. We've been through a lot tougher things than having to find a data port," Hunter said.

"Yeah, a data port guarded by soldiers armed with laser rifles who won't hesitate to use deadly force," I reminded him.

"You're the one who brought it up, Tyke, not me. But I think there are some mirror-suits around here somewhere anyway; I'm not really all that worried about the lasers," Hunter said.

"We can't wear a mirror-suit in the daytime. They'd see us coming for miles, and if they figure out what we're doing then they could cut the wires to the data port and leave us out of luck. We've got to be stealthy about this," I said.

"Then I don't know what to say, except to wait for nighttime. But you know we can't do that," Hunter said.

"Yeah, I definitely know that," I agreed.

"So what do we do, then?" Hunter asked.

"What's the terrain like out there?" I asked.

"Um. . . grass, from what I gather," Hunter said.

"Tall enough to hide us?" I asked.

"Maybe if we crawled and wore camo," he said.

"Then let's do that. I think it'll work," I said.

"You know Captain Stone would never let you go on a dangerous mission like that. If you get killed then all of them are stuck here on Venus with no vaccine," Hunter pointed out.

"Last I checked, Captain Stone has no authority over me or you either one," I reminded him.

"Well. . . true. Sometimes I forget about that," he said apologetically.

"It's easy to get in the habit of listening to him when you see everybody else doing it, but we're not his soldiers," I said.

"Then I guess we can do whatever we want to," Hunter said.

"I guess so. But the question is, do you want to?" I asked, and he shrugged.

"I'm game if you are," he said.

Hunter was right about one thing; Captain Stone didn't like the idea at all. He knew he couldn't actually stop me, but if looks could kill then I probably would have been a pile of smoking ashes on his tent floor before the interview was even half over. But once he realized there was no stopping me, his attitude changed. Some people, when they can't actually prevent you from doing something they don't like, will then console themselves by refusing to help you or by making things as difficult as they possibly can. But Captain Stone did no such thing. Furious as he might be, he realized it was in his own best interest for us to succeed if possible, or if not then to at least come back in one piece. Therefore he gave us a laptop computer with a data cord, and two suits of wheat-colored camo, and a map of the spaceport compound showing where all the external data ports were located, and anything else he could think of that might help us.

The look in his eyes promised that the conversation wasn't over if we made it back alive, but on the other hand they do say that success covers a multitude of sins. I figured if we actually pulled off the plan then it would go an awfully long way toward getting us back into Captain Stone's good graces.

And so it was that early the next morning we were dropped off just over the horizon from the spaceport, and from there we had to keep down and crawl through the short grass on all fours. That might sound like it wouldn't be too difficult, but it gets to be an awfully thorny experience after you have to do it for more than a hundred feet or so. We had to do it for almost three miles, and by the time we reached the spaceport the skin on our knees and elbows was cracked and bleeding. People aren't designed for crawling that far after we reach a certain size, and it's hard work, too; much harder than walking would have been.

Captain Stone really did us right, though; he staged a minor offensive that day to help distract the garrison inside and keep them busy while we crept up on them. And that plus the camo must have worked, because nobody shot at us.

About halfway to the compound I brought up something I'd been thinking about ever since we crossed the desert.

"Hunter, have you ever thought about becoming an Avenger?" I asked, and he laughed a little. He knew what that meant, of course; none of it had been a secret anymore since we got back from Titan. Crawling through knee-high grass on our way to single-handedly attack an enemy compound on Venus probably wasn't the ideal set of circumstances under which to ask him such a question, but realistically speaking I knew it might be the last chance I ever got. We had only the one slot left, but after seeing the way he acted when times got tough, he seemed like a good choice to fill it.

"Well, nobody ever asked me before," he said.

"You've been too young up till now. But would you want to, if I said something to Uncle Philip about it?" I asked.

"Maybe; I'd have to think about it for a while. Ask me again when we get back home," he said.

"Fair enough. It's a lot of responsibility," I agreed.

That was all we said about it, but I really hoped he might seriously consider it. Hunter was brave and noble of heart, two of the traits an Avenger most needed to have. Those things weren't enough without the selfless desire to do good and to make the world a better place, of course, but only he could decide if he had *that* or not. It wasn't an easy decision, as I well knew.

Several hours later we approached the area at the back of the compound where the data port was supposed to be. It was located right next to the air conditioning unit, and I suppose it was intended for maintenance purposes. We'd intentionally picked one in an area where there were no windows, so hopefully we wouldn't be seen as long as we stayed close to the wall. But there *was* a heavy steel access door right beside it, and I confess that part *did* make me a little uneasy. If anybody opened that door we'd be cornered like rats between the air conditioner and the wall. We both had laser pistols, true, but we also knew that if it actually came down to a fight then we'd have almost zero chance of coming out of this mission alive.

"You know they'll realize somebody hacked into the station computer, as soon as they see one of those big birds take off," Hunter said in a low voice.

"Yeah, I know that. But I hope it'll take them a little while to figure out how we did it. I'm gonna try to mask our location if I can," I said.

"You better. They'll be down on us in a heartbeat as soon as they can identify where we are. It won't even take them that long to search the whole compound on foot," Hunter said.

"I know that too. They won't know we're here at first, while I'm breaking into the mainframe. They won't know anything's going on till they see one of the ships take off, like you said. I figure we've got about twenty minutes after that point before they find us one way or another, but that should be enough time to move the ship out of range and set it down a few miles north of here on the plain. Then they can keep their crummy old spaceport for all I care," I said.

"Yeah, but is that enough time for us to get away?" Hunter asked.

"I hope so. Try to get done moving the ship as quick as you can without wrecking it, and then we'll hit the hay again. I don't think they'll find us in all that tall grass, as long as we're not right up here next to the building like this," I said.

"I'll do my best," he agreed.

"Good. Now let's get started," I said, pulling the pack off my back that held the computer and cord. It had a fully charged battery which should last for several hours, so that ought not to be a problem. I touched the keypad to activate the holographic screen, and then rapidly typed in several commands to prevent the computer from identifying itself when it made contact with the mainframe inside the building. Then I plugged the wire into the data port.

It took only a second for the computers to link up, and then I was busily at work. It would've helped if I'd had a more powerful processor to work with, but there's only so much you can do with portable equipment like that. In any case, I was finally able to break through the security system and get access to everything, and from there I immediately went to the command screen for the outermost colony ship. It was named the *Alabama,* and I figured it couldn't hurt to suck up to Captain Stone a little bit, since that's where he was from. Besides which, I figured that one would be the easiest for Hunter to maneuver.

"All right, Hunter. As soon as you press this button, it'll start the engines. I've got the screen and the keypad set up to mimic a flight simulator, so take her a few miles north and set her down again as fast as you can. You've got fifteen minutes. Then we'll grab the computer and get out of here," I said, as soon as everything was ready. Then I stepped aside so he could get in front of the screen.

"Here we go," he muttered under his breath.

Then he pressed the button, and even from nearly a half mile away I could hear the deep throb of the ship's engines and feel the vibration in the ground. I don't doubt the people inside the spaceport heard it too, and that meant the clock was already ticking till they figured out where we were.

Even I knew that normally it was proper procedure to let the ship idle for several minutes and do a complete systems check before taking off; I'd spent enough time with Jesse to know that. But we didn't have time for all the nice little procedures like that; not if we wanted to survive. So Hunter lifted off barely thirty seconds after he first started the engines, flying low over the grassy plain.

"Just get her over the horizon so they can't shoot at us anymore; that'll be good enough," I said, looking over his shoulder. He grunted, so I guess he must have heard me. Ten minutes later he set her down on the plain five miles north of the spaceport, and started to shut down the engines.

"No, leave them running. I don't know for sure that we'd get them started again; they might have programmed some kind of hidden locking system in there so we'd have to go back through the spaceport computers again. Let's not push our luck," I said.

Then I broke all the links I could find between the spaceport computer and the ship's computer, and took a few seconds to shut down the mainframe altogether. That ought to cause them some serious headache for at least the next few hours, trying to get all their systems back online. Then I yanked the cord loose, stuffed the computer in my pack, and we scrambled back into the grass.

None too soon, either. No sooner were we hidden in the grass than the door beside the air conditioner flew open, and an NADF soldier with a laser rifle stuck his head out and glanced wildly around. He was too distracted to look very closely at the grass or there's no doubt in my mind he would have seen us; we weren't far enough away from the building to be completely out of sight yet. But he only swept the area to make sure there were no obvious intruders, and when he didn't see any he slammed the door shut and locked it again.

Hunter and I had been frozen in the grass while the soldier was standing there, but as soon as he shut the door we eeled our way off into the grass as fast as we could crawl on our bloody knees.

"That's about as close as I'd ever want to cut it," I said after a while.

"Too close," Hunter agreed.

It took us several hours to crawl back to the place where Captain Stone had dropped us off earlier, weary, sore, and grass-stained, but also pretty cocky, to tell the truth. Our wild escapade had worked, and in the process we'd saved who knew how many lives that would have been lost in a direct frontal assault. To take Captain Stone's own proverb, we'd saved the whole world multiple times over. I felt like we were entitled to do a little bit of swaggering after all that.

So that's exactly what we did as soon as we got back to camp, and the way those raggedy rebel soldiers clapped and cheered and carried us around on their shoulders, you'd think *they* believed we'd saved the whole world, too. Even Captain Stone cracked a smile.

But there was no time to savor our victory for long. Everybody immediately loaded up on the captured *Alabama* and we took off as soon as possible. But before we left the planet for good, Captain Stone offered me the honor of blowing up the other ships. Missiles were already locked on target and all I had to do was press the button. So that's what I did, to great fanfare I might add, and a few seconds later we saw the other two colony ships go up in a bright red mushroom cloud.

We were free at last, and Colonel Bartow and his flunkies were trapped on Venus forever.

Chapter Thirteen

I don't think I've ever been so glad to be out in space again as I was that day, but we still had unfinished business to do before we could get back to Earth.

"I wonder what the plan is about Colonel Burns," Hunter said, not long after we launched.

"I'm not sure, other than heading over to Mars to blow up his ships. We might have to wait a while on that, though; he's supposedly bound for Jamestown right this very minute to pull all *their* chestnuts out of the fire, if what we've heard is true. I'm not sure Captain Stone wants to risk a space battle," I said.

"I don't know if it can wait, Tyke. I wouldn't put it past Colonel Burns to drop a few missiles on Kona the second we landed and wipe us out completely. But Captain Stone is a pretty good strategist, you know; I'm sure he hasn't overlooked that possibility himself," Hunter said.

"That's true," I admitted.

"I doubt Colonel Burns would have taken more than one ship to Jamestown. The other two are probably still parked on Mars somewhere, so if I had to guess I'd say we'll probably try to go destroy those first, even if we can't nail the third one yet," Hunter concluded.

"Maybe," I said.

"We shouldn't even have to land, if it comes to that. We can just bomb them to smithereens from space and then go home, hopefully," Hunter said.

"I might go have a talk with him and see what he's thinking," I said.

"Cool. But if you do, you'll come back and let me know what he says, right?" Hunter asked.

"Sure," I agreed.

It turned out that Hunter was right; Captain Stone had already made plans for attacking whatever ships were still on the ground at the Martian colony, and when I went to ask him about it he was unsurprised.

"That was already in the plans from the beginning. I'm surprised you hadn't thought of it yourself, Mr. McGrath," he said.

"I did, sort of. But I thought we might have to wait till that other one gets back from Venus so they'd all be in one spot," I said.

"I don't think so. Colonel Burns is a ruthless man, and a smart one, too. We can't allow him to have time to make preparations," Captain Stone said.

"So what do we do, then? Go to Mars and blow up the other ships?" I asked.

"Not quite. As you mentioned, one of the remaining colony ships has already left Mars on its way to Jamestown to bring relief supplies. The other two have been moved to a secret location to keep us from finding them. The one on its way to Venus doesn't concern me; we planted a nuclear device underneath the tarmac at the airport before we left Jamestown, set to be triggered when it detects the landing signal of a spaceship. There won't be anything left of *that* one but a crater in the ground," Captain Stone said, waving his hand dismissively.

"I'm shocked it didn't blow up during the battle. There were all kinds of missiles and laser beams and exploding ships crashing everywhere," I said.

"Don't display your ignorance, Mr. McGrath. Modern nuclear devices don't work that way. They can only be exploded by the ignition computer, which will only do so under the circumstances it's instructed to look for. No amount of heat or explosions would suffice," Captain Stone said.

I hadn't known that, but then military ordnance is not exactly my area of specialty. I decided it was time to change the subject.

"That's awfully close to Jamestown for a nuclear bomb, isn't it?" I asked.

"It'll be a clean one, Mr. McGrath. Jamestown is nearly six miles from the airport; there shouldn't be any lasting damage which can't be fixed. As I said before, I don't want to cost lives unnecessarily," he said.

"You don't think they'll find it before the ship gets there?" I asked.

"I don't believe so. I set the device personally, and as far as I could tell no one suspected me. We'll find out soon enough," he said.

"So what about the two other ships on Mars that got moved elsewhere, then?" I asked.

"There's nothing we can do about that immediately; not till we figure out where they are," he said.

"And how do we do that?" I asked.

"Patience, Mr. McGrath. We have soldiers on Mars just as we did on Venus. At some point one of them will be able to find the information we need. Then we'll go wipe out those ships and hopefully rescue our friends," he said.

That was the first I'd heard about rebels on Mars, though of course I don't suppose it should have surprised me. But if any such allies existed there, then naturally we wanted to rescue them and bring them back to Earth if at all possible. There was safety in numbers, at least to a certain extent.

"So there's really no way of knowing how long it might take, then?" I asked.

"None at all. But I don't expect it to take very long, actually. Give it a few days and we'll see what happens. If I hear anything, you'll be the first to know," he said.

And as a matter of fact, it was the very next day when Captain Stone called me back to his office.

"We found them," he said without preamble, and I knew immediately that he was talking about the Martian colony ships.

"So does that mean we're headed for Mars?" I asked.

"That's right. The colony ships are parked in Gusev Crater. We'll go there immediately and destroy them, and I've also made arrangements to pick up our compatriots at a secure location. Hopefully, if all goes well, we can slip in and out of there with no fighting at all," Captain Stone said.

"That would be the best thing," I agreed, even though I privately had my doubts. Things had never been that simple on Venus, or anywhere else I'd ever been. There were always complications of some type or other.

In the meantime, Captain Stone's plan to wreck the colony ship on its way to Venus went off without a hitch. We watched the nuclear explosion utterly destroy it, right along with the terminal building and most of Colonel Bartow's remaining aircraft. The telescopes on board the *Alabama* were powerful enough to focus in and let us see everything in living color.

Jamestown suffered some damage, of course; broken windows and a wall or two knocked down on the west side of town closest to the airport, but just as Captain Stone had promised, nothing that couldn't be fixed. In my heart of hearts, that was a huge relief to me.

The mission to Mars turned out to be a little more problematic.

Oh, things went pretty well at first; we slipped in and destroyed the colony ships at Gusev Crater, taking Colonel Burns completely by surprise, I think. That permanently wiped out our enemies' entire space fleet, and when we all watched it happen on the big screens in the command room, there were even tears in some peoples' eyes.

So far so good.

But there were still three hundred and twenty-six rebels to pick up and carry home with us, and that's where the trouble started. I'm sure Colonel Burns had his own ways of knowing things, and I also think he wanted to recapture the last colony ship while he had the chance, even if he had to damage it in the process.

So it was that we landed uneventfully at the prearranged meeting spot on Tharsis Tholus, and the Martian rebels quickly streamed on board as fast as we could work the airlock. It turns out Mars can't be terraformed with breeder gases in quite the same way as Venus had been; the air is too thin, and the planet in general is too small. People still wouldn't have been able to breathe even if every molecule of carbon dioxide on the planet had been converted into oxygen and graphite. The Martian colonists supposedly had a way to release oxygen from surface rocks, but that's a much longer and more difficult process. Even after fifteen years of hard work, I gathered that the results had been meager at best. So I wasn't surprised to see that everybody was dressed in space suits when we landed, and it took hours to process them all into the ship through the airlock.

I would have liked to go outside and walk around a little bit on the Martian surface if I could have, especially since it was highly doubtful I'd ever get another chance. But I knew as well as anybody else that we didn't dare fritter away airlock time on something frivolous like that. We needed to get the rest of the rebels loaded up and then slip away from there as fast as humanly possible.

So I contented myself by going down to the entrance bay with Hunter and watching the newcomers stream inside and take their space suits off. They looked a lot like the ones from Venus, at least to the extent of being young and nice-looking. They were a lot paler, though.

"Got some real grub worms in this group, don't we?" Hunter commented after a while, and I laughed.

"Oh, you noticed that too, did you? I bet they don't get much sun out here like the ones at Jamestown did. They have to live underground most of the time," I said.

"Yup; pale dudes who live underground. Grubs. Let them hang out on the beach in Kona for a little while and that'll change soon enough, though," Hunter said.

"No doubt," I agreed.

We chatted companionably about this and that while we watched the airlock disgorge ten more soldiers every twelve and a half minutes, but even after we'd been at it steadily for almost six hours, we'd still only managed to load up two hundred and eighty of the rebels.

"Slow process, isn't it?" I said, glancing at my watch.

"How much longer have we got?" Hunter asked.

"Still a little over an hour, if they keep up the pace," I said.

"Well, tell you what. Why don't we go back to the cafeteria and grab something to eat before all these roughs pile in? I'm starting to get hungry," Hunter said.

"You're always hungry, Hunter," I said, and he laughed.

"I can't help it if I'm growing fast; you know I'm two inches taller than I was when we left Earth?" he asked. I hadn't actually noticed, but I didn't doubt the truth of it. When Chris and Jesse and I were all three roughly that age Philip used to like to say that it really did his heart good to watch a teenage boy eat. . . which was a good thing, since we were about to bankrupt him in the process. He was only joking, of course, but I suppose it wouldn't have been funny if there hadn't been at least a grain of truth to it. I couldn't help smiling a little at the memory.

"Come on, then. Let's go eat something before you dry up and blow away," I said tolerantly, and we got up from our seat to head for the cafeteria.

That's when the attack started.

Colonel Burns must have been stealthy about it; I have to give him that much. But all of a sudden we heard the sound of heavy explosions rocking the ship, and almost instantly the *whoosh* of dropping pressure.

"We've got a hull breach!" I cried, and my voice was already thin and tinny-sounding. Wherever the hole was, it must have been a monster.

And that was a major problem. Once the air pressure drops below a certain value at room temperature, you will die. Not only can you not breathe, but the blood vessels in your nose will burst and your blood will start to boil the instant it runs out onto your face. If pressure keeps dropping then the vessels in your eyes and lungs will start to burst open too, and then you'll drown on boiling blood. The pressure on Mars is plenty low enough to make that happen, which meant as soon as pressure between the ship and the outside had time to equalize, then we were dead meat.

"Space suit!" I yelled to Hunter, and then held my breath to save oxygen. He must have heard me, even though it was getting hard to breathe and even harder to hear, because he rushed across the room to grab a suit. We fumbled to get inside them, our noses already bleeding like crimson fountains by then, getting blood all over everything and making the process twice as hard from slick hands and sticky zippers. Hunter had never used a spacesuit before and I'd only done it once myself, during the trip to Titan. I pushed his awkward hands away and got him sealed in from the outside, then sealed up my own suit. Just in time, too. I was light-headed and blurry-eyed, and if you think having a profuse nosebleed inside the helmet of a spacesuit is a fun experience then you should try it sometime. I felt like somebody had killed a hog inside my suit.

It was even worse when I felt the ship suddenly leave the ground. I stumbled and fell, which only succeeded in splashing the blood against the inside of my faceplate and practically blinding me. There were still almost fifty rebels down there on the surface, but Captain Stone must have realized just as well as I did that there wasn't a thing we could do to save them. A few more hits like the ones we'd already taken and we wouldn't even be able to save ourselves.

"Are you okay, Hunter?" I asked, keying my radio.

"Yeah. Bowed and bloody, but not beaten," he said wryly, and in spite of everything I had to laugh.

"Come on then, let's see if we can find our way out of here," I said. There were twelve Martian colonists who'd still been in the room with us when the attack started, and ten more inside the airlock. We quickly got those out, and since there was nobody else to do it I gathered them all together in the middle of the floor.

"All right, it looks like this deck has a hull breach, but there are four other decks on this ship and hopefully there's at least one of them that still has cabin pressure. Come on," I said, trying to sound calm and self-assured, like I knew exactly what I was doing.

They must have thought I did, because they meekly followed along behind me as I led them out into the hallway and toward the stairs. The decks on the *Alabama* were lettered from A to E, with A-deck being uppermost. The airlock was located on E-deck, so we had nowhere to go but up. As it turned out, D-deck and C-deck were breached also, and along the way we found the bodies of several newcomers who hadn't had time to get back to the entrance bay to grab a spacesuit before they bled to death.

Those were heartwrenching scenes, and I was actually glad the blood on my faceplate kept me from seeing very well. We covered them up with whatever lay near to hand at the time, but that was the best we could do for them.

The gastight doors between B-deck and C-deck were closed, which gave me hope that maybe the rest of the ship was still survivable. The *Alabama* was meant to carry a thousand people, of course, and if we'd been full to capacity then we would have had a horrifying disaster on our hands. But as it was, there ought to be enough room to cram the not quite four hundred people on board into the livable space that was left.

"Captain Stone! Can anybody hear me?" I asked, punching the intercom button beside the gas doors.

"Who is this? Where are you?" came a voice back.

"It's Tyke McGrath. I'm trapped on C-deck with about twenty-five survivors," I said.

"Have you got air?" the voice asked.

"We're suited up. C-deck is depressurized," I said.

"Is anybody injured?" the voice asked.

"No, I don't think so," I said.

"All right, Mr. McGrath. Sit tight where you are for a little while. We'll have to set up a portable airlock and that may take a few hours. But don't worry; we'll get you out," the voice said.

"Just come as quick as you can. I'm not sure how much air everybody has left," I said.

"Will do," the voice said, and that was that.

It was really only about forty-five minutes before the gastight door to B-deck came up, releasing a blast of air which knocked several of us down on the metal floor. Inside were two space-suited soldiers, and almost immediately I heard a voice on my radio.

"Hurry and come on inside; all of you. This is only a makeshift airlock and it may not hold for long," one of them said.

All of us squeezed into a space no bigger than ten by twelve feet, though it was a tight fit, and then one of the soldiers resealed the gastight doors. They must have had a way to bleed air into the space from B-deck, because we didn't get hit with a blast of wind this time. Only a gentle hissing that grew louder as the pressure rose, and finally they were able to swing open the door in what looked like a hastily-welded metal wall. I noticed as we went past that it had already started to warp from the strain, and I had no doubt it wouldn't have lasted much longer without blowing out.

B-deck didn't seem to have suffered any damage that I could tell, and I wearily shucked off my bloody suit and left it right in the middle of the floor, not caring at all about proper procedure or where it was supposed to be put. Then I went to the restroom to wash my face so I wouldn't look like the victim of an axe-murderer anymore. Hunter did the same, and I think if possible he looked even more tired than I did.

"Thanks for saving me back there. I never would have figured out how to work that suit if you hadn't done it for me. I would've ended up like those dudes we saw on D-deck," he said in a sober voice.

"You would have done the same thing," I said diffidently, embarrassed to be thanked for something like that. When your friends and the people you love need you then of course you'll be there for them, but the last thing in the world you want is to put them in your debt or to risk ruining a lighthearted and easygoing relationship by suddenly making it feel serious and awkward.

"Well. . . thanks anyway. I won't forget about it," Hunter said.

"You're welcome," I said.

"Well, I'm fixing to go lie down and rest for a while, I think. It's been kind of a rough day," Hunter said.

"Yeah, you probably should. I think I'll go talk to Captain Stone for a minute and then I'll probably do the same thing," I agreed.

So that's what I did, and Captain Stone looked almost as haggard as Hunter had.

"Congratulations on your quick thinking today, Mr. McGrath. It's much appreciated," he said when I came into his office.

"Thank you, sir. I'm just glad to be back among the living," I said, and he nodded.

"Undeniably. We're all lucky to be among the living, if the truth be told. Colonel Burns caught us by surprise after most of our people were trapped inside the ship and couldn't return fire. Two of the *Alabama's* six engines are badly damaged, and that leaves us with some serious questions about whether we'll have the power to reach escape velocity. We think it'll work out, but it's very borderline," Captain Stone said.

"I see. Is there anything I can do to help?" I asked.

"Pray, Mr. McGrath. That's all you can do," Captain Stone said.

"I will, sir," I said, and he nodded.

I left him alone then and went to my new cabin. My old one had been on C-deck, but I hadn't left anything in there that I cared about losing. All I needed was a soft spot to sleep and I was good to go.

I did as Captain Stone had asked and said a prayer before I went to sleep, and then for several hours at least I was able to escape from the cares of living.

The next morning at breakfast I heard that thirteen people had died from pressure loss and laser burns during the attack, and that the engineers were still trying to squeeze out every last possible drop of power to get us over the hump and into space. If Mars had been a heavier world with a higher escape velocity then we never would have been able to break free. As it was it took literally *days* to struggle our way up out of the planet's gravity well, with intermittent attacks from Colonel Burns the entire time. He didn't have time to drag his heavy lasers into position while we were moving, and his jets were no match for the *Alabama's* guns, but that didn't keep him from harassing us. When it became clear that we'd ultimately succeed in getting away, I think everybody on board let out a long sigh of relief. I know I did. But even then we had to limp away with damaged engines, which meant a trip of nearly three weeks to make it back to Earth instead of six days.

Instead of attacking our soldiers when the battle first began, Colonel Burns had immediately started firing heavily on the *Alabama's* engines. It had been a diabolically smart move on his part; if he could have stranded us on Mars then he could have starved us out at his leisure and then gone in to repair the ship for his own use later. And there would have been *nothing* we could have done about it. Only Captain Stone's quick thinking had saved us, and even that only by the skin of our teeth.

Three weeks later we landed the *Alabama* at the airport in Hilo, and walked back out into a world I'd almost forgotten. I didn't think our faithful ship would ever fly again, but that was all right. She got us home, and that was all that mattered.

Chapter Fourteen

We rode several tour buses across the mountains to Kona, and once there I made the worrisome discovery that the town was completely deserted. Philip and Joan and the others were nowhere to be found, and from the way the weeds had grown it didn't look like anyone had been there in months at the very least.

But even as scary as that was, I couldn't do a thing about it. As soon as we got into town I had to immediately run to my lab at the university to start manufacturing Orion vaccine as fast as I possibly could. There was no telling when and how many of the newcomers had already been exposed to spores, but I had to behave as if every single one of them had been infected the second they set foot at the airport in Hilo. I had thirty-six hours from that moment to get everybody on the island inoculated, and that's a tall order. I couldn't do *anything* else till that got done.

It gave me unpleasant flashbacks to that original marathon research session in Tampa when I had to find the tiny needle of a cure somewhere inside the massive haystack of Josh Hampstead's DNA. This time all I had to do was multiply the genes and get the retroviruses ready to deliver them, and while I did all that I thought wryly to myself that every human being on earth from now on and forevermore will have a little bit of Josh Hampstead in them. Not to mention every bird and every whale, every cat and every deer, and all things else that draw breath with a warm and beating heart. God bless him and may he rest in peace.

But all that work took time, even though I knew exactly what to do. I didn't get a wink of sleep that night, too busy manufacturing vaccine and giving doses to the hundreds of people standing in line outside my lab. Even with some of the newcomers who had medical or scientific training to help me, we still didn't get finished till mid-afternoon the next day; just barely in time. Several people had already started to get sick by then, and those folks we moved up to the front of the line so they could get treatment first. Nobody died, but quite a few of them were in bad shape for several days afterward. Eight people ended up having mild to severe reactions to the vaccine itself, and for a while we were occupied dealing with those issues, too.

While I was busy in the lab, Hunter and Leah had a full time job helping the newcomers to get resettled. Kailua Kona originally had a population of something like ten thousand, I believe, so there were plenty of empty houses for them to occupy. Everybody picked a place they liked, just as the rest of us had done when we got there two years ago, but Hunter and Leah had to take down names and addresses, and get water and lights and phones turned on, not to mention answer a million repetitive questions.

But eventually it was all done, and then we were finally able to consider the matter of what could possibly have happened to our missing friends and family members.

"Where do you think they could be?" I asked, as soon as I had a chance to sit down with Hunter and Leah alone.

"You don't think they recaptured them, do you?" Hunter asked.

"Maybe," I said, frowning. I had no idea what might have happened at Southern Command after the soldiers stunned me. I liked to imagine that everybody had gotten away, but I knew all too well that that might not be the case. Some or all of them might have been caught or even killed while I was knocked out, or possibly later on while I was en route to Venus with Hunter and Leah. The thought of them being locked up under guard somewhere I could cope with; the other idea I didn't even want to think about.

"If they did then don't you think they'd still be at Southern Command? That should be the first place we look before we think about anything else," Leah pointed out, and of course there was some sense to that suggestion.

"Let's go find out, then. We'll take some soldiers with us just in case we run into a nasty situation. Hopefully if they're still locked up then Colonel Bartow's henchmen will realize they're trapped here with no possible help. They might see reason and cut a deal to turn everybody loose," I said.

So the three of us boarded the *Pineapple Express* along with a contingent of forty soldiers Captain Stone assigned to the task. They were mostly grubs; Hunter's silly name for the pale-skinned Martian colonists, which I found myself using half the time in spite of all my efforts not to. I didn't know them nearly as well as the group from Jamestown, but they were unfailingly courteous and I didn't doubt they were competent. I suspect Captain Stone wanted to give them a chance to prove themselves after the debacle at Tharsis Tholus; he was a good leader that way.

Anyway, Hunter landed us at the airport in Atlanta, and then we had to find a functional bus in the parking lot to get us to Southern Command. That might have been a problem if we'd had to depend only on Hunter and Leah and me, since none of us had ever driven something that big and bulky before. But one of the grubs knew how, so before long we made it across the city and pulled in to the headquarters building.

My first thought was to be creeped out at having to visit the place again, considering what all happened last time I was there. But the place seemed tranquil and silent, and nobody shot at us at least.

Even as big as it was, it didn't take long for forty soldiers to comb the building and verify that it was deserted. Most of them were at least semi-familiar with the place, since they'd worked or visited there occasionally before the plague. We could be reasonably sure they hadn't overlooked some squirrelly little corner where Colonel Bartow's goons might be hiding.

But that only made things even more puzzling than before, actually. I couldn't fathom why Colonel Bartow's soldiers would have taken our people anywhere else if they still held them captive.

But then on the other hand, I couldn't fathom why Philip hadn't taken them back to Kona if they were free. It didn't seem to make any sense.

"So what now?" Hunter asked as we stood in the parking lot.

"I don't know; let me think a minute," I said, waving him off. The soldiers stood quietly talking among themselves next to the bus, seemingly content to wait for whatever orders might come. I didn't really expect them to have any suggestions when they knew so little about the circumstances, but it sure would have been nice.

"Maybe Jesse got hurt and couldn't fly them home," Hunter said after a little while, and much as I didn't like that idea either, it was at least logical.

"So what would they do in that case?" Leah asked.

"I think they wouldn't have stayed in Atlanta for long. They would have seen the ship take off, and if they came back after that and searched Southern Command like we just did and found it empty then they would have known we were gone. But Philip would've been afraid to stay too close, just in case they came back with more soldiers. He has to think about everybody," I said, feeling my way along.

"But that still doesn't tell us where they might have gone," Leah pointed out.

"I think. . . he would've taken them somewhere we might think to look but no one else would think of, just in case we somehow managed to escape on our own," I said.

"Tampa, you mean?" Hunter asked.

"No, I don't think it would've been Tampa or anywhere in that vicinity. It's common knowledge that's where we used to live. The NADF could just pull it up on some database and that would be that. Tampa wouldn't be any better than Atlanta. Neither would Kona, for that matter," I said.

"So where, then?" Leah asked.

I tried to think of places that had some kind of special significance which Philip would have known I'd know about. Try as I might, I could only think of a handful.

"I can only think of three places like that," I finally said.

"What are they?" Hunter asked.

"Well, there's my grandparents' old ranch outside Linden, Texas. My father grew up there and Philip and Joan are from that general vicinity, too. But I don't think that's something anybody else would ever know or guess," I said.

"And the others?" Hunter asked.

"There's also the Avengers' library, in Natchitoches, West Louisiana," I said.

"And the third?" Hunter asked.

"There's a place we used to go on vacation now and then to stay with some of Philip and Joan's friends, way up in the mountains in North Carolina," I said.

"Well. . . that's the closest place to here; we should probably check that one first, don't you think?" Leah asked.

"Yeah, probably. It's called Maggie Valley; it's right outside the Great Smoky Mountains National Park, maybe twenty-five, thirty miles west of Asheville. No more than a little spot in the road," I said.

"We better go see, then. If they're not there then we can go check the others," Hunter said.

"Good enough," I agreed.

So that's what we did, flying the *Pineapple Express* to Asheville and then driving the rest of the way. We left the soldiers at the airport to guard the plane since we didn't expect to have to do any fighting, and it was easier to drive one car than to have to lead an entire troop convoy. I remembered the route very well, from a hundred road trips as a kid. Everything was starting to crumble and disappear into the overgrowth, of course, but it was still recognizable if you knew what to look for.

Luther and Jenine Anderson's old place was a farmstead, complete with a red barn and a little lake surrounded by heavily wooded mountains. We all used to love that place when I was little; digging tunnels in the snow at Christmas and jumping off the rocks into the lake if it was summertime. Aron Anderson had always been the kind of kid who cared no more for the great outdoors than he would have cared for a tin can in the ditch, and Chris and Jesse and I had had many discussions over the years about what a pity it was that such an awesome place should be wasted on a boy who didn't appreciate it.

Luther and Jenine still kept the place even after they moved to Tampa, as a vacation home I guess. But they'd never minded us using it whenever we liked, even though they didn't live there anymore. And we had, right up till the plague came along. I think the last time we visited the place was sometime during the summer before I turned sixteen, when Florida had been hot as blue blazes and the mountain air had felt pretty good for a change.

The taste of nostalgia is sweet sometimes.

At first I was afraid I might not remember the way after we got off the main road; things looked different, and five years is a long time. But after a little bit of hesitation and one or two false starts I managed to find the right turn.

The farm was at the very end of a gravel road, behind a metal gate that was intended to keep cows inside, even though the Andersons had never actually owned any. We had to stop there and walk the rest of the way since I didn't have a key to open the lock, but that was all right since it wasn't very far.

At last we came around the last turn and saw the lake and the barn in front of us, and hope filled my heart when I saw that the grass had been mowed sometime not all that long ago.

"Somebody's here; see the grass?" I asked.

"Let's see," Leah said, and hurried forward.

They must have seen us coming, because the door opened before we were even halfway there, spilling out all those dear and familiar faces we hadn't seen in so long.

As soon as I spotted Danielle coming outside with Derrick and Josie I ran across the yard and swept up all three of them in my arms. She hugged me tightly for a long time without saying a word, and when she finally let go the light in her eyes said more than words ever could have.

"You sure did take long enough, mister," she finally said, with a little smile on her face.

"I did the best I could," I said awkwardly, and she laughed.

"I'm only joking, baby. I don't care about any of that, as long as you're back home now. I'm so glad to see you I can hardly stand it," she said, throwing her arms around me again.

"Me too," I agreed, hugging her back. It was springtime in the high Appalachians, tender green and full of flowers, and maybe it's true after all that love and beauty are linked forever in the heart of man. That was something my grandma Lisa always used to like to say, or so I'm told, and she must have been a wise woman because I don't think I could possibly have loved Danielle any more than I did at that moment. It may sound strange that the bright red roses and the whispering wind should enlarge my heart beyond what it already was, but it's true nonetheless.

"So where have you been all this time?" Danielle said, when we could breathe again.

"Venus, mostly. It's beautiful there," I said truthfully.

"You'll have to tell me all about it, then," she said.

"I will, but right now I'm more interested in you and Josie. She looks like she's twice as big as she was when I left," I said, staring at her in mild amazement.

"Babies tend to do that, you know. Your daughter is fond of eating," Danielle said, laughing again.

"I bet she is," I said, and tried to pick her up. She started to cry, so I gave her back to Danielle.

"Don't worry; she'll remember you soon enough," Danielle said.

"I'm sure she will," I agreed, even though it disappointed me a little.

"*You* remember me, don't you, sport?" I asked, getting down so I was even with Derrick.

"Yup," he agreed, so I smiled and picked him up instead.

"Well good; I would've felt bad if *everybody* forgot about me after only six months," I said.

"Nope, we didn't forget," Derrick said.

"So what happened to everybody, then? I don't know anything from the time they knocked me out," I said.

"Well, there's not much to tell, really. They stopped chasing us after they caught you again. I don't think they cared much about the rest of us, as long as they got you and Hunter and Leah," Danielle said.

"Yeah, that makes sense. Hunter and Leah's father is the NADF commander on Venus who ordered the raid in the first place. He wanted me to give him the vaccine against the Orion Strain," I said.

"That makes sense, then. Anyway they let us go, and Philip hid us in an empty building for a little while. We saw the spaceship take off, and then when he and Chris went back to Southern Command they found out everybody was gone. It didn't take much to figure out they'd taken you and left the planet. So he brought us here so we'd be safe," Danielle said.

"But why didn't you go home? Was he afraid the soldiers might come back?" I asked, and a cloud passed over her face at that question.

"Tyke, I. . . " she began, and I felt a creeping dread start to rise in my gut. People don't look like that or sound that way unless they're about to tell you some really bad news.

"What is it?" I asked.

"It's Jesse. They shot him in the head with a stunner before we could get away. I'm so sorry, baby," she said, her eyes full of compassion.

"How bad is he?" I asked, surprising myself at how calm I could be.

"He can walk and talk, and feed himself, and things like that. He remembers who we are. But he can't fly anymore, and most of the time he'll just sit there and stare at the wall unless you show him what you want him to do. Joan has been trying to teach him how to read and write again, but no luck so far. I don't think he'll ever be the same as he used to be," she said.

"It seems like he should have been out of range by the time they knocked me out; I know he was way up in front of me, and he's a fast runner," I said, and all of a sudden she looked away and wouldn't meet my eyes anymore.

"What is it? Tell me," I said, and she sighed.

"I'll tell you because I know you'll find out anyway, but I don't want you to blame yourself," she said, grasping my hands.

"Just tell me. Please," I said.

"He saw you fall, Tyke. He went back to try to save you, and that's when they shot him and left him to die. I think he would have, if they hadn't snatched you and gone right back inside so we could go get him. Joan had to start him breathing again," she said.

It took a second for her words to fully sink in, and then I had to turn my face away toward the lake so no one would see me start to cry. God knows I hated Luke Bartow at that moment with every ounce of my being, but that only made it hurt even worse. Danielle knew, of course, and knowing me as she did, she handed Josie to Derrick and slipped her arms completely around me to hide my tears from the others. I'm sure they would have understood; it's just that there are certain things a guy doesn't want anyone to see. I don't know why; it's just the way it is.

I was really good about keeping it all together when I saw him later, in spite of the way he was. Oh, he smiled when he saw me and gave me a hug and we even talked for a little while, but he wasn't the same; I could tell it immediately. The sharp edge of his mind was gone, and along with it all the quick humor and depth of life that I was used to. He was like a shadow of the Jesse I remembered, a person who looked and sounded the same but whose soul was forever dimmed. And although I supposed I might in time come to love this new individual almost as much, in the meantime I missed the old one terribly.

Leah would have the hardest time of us all, I suppose; life had dealt her a cruel hand with all this. I didn't doubt she'd take care of him, and of course he might eventually recover somewhat more than he had thus far. But nevertheless, her life would certainly never turn out the way she'd probably always hoped and dreamed it would.

The next day we gathered up such things as everyone had, and rode back to Asheville in somber quiet. It should have been a joyous occasion, I suppose, and maybe in time I'd be more inclined to feel that way. But not quite yet.

The grubs caught the mood immediately when we reached the airport, and made no attempt to joke or laugh.

"Let's go home, babe; I've had enough adventures for a while," I said to Danielle as we first got out of the car on the tarmac.

"Amen to that," Danielle agreed, and without another backward glance we all boarded the *Pineapple Express* for the long flight back to Hawaii.

Chapter Fifteen

Things settled down pretty quickly after we got back to Kona. Three hundred and fifty-four surviving soldiers plus the twenty-two of us who were already there to begin with turned out to be just enough to form a cozy little community. There were actually enough of us at that point to keep the whole town clean and mowed and looking good for the first time since we moved there.

That one fact alone did all of us an amazing amount of good, I have to say. I felt like we'd stepped back into the real world again for the first time since the plague, and that's an incredibly wonderful thing when you've spent so long feeling like castaways on a desert island. It made it easy to forget sometimes that the rest of the world beyond this one little city still lay empty and desolate.

It turned out that Captain Stone already knew my father from somewhere, and before long you couldn't have pried those two apart with a butter knife. I didn't pay it much attention at the time, though; I was still sad and preoccupied about Jesse, despite the fact that there was nothing I knew of to do about that situation except learn how to live with it.

At least, not till I spoke to my father one day.

"Tyke, do you believe in miracles?" he asked me one morning. It was Saturday, and since he wasn't teaching that day he had a few

hours to spend with me at my lab. There's no way to completely
make up for fifteen lost years, of course, but I liked those quiet
Saturday morning talks very much. Biology isn't his passion and
astronomy isn't mine, but there are certain areas of common
ground where we could both show some interest, like terraforming
for example. A seamless blend of biology and space science, and
one which I happened to have quite a lot of experience with over
the past few years. Or sometimes he'd ramble on about his family
and the place he grew up back in Texas, and those were good things
to know, too. It's nice to feel rooted somewhere, and those stories
he told me fed a craving I'd only dimly realized I had.

But we didn't often talk about theology and metaphysics, so for
him to bring it up now made me curious.

"Sure, I guess. Natural laws are just a pattern to which events
have to conform. If God is real then it would be silly to think He
couldn't do things if He liked, just the way we can. He has more
power than we do, of course, but I don't see any intrinsic
impossibility to that kind of thing. Why do you ask?" I asked.

"I was thinking about Jesse, that's all," he said.

"What about Jesse?" I asked.

"Well, I've never told you the story before, but a long time ago
when I was young, there used to be a pool of water on my parents'
ranch, maybe thirty feet across and a little less than ten feet deep.
They called it Cadron Pool, because there was a spring at the
bottom of it that fed a creek of the same name," he said.

"Okay, so what about it?" I asked.

"Once in a while people would come to the ranch, with things no
medicine could heal, and then Mama and Daddy would take them
to that pool and pray over them, and then wash them in the water.
I saw things I can't explain any other way than to say they were
miracles. I saw blind men see. I saw people with end-stage cancer
walk out whole. Things most people would never believe, Tyke,"
he said soberly.

"Really?" I asked.

"Yeah, really. I don't know for sure if it's still there or not;
Daddy always said it was only meant for he and Mama to guard and

to use. But if it is, then you might take Jesse there. If you have the courage to believe, that is," he said.

"Why me?" I asked.

"Because you're the last McGrath. You're their grandson, so it might be acceptable for you to do it," he said.

"What about you, then? You're their son; it looks like you'd be an even better choice than I would," I said.

"Maybe I would have been at one time, Tyke. But I turned my back and said I didn't want the place or anything to do with it. Sometimes that's the kind of choice you can't take back. But *you* never said any such thing," he said.

As I've said before, I don't like things which I don't understand. And even though I didn't intrinsically disbelieve in the kinds of things Daddy was talking about, I was pretty hard headed about specific examples. Like this one, for instance.

I almost told him so, but then I thought about Titan and the words died on my lips. I'd seen with my own eyes something which could only be described as a miracle, after all. I remembered my dream of a mountain of ice in a black jungle, and the ancient prophecy N'grumth had shared with me, which I'd later fulfilled with my own two hands on the summit of Muwamanth. All that together couldn't be simply coincidence, and it shook my hard head at least enough to make me wonder.

But nevertheless I remembered all too well something Philip had told us many a time, that a faithless and double-minded man should never expect to receive anything from God. I couldn't go to Cadron Pool just on the off chance that something might happen, as if I were rolling dice. If I had that kind of attitude then I might as well not go at all. I had to go there with complete certainty in my heart that something great would be done, and God knows that was hard. I was much more comfortable with scientific matters which could be tested, and God can't be. Asking for a miracle is like asking your father for a dollar. The choice is up to him, and whether he'll do it or not isn't a question that science can answer.

But on the other hand, Jesse had loved me enough to risk his own life rather than leave me behind in Atlanta, and he'd ended up paying a dear price for that. What kind of friend would I be, if I couldn't even do this much for him in return? Or at least try?

I touched the Avenger's ring on my left middle finger, and that decided me.

"All right, I'll go," I said quietly.

I felt like I ought to tell everybody what I was doing, sort of as a proof of good faith, you know. So I gathered us all together in front of the Mo'Kuai'Kaua church, all three hundred and seventy-six of us, and told them the story Daddy had told me and what I meant to do, and asked them to pray for me.

Only twelve of us went. Philip and Joan, Chris and Emily, Hunter, Veronica, my mom and dad, me and Danielle, Leah, and then Jesse himself, of course. All the people who were closest to him. Well, other than Davy, I suppose, but we all agreed it wasn't the time or the place for babies.

Hunter flew us to Shreveport in the *Pineapple Express,* and from there we drove a little more than an hour or so to Linden, and from thence out to Goliad. I'd never seen the place myself, even though Daddy had told me about it many times. There wasn't much to see except thick woods, honestly; even the gravel road was starting to sprout little saplings.

"I don't think we can go any farther," I finally said. A sweet gum tree as big around as my arm was growing right in the middle of the road, and I was pretty sure we wouldn't be able to make our way around it. We'd had to drive a van from the airport so there'd be room for everybody to ride, and that's a far cry from a dirt bike or even a 4x4. Getting stuck in the ditch and having to walk five miles back to town in the sweltering Texas heat was not at all my idea of a good time.

"It's all right, we can walk it from here. See that hill over there?" Daddy asked, pointing through the trees. I could barely make out something vaguely like a hill, so I nodded.

"Yeah, I think I see it," I said.

"That's where we have to go. Cadron Pool is right at the foot of that hill," he said.

So we all got out of the van and headed off into the thick woods, and I'm sure if we hadn't had the hill to guide us we would have been lost in ten minutes. In the old days we would have been covered in ticks and swarmed with mosquitoes in no time, but happily all the little blood-suckers were extinct. It's not often when I find occasion to be glad for the Orion Strain, but that was one of them. We still had to contend with the saw briers and the heat, and that I can assure you is quite enough.

I didn't complain, though, not even under my breath. We were there for a reason, and I didn't grudge what we had to go through for that purpose.

And before very long, we reached the place. Cadron Pool was about thirty feet across, just as Daddy had said, and ringed with a short rock wall about a foot high and flat on top. The water was smooth as glass, reflecting the sky like a mirror, and it quietly spilled out over a low spot in the ledge to flow away into the woods somewhere. Trees grew right up to the edge of the rock wall, but in spite of that the pool was clear instead of being dark from fallen leaves as you might have expected.

"This is the place," Daddy said.

"What should I do?" I asked.

"I only know what I saw. Put your hands on his head and pray over him, then strip him down and have him swim in the pool, making sure he gets completely under," Daddy said.

"He's got to be naked?" I asked skeptically.

"I only know what I saw," Daddy repeated, shrugging.

It seemed silly, and I had to remind myself I wasn't necessarily here to understand, I was here to trust. There's a difference.

So I put both my hands on his head, feeling intensely self-conscious, but the way he stared at me with that vacant look in his eyes was enough to make me forget about my own discomfiture. I looked up to the sky, just as I'd done on the spire of Muwamanth long ago, and prayed aloud that he'd be made whole and healthy again. Then I stripped him down and led him by the hand up onto the lip of the pool.

"Go swim in the water, Jesse. Wash off," I said, feeling like I was talking to a puppy. He obediently dived in, while I tried with my whole heart to believe.

He was under there for a long time, and when he finally came up I thought at first that nothing had changed. Then he looked at me, and I was almost sure there was a keenness in his eyes that hadn't been there in a very long time. He didn't say a word, but sometimes you say the most when you say the least.

I shut my eyes and whispered a silent prayer of thanks, and then he was climbing out of the water and hugging Leah, apparently not perturbed at all to be walking around in his birthday suit. I think I would have been a little more reserved, myself, but to each his own I suppose.

"Hey, Tyke, toss me those clothes," he finally said, so I balled up the jeans and threw them at him. He caught them and slipped them on, then came to fetch his shirt and socks. Before long he was dressed, still wet from the pool but seemingly fit as a fiddle.

"Are you okay?" I asked in a low voice while he was putting his shoes on.

"I am now," he said soberly, pausing for a second with his shoe half on and half off.

"I'm glad. I've really missed you, buddy," I said, and he laughed.

"Of course you have. Who wouldn't?" he asked, and I laughed a little myself. That was more like the real Jesse; always a smart aleck. I think it was then that I was finally a hundred percent sure he was really well. If he could tell stupid jokes again then he was fine.

In fact he was a real chatty cathy on the way back to Shreveport; he didn't seem to remember much of anything since the day he got nailed in the head at Southern Command and I guess I couldn't blame him for wanting to know everything that had happened since then. But honestly, I almost wanted to tell him to hush for a while and let somebody else get a word in edgewise. He wouldn't even slow down long enough to let one person answer a question before he was already asking somebody else another one.

But by the time we made it back to Kona he'd settled down a little bit, enough to be amazed by the sight of so many new people and so much work that had been done.

But not half so amazed as the grubs were of *him*. They stopped and stared in silent awe, in the oldest and fullest sense of the word. The way you might feel if somebody told you there was a mighty angel with a flaming sword standing in the next room and you fully believed it. *That* kind of awe.

I'm not so sure but what I didn't share the feeling a little bit, come to think of it.

But Jesse was plain old Jesse again, and it's hard to maintain awe for any length of time when you see somebody every single day. And even though in my heart of hearts I thought quite a lot about Cadron Pool and what it might mean that it was entrusted to me, I refrained from saying anything about it. I still had a lot to ponder.

"It sure is a lot different with all these people here now," I said to Danielle one evening while we were alone on the beach a few weeks later. That was getting to be something of a rarity as the newcomers got settled in and started using the place, too. But every now and then we still had a little bit of the old solitude.

"Yeah, but I think it'll be a good thing overall. I've been talking to some of the girls and getting to know them, and it's really nice to have some new friends. You should get out a little more and make some of your own," Danielle said.

"Maybe I will," I said, and she laughed.

"We both know you probably won't, but I'm just saying I think it would be good for you, that's all," she said.

"I've got Jesse and Hunter, you know. That's plenty," I said.

"If you say so, baby. Whatever makes you happy," she said, kissing my forehead.

After a while I grudgingly decided she might have a point. I am not and never will be a social butterfly, but I suppose it never hurts to expand your circle of acquaintances.

So I tried, hard as that is for me, and I soon found that I was looked upon as a minor celebrity amongst the soldiers. I'm not used to being viewed like a movie star, honestly. But it made socializing an awful lot easier; I do have to say that much. Those soldiers seemingly never got tired of hearing about my adventures on the Moon, and on Titan, and most especially on Mars and Venus. I didn't mind, though; they were pretty likable folks once you got to know them.

As I mentioned before, none of them were older than about thirty at the very most, and they were almost evenly split between males and females. Colonel Burns must have had similar ideas as Dr. Weiss, when it came to repopulation. But then I suppose if you start with the same basic set of facts and the same ultimate goal then it's difficult not to arrive at the same general strategy for accomplishing it.

They had all kind of jobs, but mostly of the practical types: radar and computer techs, mechanics, agronomists, scientists of one type or another, doctors and nurses, engineers, and even a few psychologists and child development specialists, plus a smattering of all kinds of other things. And I must have been right about Colonel Burns' determination to pick only the best; besides being good-looking, they were almost without exception the most intelligent and well-adjusted individuals you'd ever want to meet.

I discovered something else in the course of my socializing, too, from a stray comment I heard one day about how every soldier had had to undergo genetic testing before they were allowed to join the Mars and Venus expeditions. That piqued my curiosity, naturally, so I had a few volunteers come in and let me examine their DNA.

And what I found absolutely horrified me.

Every human being carries two copies of each gene in his or her genome, and all of us normally have something like five or six distinct recessive genes which would have been lethal if we'd ended up with two copies of any one of them. Inheriting the same fatal gene from both parents is one of the major causes of death in babies. Not only that, but each person also typically carries another twenty to thirty harmful genes which wouldn't actually be fatal. Things like baldness or varicose veins or certain kinds of mental illness or various other problems like that.

None of the soldiers I examined had *any* of those genes, and not only that, but when I looked a little closer I discovered that their DNA was chock full of clip-tags. They hadn't had genetic *testing;* they'd had major genetic *surgery.* Someone had gone in and deleted every lethal or harmful gene they possessed, no doubt with an eye toward the long-term future of humanity. Whatever traits Colonel Burns and his staff couldn't select for by being choosy, they simply went in and fixed. Apparently without even informing anybody what they were doing.

That may sound all fine and peachy keen, but as I've said before, genetic therapy has some serious risks. It can result in crippling autoimmune disorders and even death, and that's just from replacing *one* gene. The fact that the Defense Forces had deliberately and brazenly cut and pasted these people's genetic material on such a massive scale chilled me to the bone. Yes, it turned out well enough for the ones who survived, but God only knows how many others they must have killed in the process. Hundreds at the very least, if not thousands. It was the most shockingly immoral thing I'd witnessed ever since I first discovered that the Orion Strain was purposely designed.

In fact, when I examined my own genetic fingerprint in a sudden fit of suspicion, I discovered they'd done the same thing to *me* at some point. My mind instantly jumped to all those tests and procedures back when they first hauled us in as captives at Southern Command, and Colonel Bartow's chummy words about wanting us to join his little society if only I'd give him the vaccine. He must have wanted to make sure we were fit specimens to join while he still had the chance, just in case he got me to agree at some point. Playing chess again, just like always, making sure every base was covered and no stone left unturned.

I tested the others with a cold sense of foreboding, and sure enough, we'd *all* had our bad genes deleted. Even the babies.

That was an even more unspeakable sin than experimenting on adults; one which I didn't even want to think about.

But it did leave me with a renewed and unshakable certainty that we'd done the right thing not to let those ghouls come back to Earth. Anyone with no more respect for life than that is someone I'd be afraid to have living next door. It was people just like that who created the Orion Strain, and even though the motive may have been different the reasoning and the attitude were exactly the same; that life is cheap, and individuals don't matter, and it's worth inflicting terrible harm in the name of some greater good. That kind of thinking is nothing but pure evil.

I immediately told Philip and everybody in town what I'd discovered, of course, and once the initial wave of anger and disgust had passed, it was replaced almost at once by fear. I was kept busy for days trying to reassure everybody that nothing bad would happen to us at this point because of what had been done, that we were all safe and it was instead an untold slew of NADF soldiers who had already paid the cost in blood for this despicable scheme.

Then there was only sorrow.

I suppose it might have festered and poisoned peoples' minds for a long time if nothing had been done. But when Philip stood up in church the next week and suggested that at the very least we should build a monument to those peoples' memory, the idea was met with enthusiasm.

Thus it was that we made a special trip back to Atlanta to bring back a huge block of Georgia marble, for the purpose of having our one and only sculptor carve a memorial out of it. It seemed fitting to use a piece of stone from the same vicinity where all those nameless victims had died in the labs at Southern Command. The sculptor's name was April Lemley, and she ended up carving a statue of an unknown soldier out of that chunk of white marble, which we then placed reverently atop a pedestal on the main square in Kona. It looked thoroughly out of place alongside the jet-black paving stones of Hawaiian basalt, but maybe it was fitting that it should draw so much attention to itself. And since we didn't know any names, we engraved the stone with a simple motto instead:

Never to Forget

God willing, we never will.

Epilogue
Sunday, November 18, 2158

Today was Hunter and Veronica's birthday again, and it's amazing how much things can change in only a year, isn't it?

There isn't really room on Kona Beach for everybody in town to come down for birthday parties and cookouts anymore, although most of us still do. But this year when Veronica danced for us on the sand she had an audience larger than she's ever had since the old days when she used to do cheerleading back in Clearwater. I think she was even more lovely than last year if such a thing is possible, and a more accomplished dancer too. She finished up her routine this time by kissing Hunter right in front of God and everybody, to the sound of many hoots and cheers from the watching soldiers. I'm sure that was exactly what she was hoping for, of course, lover of the limelight that she is. I'm not sure what Philip and Joan thought about the incident, but they refrained from saying anything at least. They may have raised a sweet and beautiful daughter, but I think modesty was somehow completely left out of her makeup.

Philip has the devil's plenty of other issues to think about already, I suppose, now that he's the leader of almost four hundred people instead of just twenty. Captain Stone refused any kind of leadership position except for his soldiers, pointing out that there needed to be civilian government if we hoped to build any kind of good society. Therefore in the ancient and formal tradition of the Defense Forces he knelt and offered his ceremonial silver sword to Philip, swearing allegiance to whatever he should be asked to do. I think Philip was kind of bemused by the whole thing, but he accepted it just as solemnly as it was offered. But then, what do you say when you've basically just been made President of the Republic, or possibly even King of the World?

Hunter wore his Avenger's ring for the first time tonight after deciding to accept the offer to join, so now we've got a full membership list for the first time since before the plague. For a long time I wasn't sure whether he'd do it or not, but he's a kid who takes his promises seriously and I can definitely respect that. I think he'll remember his oath and try his best to keep it, and that's all we have any right to ask or expect of him. There may not be quite as much evil in the world to fight as there once was, but there's still plenty of good to be done.

I was reminded of that fact pretty sharply not too long ago, in a way I certainly never anticipated. You see, it turns out that April Lemley had another project up her sleeve, too. Believe it or not, she actually saw fit to cast a life-sized bronze statue of *me*, with my right arm raised up to Heaven and a bravely noble look on my face. I didn't even know about it till they unveiled the thing on my birthday, standing right there atop a big granite pedestal in front of the university. There was a bronze plaque right below my feet which read:

Tycho Nicholas McGrath
Defender of Life

Some people might have been thrilled, I suppose, but truthfully I don't think I've ever been so mortified in my life, and especially by that last line on the plaque. Everybody in town was there for the unveiling, and all I could do was mumble a thank you while trying not to blush bright red. My first impulse was to tell them to take it down because I didn't deserve such an honor as that, but then Philip quietly pulled me aside and told me to be generous and not to deny people their heroes.

Maybe so, although I'm still inclined to think you really ought not to build statues of people until after they're decently dead and don't have to be embarrassed every time they walk past the dadgummed thing. I guess if they want to make a hero out of me then I'll shut up and let them, even though I still can't go to the university without turning red. Sometimes the good deeds you're asked to do end up being things like *that*, which might not even be a sacrifice at all to anyone except yourself but which are not a bit less difficult just because of that.

I remember comparing myself to Howard Ricketts while I was working on the Orion vaccine in Tampa and wondering if somebody might build a statue of me someday, but I can honestly say that I never imagined it would really end up happening. If I'd ever suspected somebody might actually do it then I never would have wished for such a thing. But on the bright side, I suppose if nothing worse than public embarrassment happens to me for the rest of my life then I'll be doing pretty well for myself.

I often wonder how those folks on Mars and Venus will get along, considering what a tight thumb Colonel Burns and Colonel Bartow seem to like to keep on things and how cruel and ruthless they seem willing to be. Those two won't live forever, of course, and after that it's an open question what will happen next. Sadly, an unbroken string of absolute dictators is what I strongly suspect. But if no other good ever comes of the Orion Strain, then at least mankind will have three worlds to live on now, and not just one anymore. Still, I'm deeply thankful they're stuck firmly where they are and we'll never have to worry about them swooping down in the middle of the night to drag us off in chains ever again. It might sound cheesy to say it, but I don't think I'll ever take freedom for granted again after that experience.

I also wonder very much what ever happened to those fifty or so rebels we had to abandon on Mars; whether Colonel Burns killed them, or put them in prison, or whether they fled out to die in the desert. I guess we'll never know.

In my heart of hearts I still struggle sometimes with what the NADF did to us, cutting and slicing our DNA like celery sticks and almost killing Jesse in Atlanta, let alone everything else. That's hard to forgive. It's bad enough that they did it to me, but endangering all the people I love makes it ten thousand times worse. And even though I know I *said* we wouldn't have any health problems from what was done, all those clip-tags in our chromosomes still worry me. A *lot*. Nobody ever experimented with human subjects on such a massive scale before, and the long-term effects of that are simply impossible to know at this point. We're walking in completely uncharted waters.

But Philip has said many times not to let bitterness canker our hearts, and I'm trying to forgive them and even to pray for them. The very first thing Philip did after Captain Stone swore allegiance to him was to have all three hundred and seventy-six of us get down on our knees and swear allegiance to God and promise that we'd do our utmost to build a Christian society of peace and love in this place. The grubs were still so awed by what happened to Jesse that they were glad to make such a promise. So I'll try to do my own little bit to make that happen, and part of it means not hating anybody. Philip likes to say that love is easy for those who do it, and maybe someday I'll reach the point where I can say the same thing. But I have to confess I haven't quite reached that level yet.

I'm still not sure what I'll do about Cadron Pool. It's a long way off, and there aren't often many accidents like what happened to Jesse. But it's good to know it's there, and I think we might go back once a year or so to keep it in good shape. Beyond that I can only wait and see. One thing I do know is, it's given me a lot of food for thought and softened my heart when it comes to miraculous things. The world is full of more wonders than I ever dreamed, back in the days when I thought I knew it all. *Credo ut Intelligam; I believe so that I may understand.* Old Professor Brooke was so very right after all.

I have a lot more time on my hands to think about such things than I used to. Since there are so many of us now, that means we all get to do our own jobs for a change and nobody has to wear two or three hats anymore. I can work in my lab on the species repopulation project with nothing else to divide my attention. I'm making slow but steady progress, with more and more animals coming back to life. Someday, if things keep going the way they are, the world might end up almost normal again.

But in spite of all the changes lately, there are certain other things that haven't changed at all. The town still feels like a nursery school, for example. All the soldiers are settling down to have families, and even Philip and Joan are expecting a new baby in June. So are my parents, believe it or not, so I guess my days of being an only child are over. I don't know if it'll be a brother or a sister yet, but we'll find out soon enough. I think Danielle and I are content with just one for now, at least till next year sometime.

In the meantime, I hope I'm done with adventures for a while. My grandpa Cody used to say that he didn't mind fighting when he needed to, but he'd much rather be the sunshine and the rain that makes little things grow strong, a steady rock to shelter the weak. Daddy told me that story last Saturday, and I'm inclined to think maybe some of Cody's heart is in mine. I guess I am what I am, however it came to be, but as I said before it does feel nice to have that sense of rootedness sometimes. I hope I can give the same thing to Josie when she's older.

The four of us went for a walk at Papalokea the other day, with Derrick up on my shoulders and Josie in the baby carrier around Danielle's neck. It was windy, and the salt spray splashed us now and then while our bare feet left a long string of prints behind us on the deep green sand. We didn't talk much, just held hands and laughed when we got wet.

It was a beautiful afternoon, and maybe it's true that beauty calls to beauty, because I found myself thinking about all kinds of things as we walked, of the Summer Isles in the Sea of Tranquility and the Temple of Muwamanth on Titan, of the towering peaks of Venus and the changeless light of an unclouded day.

But you know, out of all the places I've ever been, and all the grandeur I've ever seen, I can still say one thing with perfect truth: none of those things could ever compare to the simple pleasure of walking barefoot on the sand with the one that I love, and hearing her sweet laugh.

And feeling free.

The End

Continue reading Tyke's story in

Elysium

Book Five of the Tyke McGrath Series

Sample of

Elysium

The Tyke McGrath Series: Book Five
By William Woodall

Chapter One
Sunday, December 2, 2158

"There's something I need to ask everybody," Captain Stone said.

We were all sitting around the table in Aunt Joan's kitchen for our weekly Avengers meeting on Sunday afternoon, and all six of us turned to look at him expectantly. Even though he wasn't technically a member of the group, he was a trusted advisor who often attended meetings anyway. Given that our sworn purpose is to fight evil wherever it rears its ugly head, my first thought was to wonder if Captain Stone had found some fresh trouble for us to fix. As it turned out, I was more or less correct.

"Sure. What's on your mind, Brandon?" Uncle Philip asked, swiveling his chair around to face the man.

"It has to do with Mars. You see, ever since we got back from Tharsis Tholus I've been trying to come up with a workable plan for how we might rescue some of the soldiers we had to leave behind. It didn't seem possible at first, especially since we lacked a reliable ship and couldn't even be sure that any of the rebels had survived the battle in the first place. Nevertheless, I've been directing several projects over the past few months with the aim of eventually leading a rescue mission if such a thing turned out to be feasible. I believe that time has finally come," Captain Stone said. There was a rare smile on his face, and his fiery red hair seemed to add its own bit of dramatic flair to the announcement as it glinted in a passing shaft of sunlight from the window behind him. He looked even younger than usual that day, like a high school kid who just won the biggest game of the season.

"Really? Seems like there wouldn't be much hope left for survivors after all this time," Jesse said. I'm sure he didn't mean it to sound quite as skeptical as it did, but honestly I couldn't blame him. It *was* awfully hard to imagine that any of the rebels were still alive after being stranded in the Martian desert for six months. The Red Planet isn't a very forgiving kind of place, even after all the terraforming work that Colonel Burns and his scientists have done.

"It might seem that way at first glance, Jesse; I'll get to that part in just a minute. But first let me say that we *have* solved the transportation problem. It wasn't possible to repair the *Alabama*, unfortunately, but I've had a team of technicians working to upgrade and refurbish at least one of those old XR planes at Hilo. It's been a major undertaking, but as of yesterday, the *Susie Q* is officially spaceworthy again," Captain Stone said.

That announcement at least was met with applause and cheers of congratulations, but before long Captain Stone raised his hands for quiet and we settled down again.

"Now as for the point Jesse made, that's required some serious investment of time and energy also. It obviously wouldn't be worth making a trip to Mars unless we had some kind of evidence that there were actually survivors to be found. But Mikey and I have been working on that, and we've come to the guarded conclusion that it's very likely there are at least a few rebels left," Captain Stone said.

As usual, it puzzled me a little bit to hear the chummy way he referred to my father, as if they'd known each other since they were toddlers. Most everybody in town referred to my father as Dr. McGrath, or at least Micah. In fact I couldn't think of *anybody* other than very close family who ever called him Mikey, and even then not often.

But it wasn't really the time to get sidetracked by irrelevant issues like that.

"But how could they have survived? Do you think Colonel Burns might be holding them captive?" Jesse asked.

"Certainly not. Colonel Burns wouldn't have taken prisoners. He would have executed them right on the spot for treason," Captain Stone said coolly, and I flinched a little. I'm a molecular biologist, after all; not a soldier. Things like that are way outside my comfort zone.

"So how *could* they have survived, then?" I asked.

"Well, we're still not *sure* any of them did. But we found some interesting signs of possible occupation near the old Redoubt in the Mountains of Tantalus," Captain Stone said.

"What's the Redoubt?" Jesse asked.

"It's a secret refuge which the Martian rebels built several years ago, stocked with weapons and supplies so they could survive and defend themselves if that ever became necessary. It would have been the logical place for any survivors to go, if they could make it that far," Captain Stone said.

"How come nobody ever mentioned it before?" Hunter ventured to ask. He was just barely seventeen, four years younger than the rest of us, and he didn't normally talk much at meetings.

"Would there have been any point till now?" Captain Stone asked. He had a way of being brutally honest like that which had been hard to get used to at first, but once you got to know him for a while you realized he was never spiteful, just very blunt sometimes.

"No, sir. . . I don't guess there would have been," Hunter admitted meekly.

"All right, then. What I have in mind at this point is to head out to Mars immediately on board the *Susie Q,* scoop up any survivors from the Redoubt, and then get off the planet as quickly as possible. With a little luck, it won't take more than a few hours on the surface at most; I prefer not to give Colonel Burns any more time to notice our presence than absolutely necessary. It'll be a difficult and risky mission all the way around, which brings me to the question I actually came here to ask. I'd like for at least a few of you to consider joining me," Captain Stone said.

"You're going?" I asked skeptically.

"Of course. Surely you don't think I'd ask men or women under my command to take risks I'm not willing to venture myself, do you?" Captain Stone asked.

"No, it's not that. I just thought. . . " I said, and then trailed off, not quite sure what I *did* think. Brandon Stone had a long history of shattering every preconceived notion I'd ever had of an NADF officer; I don't suppose I should have been surprised by anything at all he might have said or done at that point. It just seemed odd that a high commander would get personally involved with a dangerous mission like that, you know. I'd read about such things in history books, of course, but it hadn't been a common attitude in centuries.

"I'm sure you probably thought commanders should stay safely behind the scenes and push pencils, no doubt. I've seen quite a few of that type myself, more's the pity. And maybe if this weren't such a critical and sensitive mission then I might stay home and assign a few trustworthy lieutenants to handle things. But I can't in good conscience order anyone to risk his life for nothing but a maybe. This will be a mission only for volunteers, and even though I've got soldiers with greater technical skills and combat specialties than anyone in this room, so does Colonel Burns. We can never hope to match him toe-to-toe like that. Our most valuable asset at this point is the ability to think outside the box, and unfortunately that's something none of my soldiers can give me. All of them were trained under the same teachers at the same military academy. Colonel Burns knows the way they think inside and out. At all costs we can't be predictable, and that's why the six of you came to mind instead. Besides which, I've already had the opportunity to see several of you in action, particularly Tyke and Hunter during the battles at Barbados and Jamestown. They both comported themselves with exceptional courage and resourcefulness even in the face of very difficult odds, and I've heard similar stories about the rest of you. Those are exactly the kind of people I want to have at my side during a mission like this," Captain Stone said. Such high praise was uncomfortable to hear, but I noticed Aunt Joan watching me and remembered my manners just in time.

"Thank you, sir," I said, and Hunter mumbled something likewise. Danielle reached across the table to squeeze my hand encouragingly, her diamond wedding set sparkling in the sunshine. In two and a half years that ring had never once left her finger.

"I believe in giving credit where it's due, that's all," Captain Stone said.

"So what's this evidence you mentioned that led you to think there might still be survivors?" Uncle Philip asked.

"It'll be easier to show you than tell you. If y'all have time to come up to the observatory for a little while tonight then I'll be glad to show you what we found," Captain Stone said.

"Would eight o'clock be all right?" Danielle asked.

"Perfect. Will that work for the rest of you?" Captain Stone asked.

"Fine with me," Jesse said, and Hunter sort of shrugged as if it didn't much matter.

"I think Joan and I might have to pass on this adventure. We have too many responsibilities already, and besides that it wouldn't be a good idea for us to go out in space right now; not with a new baby coming soon and all that. The others can see what you found and then decide for themselves whether to go or not. I give them my blessing, if they're willing," Uncle Philip said.

No one questioned his decision. Philip is the undisputed leader of all three hundred and seventy-six human beings still left alive on earth. We all live together in the little town of Kailua Kona on the island of Hawaii, after a man-made plague known as the Orion Strain wiped out every warm-blooded species on the entire planet just five years ago. A few of us had managed to escape to the Moon or other places, but the Earth itself was still infested with deadly spores. Some of us had been able to come home again after I discovered a workable vaccine, but we still had some vicious enemies on Mars and Venus who would have liked nothing better than to kill us and take over the world for themselves. After some fierce battles we'd destroyed their spaceships and left them stranded on their own worlds, but a handful of our own people were still unaccounted for on Mars. Those were the ones we'd been talking about.

"Thanks, Philip; I appreciate that. There's no rush; they can think about it for a day or two and let me know if this is something they want to be a part of. In the meantime, I'll see everybody tonight," Captain Stone said.

The meeting didn't last much longer, but as we walked home along the beach I couldn't help thinking about Captain Stone's request for volunteers. I could understand Philip and Joan not wanting to go on such an expedition, but Danielle and I had children to think of, too. So did Jesse, and he'd already been badly hurt the *last* time we tangled with Colonel Burns and his flunkies. I wasn't eager to sign up for a second round.

But then on the other hand, we really *did* have a moral obligation to go back for the ones we'd left behind, if there were any of them still alive and if it were actually possible. It was exactly the kind of mission any Avenger should have been proud to take on, if his heart was in the right place. My hesitation seemed unworthy of the oath I'd sworn, but that still didn't keep me from feeling it.

"So, what do *you* think about all this, beautiful?" I finally asked. Danielle hadn't uttered a peep about her own thoughts yet.

"I think we might as well go up to the observatory tonight to look at the evidence before we decide anything for sure. If it's convincing enough then yeah I think we should probably go," she said.

"You do?" I asked, kind of surprised that she'd made up her mind so easily when I'd been twisted in knots myself.

"Yeah, I do. Captain Stone has a good point about choosing people who might be more likely to see things outside the box and not be too predictable. There's nobody else who fits that description except us. Besides that, we *have* been through a lot of hard times together and faced down a lot of dangerous situations. We're probably the best team he could hope to find, all things considered," she said.

"But what about Josie and Derrick?" I asked, referring to our eighteen-month-old daughter and ten-year-old nephew.

"Yeah. . . that's the really hard part, isn't it? But if all goes well then we shouldn't be gone longer than a few weeks or so, and in the meantime we can leave them with your parents for a little while. They like going over there anyway," Danielle said.

"Well. . . okay. What do we do with them tonight while we're up at the observatory, though?" I asked.

"Already got that one covered, too. Your Aunt Joan said she'd watch them till we get back," she said.

So that's what we did, and late that evening after the sun went down we dressed in warm clothes and drove up the mountain to see whatever there was to be seen. Jesse and Hunter rode with us in the back seat, since there was no reason to waste fuel by driving two vehicles. My father's car was already parked in the lot when we arrived, and I silently pulled up beside him.

"I didn't know your dad was supposed to be here too," Danielle said as soon as I killed the engine.

"Neither did I, but maybe Captain Stone needed him to run the telescopes or the computer or something like that," I said, and she shrugged noncommittally.

Sure enough, Daddy and Captain Stone were huddled together over the computer screen when we got inside, but they both looked up when they heard the door open.

"Well, here we all are, and just in time, too! I'm glad everybody could make it," Daddy said, getting up from his chair to give all four of us a bear-hug before he sat back down.

"Captain Stone said there were some things he wanted to show us," Danielle said.

"That's right; time to show off our detective work, Mikey," Captain Stone said.

"Sure thing. Y'all come closer where you can see," Daddy said, and we quickly gathered round the screen. I wasn't quite sure what we were seeing at first; just a reddish, dusty landscape scattered with darker red rocks.

"What are we looking at?" Danielle finally asked.

"This is the southern slope of Tharsis Tholus, about three quarters of the way up to the summit. That was the rendezvous point where the *Alabama* landed and where the battle took place," Daddy murmured.

His words reminded me unpleasantly of everything I'd seen during that battle. Colonel Burns had caught us by surprise while we tried to evacuate the Martian rebels, almost destroying our ship and nearly killing all of us in the process. I could still remember our noses starting to bleed like fountains when the flight deck lost pressure from a hull breach, and then seeing the blood start to boil on the faces of those who couldn't get suited up fast enough. We'd barely made it out of there alive, and even then only at the cost of abandoning dozens of the very people we'd come to save. The memories weren't nice ones.

"What are we looking at that place for? I'm sure any survivors would be long gone from *there* by now, no matter what happened," Jesse said.

"You're absolutely right, Jesse. Colonel Burns would have killed as many of them as possible immediately, but one of the first things we needed to know was whether anybody escaped the battle or not. For that we had to examine the battlefield itself, and there are a lot of bones, I'm afraid. Colonel Burns never took the trouble to bury them," Captain Stone said.

That was kind of a gruesome thought, actually, but I told myself I'd seen worse things. So I kept my eyes glued to the screen while Daddy fiddled with the controls until he found the exact spot where the battle had taken place. Sure enough, there were space-suited mummies lying everywhere on the red ground.

"There they are," he said wryly, and I felt a wave of pity come over me at the sight even though I knew those poor people had been dead for months already by then. Colonel Burns really could have had the common decency to bury them, one would think; even enemies in war did that much. It looked like a few of the suits had been robbed for usable parts, but I guess most of them were too damaged to be worth the trouble.

"That can't be all of them. How many did you say were left behind? Fifty?" Danielle asked.

"Forty-six, to be exact," Captain Stone said.

"There's no way that's forty-six bodies," Danielle said, and after scrutinizing the field I had to agree. They were piled and strewn all over the place, with a few of them half buried in wind-blown dirt.

That made it hard to tell *exactly* how many there were, but it sure didn't look like forty-six.

"Precisely. That's our first bit of evidence for survivors. Some of the rebels must have escaped or else they'd all be lying there together right now. Count them and see how many you come up with," Captain Stone said.

"I count thirty-one," Danielle said after a while.

"I only got twenty-eight," I admitted.

"Well, just to be conservative, that still leaves at least fifteen of them unaccounted for. Maybe more," Jesse said.

"Yes, but it doesn't necessarily mean they *survived*. All it means is that they didn't die at that particular place and time," I pointed out.

"I told you we couldn't be *sure*, Tyke. I only said we had some evidence," Captain Stone reminded me.

"How did they get to the rendezvous point to start with? If they *did* escape, that's probably how they got away," Danielle said.

"Good point, my dear. That's the next thing on our list of sites to see. But to answer your question, they had land rovers," Captain Stone said.

"Don't you think Colonel Burns would have either taken those or destroyed them during the battle?" I asked.

"Maybe, if he wasn't too busy with other things. He was so intent on capturing the *Alabama* that I doubt he paid much attention to anything else," Captain Stone pointed out, and I shrugged; that was possible, I supposed.

"Here's what's left of them," Daddy said after a while, pointing out a field strewn with the wreckage of at least a dozen large rovers.

"Do you think that would be enough to carry three hundred and twenty-something people?" Danielle asked.

"It's hard to say, with them blown to pieces like that. But we're not trying to figure out if any of them are missing or not; I just wanted you to see them so you'll have at least a general idea of what they look like. Show them the Redoubt, Mikey," Captain Stone said, and Daddy quickly shifted the view about three hundred miles north to a spot on the western fringe of the Tempe Hills, at their highest and most rugged section in the Mountains of Tantalus.

That still isn't saying a whole lot, to be sure; they wouldn't have seemed like much more than steep and knobby hills if it hadn't been for the fact that they looked out to the northwest across an utterly flat and featureless plain extending for hundreds of miles in every direction and ending eventually at the North Sea. All that flat nothingness made them look bigger in comparison than they really were.

But my musings were interrupted.

"There it is. And there's the rover they took. We *think*," Daddy murmured, pointing it out.

It didn't look like much to me; just a glint of metal down inside one of the many cracks and canyons in that region, something you'd never even notice unless you knew exactly where to look. It might have been a rover or it might not have been, for all I could tell. We simply couldn't get enough resolution on the image to be sure.

"So where's the Redoubt itself? I don't see anything but empty land," Hunter said.

"It's underground, dug back into the walls of the canyon down at the bottom where snoopy spy satellites can't find it. I promise you it's there," Captain Stone said.

There was nothing we could do except take his word for it, since there was absolutely nothing to see. The only tell-tale evidence of human hands was that bright little glint of metal coming from a place where it shouldn't naturally have been, and that was meager proof at best.

"So let me get this straight. You think maybe fifteen or twenty rebels escaped the battle and possibly went to this Redoubt to try to survive?" Jesse asked.

"We hope so, yes," Captain Stone agreed.

"It seems to me like Colonel Burns ought to have noticed anybody escaping in a rover, you know. There's not much cover between Tharsis Tholus and the Tempe Hills, and it's a fair distance, too. They would have stuck out like a bug on a plate, if he bothered to look for them at all," Jesse pointed out, and Captain Stone nodded.

"We already thought of that, Jesse. Unfortunately you're right; there's a very real possibility that Colonel Burns *did* notice, and then deliberately allowed them to escape for the purpose of using them as bait to draw us back there," Captain Stone said.

"And we're going to walk right into a situation like that, knowing full well that it could be a trap?" Jesse asked.

"It's one potential risk among many others that we'll have to face on this mission, Jesse, no more and no less. I've said from the very beginning that it might be dangerous; that's why this is an all-volunteer expedition," Captain Stone said.

"Yeah, I know," Jesse admitted.

"One thing I want to mention to all four of you before anybody makes up his mind whether to go or not. Under no circumstances can we allow a spacecraft of any kind to fall into Colonel Burns' hands. That's why the *Susie Q* has been fitted with a self-destruct circuit so that it can be destroyed by remote control should that prove to be necessary. If any or all of us are still alive after that, it may mean we'll be stranded on Mars for the rest of our lives, which are likely to be very short ones. That's the brutal reality, I'm afraid," Captain Stone said.

"You're painting it awfully black, aren't you?" Danielle asked.

"Only being realistic, my dear. Any or all of those things could certainly happen, and we have to be prepared for them. But I wouldn't even suggest a mission like this if I thought it was impossible. I believe there's a good chance we'll find at least a few survivors at the Redoubt and bring them safely home again without any trouble at all," Captain Stone said.

That was a much more cheerful way of looking at things, to be sure, but the specter of finding ourselves permanently stranded on Mars was enough to shake anybody's courage. I remembered enough about the conditions on that cold and dusty world to know that it was a forbidding destination even at the best of times. Our short experience on Tharsis Tholus proved *that*.

It did help somewhat that Mars was only two or three months short of opposition at the moment; that is, its time of nearest approach to Earth. That would shorten the trip considerably and also make it much easier to stay in touch with the folks back home since there wouldn't be as much radio delay. It also happened to be late summer in the northern hemisphere, which meant it shouldn't be impossibly cold. The Mountains of Tantalus are located about 35 degrees north of the equator, or roughly the same latitude as South Carolina. That's just about the northern limit of survivability on Mars; any farther from the equator than that and you'll freeze to death when winter comes. It gets so cold then that even the atmosphere starts to freeze into huge slabs of ice. Much better to stay in the tropics, if you're smart.

Not exactly the kind of place you'd want to spend the rest of your life.

But actually, in a strange kind of way I think it was that very fact which convinced me to go. In the back of my mind I couldn't help thinking that if *I'd* been the one abandoned in such a horrible place, I surely would have hoped that somebody might find the courage to come back after *me* if they could have.

Philip likes to say that most moral questions are really very simple things. It's usually when we're looking for an excuse to keep from having to do the right thing that we end up making them complicated. Maybe so. All I can say for sure is that when all the fat was sliced off the bone, it was mostly the plain old Golden Rule which ultimately settled the issue as far as I was concerned. I glanced at Danielle, and she nodded slightly.

"Danielle and I will go," I said, and it wasn't long before Jesse and Hunter added their own agreement.

"Good. I knew you'd all come," Captain Stone said, just like he'd never doubted any of us for a second.

"So when are we leaving?" I finally asked.

Chapter Two

We left the very next day, actually; Captain Stone already had everything stowed and ready before he even asked us.

Only the five of us went: me, Danielle, Jesse, Hunter, and Captain Stone himself. Our hope lay in speed and stealth, not in pitched battles, and for that a small group suited our purposes much better. Besides which, those little XR-227 planes from the old days were only built for fourteen people originally, and we didn't know how many survivors (if any) we might need to bring back with us. I noticed immediately that the *Susie Q* had been modified to carry an additional six passengers by dint of bolting an extra seat onto the end of each row. That was good as far as it went, except for the fact that it also made the center aisle so narrow that we had to turn sideways to squeeze through. It left us with fifteen slots for survivors, and I suppose in a pinch we could have carried a few more; somebody could sit in the bathroom, and others could squeeze along the walls if necessary. It wouldn't have been *safe,* exactly, but it could be done. The grubs are really good at making do with only a little when need be.

I guess I should mention that *grub* is a slangy word for *soldier,* just in case you never heard it used that way before. There are a lot of them in Kailua Kona, not to mention on Mars and Venus. Most of our techs and workers are grubs, survivors of Mars and Venus who rebelled against the tyranny and oppression in those places. Captain Stone is the high commander of all such rebel forces, even though he defers to Uncle Philip on most things.

Anyway, the grubs had done a good job refurbishing that old ship; it looked almost like a new one, inside and out. I don't doubt they upgraded and repaired as much of the mechanics of the thing as humanly possible, too. Nevertheless, fifty year old equipment is still fifty year old equipment; it's not new, and it won't take as much abuse as a new one might. That was something we had to keep firmly in mind. There wouldn't be any gravitational slingshot maneuvers or harsh takeoffs in the *Susie Q;* she was a grand old lady who had to be respected.

That said, the five-day trip out to Mars was fairly dull. We spent most of it irradiating every square millimeter of the ship and ourselves with an intense ultraviolet lamp to kill any stray Orion spores which might have been carried onboard. The very last thing we wanted was to spread the infection to a whole new world. The techs back in Kona had promised us that the lamps would work just as well as nitric acid to kill spores, and be much less messy to boot. They were tedious to use, true, but still a vast improvement over what we had to endure on the way to Venus.

Other than that there were no serious problems to have to contend with and everything on the ship seemed to work exactly the way it should have.

We set down on the smoothest and flattest place we could find at the edge of the northern plains, and Jesse timed the landing so we'd have a whole day to explore before we had to be back to the ship. It was a fairly rough landing in spite of the relative smoothness of the terrain, and I could hear Jesse muttering about tearing up the landing gear if we weren't careful. But we must not have, because he didn't say anything else about it once we were down.

In the old days we would have needed space suits to go outside on the surface even for a few seconds, but Mars had already changed a lot since the old days. Colonel Burns' scientific team had been busily modifying the atmosphere ever since they first arrived, although that was unavoidably a much slower process than it had ever been on Venus because there'd been so little atmosphere to work with in the first place. They had to go the biological route, using genetically engineered bacteria to attack the red hematite soil, releasing oxygen and leaving behind iron dust. Not the most ideal solution in the long-term, but in the meantime it had produced a thin atmosphere of 95 percent oxygen and 5 percent assorted other things, including 3 percent carbon dioxide.

The air pressure was still dangerously low, to be sure; only about 200 millibars even at sea level, which is only about one-fifth of the pressure on Earth. Almost all of that was pure oxygen, of course, so we *could* take off our masks and breathe for a while if we liked, at least down there at the lowest elevations. But not indefinitely. Three percent CO_2 is roughly a hundred times the amount we would've been breathing back home on Earth, and that's on the very verge of reaching poisonous levels. It wasn't quite enough to do us any serious harm immediately, true, but it was enough to make us feel constantly drowsy and short of breath, not to mention raise our heart rate and blood pressure to unhealthy levels.

The environment was dangerous in other ways, too; that oxygen-rich atmosphere meant we had to be *extremely* careful about sparks and fire, because anything flammable could be dangerously explosive under those conditions.

But discounting all those hazards, we wouldn't die just from exposure as long as it wasn't too cold outside and as long as we didn't venture too far above the lowlands. Unlike on Venus, the mountains and the high plateaus of Mars were not at all places you'd want to visit without a space suit. Up there the pressure quickly fell to deadly levels, and that's why we had such a horrifying experience at Tharsis Tholus; we'd been *way* up beyond the safety zone.

Our landing spot that day was roughly ten thousand feet above sea level, nowhere near as high as Tharsis Tholus, and as a result the pressure gauge read close to 150 millibars when we landed. Plenty enough not to need a space suit, but still much too thin for us to breathe without an air tank and a face mask for more than a minute or so.

Oh, I suppose if we'd been Incas from the high Andes then we could have handled it pretty well, or even if we'd lived in the

Rockies or the Sierras for a while. The body responds to low oxygen pressure by producing more red blood cells than usual and enlarging lung capacity, so that after a while you become adapted to those kinds of conditions and they don't affect you as much anymore. But it does take a while; your body can't adjust instantly, and that's why a person who's accustomed to sea level conditions (such as ourselves) can't simply drive up to a village high in the mountains and expect to run a marathon like the locals do. You're liable to wind up sick or even dead if you try it. There's a real and measurable physical change that has to take place first.

I guess you could say walking around on the Martian surface was something like going for a long hike in the Himalayas while wearing a paper sack over your head, and none of us had had time to adapt to that kind of environment yet.

It'll get better eventually, of course. Give it a few more decades and you'll be able to breathe without an air tank all the time, even in the mountains. But for the moment, I guess it could have been worse.

It was strange to use the air lock without any kind of protective gear on. We weren't wearing anything but ordinary street clothes, with a warm jacket over the top. I have to confess that I was just a bit nervous about opening the door, in spite of what the air gauge read. I remembered the incident at Tharsis Tholus all too well, and I was sure Hunter in particular hadn't forgotten it either. The last thing I wanted was a repeat of *that* experience. But Jesse seemed to have no doubt about it, so I took a deep breath and cracked the door.

It was a crisp and chilly 45 degrees when we first set foot on the reddish dirt at nine o'clock in the morning, headed for a high of around 70 later that afternoon. It really does get pretty warm on Mars sometimes, at least during the summer. I couldn't resist the temptation to unlatch my mask and take a breath of Martian air, even though I knew I'd have to be quick about it. The short whiff that I got smelled dry and dusty and vaguely metallic, like rusty pipes. Not to mention noticeably and uncomfortably thin, and it didn't take more than a few seconds before I was ready to put my mask back on.

We crunched our way eastward across flat hardpan desert scoured clear by the wind except for a few pebbles and larger rocks here and there. Almost everything we saw was some shade of red; dull crimson dirt, pinkish sky, rocks that varied anywhere from burnt ochre to butterscotch, and the towering spires of the Mountains of Tantalus themselves in the distance, a reddish smudge against the horizon. It was an easy walk, even if not a terribly interesting one. The gravity was only a little more than a third of what it would have been on Earth; just enough weight to be surefooted but still wonderfully light. There was a mild breeze blowing from the west, and even though it was chilly enough to have a bit of a bite to it, the exercise soon warmed us up.

"So what if they're not here?" Hunter finally asked.

"We'll cross that bridge if and when it arrives, okay?" Captain Stone said, which of course was another way of saying he didn't know. We didn't have the time or the resources to mount a planetwide search operation, especially right under Colonel Burns' nose. If there were no survivors at the Redoubt, then it was likely we'd have no choice but to turn around and go home empty-handed.

We made it to the canyon about three hours after leaving the *Susie Q,* and by then the sun was already climbing towards noon. One of the nice but also aggravating things about Mars is that it has a day and night cycle which is only about 40 minutes longer than Earth's. It's nice because it feels normal, physically speaking; 40 minutes is not enough extra time in a day for your body to notice.

But it's aggravating for timekeeping purposes, because even if your body doesn't notice the change, your clock certainly will. Trying to stay on a 24-hour day when the sun disagrees with you is highly annoying and inconvenient. It doesn't matter so much if it's daylight or dark for weeks on end, like it was on Venus or the Moon. But on Mars it's just enough off kilter to be jarring, and there aren't many good options for dealing with it.

You can ignore the difference, of course, and in that case it'll be 40 minutes earlier by the sun every single day; sort of like daylight savings time on steroids. Or you can adjust the length of your day to accommodate reality and then you'll be out of whack with Earth time, and even worse, out of whack with the calendar before long.

Or if you don't like *those* options, then you can always keep two completely separate clocks and calendars, with all the possibilities for mistakes that that involves. No matter what you choose, it's still a headache.

According to the files at Southern Command, the Martian colonists had decided to split the difference. They used the simple expedient of setting aside 40 minutes every midnight which wasn't allowed to intrude on the 24-hour cycle; that was as close to pretending it didn't exist as possible. It would have gradually ended up adding ten Earth-days to the calendar every year as that extra time accumulated, so they dropped the last day of each month except February and December. That arrangement kept things in line so the time and date were never more than a few hours different from Earth; no worse than a time zone switch.

Our watches were set for the correct time of day at the Redoubt, and it felt like a normal summer afternoon when we finally arrived at the canyon; warm enough that I was ready to shed my jacket by then. There was no sound except the faint whistling of the wind across the desert, and no obvious signs of life.

"So where are they?" I asked, staring at the canyon.

"I told you; down at the bottom. They have to keep things concealed from Colonel Burns, you know," Captain Stone said.

No doubt they did, but that made it hard for *us* to find them, too.

We soon found a gully which led down into the canyon, and then gingerly picked our way along it until we reached the bottom. Like many such places on Mars, it bore unmistakable traces of flowing water at some point in the past. It was hard to say how long ago that might have been; it could have been only a matter of days, for all we knew. The Martian weather cycle had started to reestablish itself as the atmosphere thickened and the temperatures rose, and that meant rainfall at least now and then, sometimes heavy. The thought made me kind of uneasy, actually; I didn't feel like getting caught in a flash flood at the bottom of a canyon if I could help it.

I glanced up at the sky just in case, but there wasn't a cloud to be seen at the moment. I told myself not to worry about it unless I had reason.

The walls of the canyon were only about as far apart as three cars parked end to end, and in most places they were sheer cliffs, rising almost two hundred feet from floor to rim. Not terribly deep or impressive compared to certain others, maybe, but by the time we reached the bottom it felt like we were on a journey to the center of the earth. It was awfully cold too, down there where the sun never had a chance to shine. It didn't take me long to decide I still wanted my jacket after all, and I zipped it up a little closer around my throat.

Captain Stone seemed to know which way he was going, so we let him take the lead and the rest of us followed. Danielle and I brought up the rear, holding hands partly for warmth and partly just because we wanted to. I'd seen several prettier (and uglier) places than Mars, but I'd rarely had a chance to share them with her except by telling stories after the fact. This was in some ways a rare treat.

We hiked for about two hours along the rock-strewn floor of the crack until we reached a somewhat wider area where the walls drew apart just a bit, and a wider and longer gully came down from above. That's where we found what must have been the glint of metal we'd seen in that satellite image at the observatory; a dusty land rover.

"I *knew* that's what it was," Captain Stone said in satisfaction, patting the fender with one hand.

"Yeah, but where's the Redoubt?" Jesse asked.

"Just a little bit farther. Not very much," Captain Stone said.

The canyon narrowed again past the place where the rover was parked, and it was during a particularly constricted section that we stumbled into the booby trap.

It shouldn't have surprised anybody, I don't suppose; I'm sure Captain Stone suspected there might be things like that in the vicinity. That's no doubt why he went first in line. But the Martian rebels must have been awfully clever about the way they set it up, because I think they caught even *him* off guard. In any case, we suddenly found ourselves in the midst of a rain of falling rocks, some of them awfully sharp and heavy ones. And even though the gravity was low, a rock that would have weighed a thousand pounds on Earth will still weigh 380 on Mars. That's plenty enough to either kill you or do some serious damage, thank you very much.

Everybody scattered without thinking; you don't have time to make plans during something like that, you've only got time to dodge boulders and try to stay alive. But there was nowhere to escape the deadly barrage, and one by one it got us all. I felt something hit me on the back of the head, and for a few seconds I blacked out.

When I woke up I was covered in wet blood from a gash on the back of my head, and I was half buried in rocks and dirt. The air was full of red dust, gradually settling out even as I watched.

I think if we'd been on Earth, the weight of the rocks would have been too much for me to get out from under, at least without help. As it was, I still had to struggle to shove aside some of the bigger and heavier ones. I soon discovered cuts and scrapes and bruises everywhere, and when I tried to stand up I found I couldn't put weight on my left ankle. I couldn't tell what I'd done to it, whether it was broken or just badly twisted or what, but whatever it was, I could only hobble on one foot.

Danielle was buried nearby, and even though she'd been knocked senseless by another falling rock, it didn't look like she was any worse off than I was; just a bunch of cuts and scrapes. No doubt we'd both be too sore even to lift a finger by the time tomorrow rolled around, but in the meantime it was nothing life-threatening.

I soon realized that *we* must have had it fairly easy, though. We only caught the tail end of the rocks, last in line as we were. The others must have had it *much* worse, and no sooner did I grasp that fact than I hobbled forward to look for them, leaving Danielle as comfortably arranged as possible on the rocky ground.

Hunter had been right in front of us, and he was the one I found first. He was lying on the ground under a massive boulder, with his head turned to one side and a thin trickle of blood running out of his mouth. At first I thought he was dead, but when I got closer I could see him gasping for air like a beached whale. His oxygen mask had been knocked off when he fell, and I quickly replaced it so he'd get enough air. I suppose if I'd taken very much longer to find him then he probably would have suffocated.

But that was the least of his problems. I didn't know if I had the strength to move that huge chunk of stone off his body, and I wasn't actually sure if I should try. As I've said before, my specialty is molecular genetics, not medical science or first aid. What little I knew about *those* subjects I'd mostly picked up from Joan, and she'd never taught me what to do in case somebody gets crushed by a falling boulder. That's not exactly a common medical emergency, you know. All I knew was that he looked really bad, and way down deep I felt the first cold prickle of fear that he might not make it.

There was nothing else I could do for him without help, so I stumbled on ahead to see if I could find Jesse or Captain Stone. Jesse must have been buried under so much rubble that he wasn't visible, but presently I spotted part of Captain Stone's hand sticking out of a pile of rocks. I knew it was him right away because the skin was so pale. Like many people with red hair, Captain Stone is white as milk and couldn't tan even if he tried. He doesn't even have any freckles.

I started moving rocks from around his hand as fast as I could, following his arm downward into the pile until I reached his body. He was buried pretty deep, but he was still alive and even awake; he'd just been covered with too much debris to get out.

"Are you okay?" I asked him as soon as we could speak.

"I think so. Don't feel too good but I don't think there's any major damage. What about everybody else?" he asked.

"Danielle's okay but still knocked out, I've got a twisted ankle I think, and I can't find Jesse under all these rocks. Hunter's got a boulder on top of him which is too heavy for me to move; he's in pretty bad shape but I didn't know what to do," I said. The truth was probably even less kind than that, actually; out in the middle of the Martian desert, with no help at hand, it would be a miracle of the first degree if Hunter survived long enough even to make it back to the spaceship. He might not even last long enough to get out of the canyon.

"Come on, then. Show me where he is," Captain Stone said, crawling out from under the last bit of dirt. He had a few cuts and scrapes, but he must have been in better shape than I was. He didn't limp when he walked, and he made to Hunter long before I did. Indeed, by the time I came in sight of him he'd already pushed the boulder away by himself.

Hunter's body was a bloody mess underneath it. As I've said before, a little blood doesn't bother me, but *lots* of it does. The kid's clothes were soaked with it, and so were the rocks all around him. But before I had a chance to get sick, I saw Captain Stone lay both his hands on Hunter's head and look up with his eyes closed, for all the world like he was praying. Which maybe he was, for all I could tell; I suppose it wouldn't have been such an unreasonable thing to do, under the circumstances.

He hadn't noticed me yet, and I hesitated, not wanting to interrupt. When he was done he stood up to head back in my direction.

"He'll be fine, I think. The boulder didn't do as much damage as it looked like at first. Just a few cuts and bruises," he said lightly, after he saw me.

"It didn't?" I asked, too shocked to think of anything else to say. Then I glanced past him to see Hunter trying to pull himself up into a sitting position next to the bloody boulder, unbelievable as that seemed.

"No, it looked a lot worse than it really was. Don't worry about him anymore; he'll be all right. Let's go find Jesse," he said.

Now I might be a lot of things, but I'm not an idiot. I'd seen what kind of shape Hunter was in with my own two eyes, and even though I was willing to admit that it might have looked worse than it really was, I knew perfectly well he had some serious injuries if nothing else. There had been way too much blood for it to come from only a few little cuts and bruises.

But on the other hand I knew Captain Stone wasn't crazy, and I couldn't imagine why he'd lie about such a thing or how he could possibly be mistaken, and besides that I could actually see the kid sitting up right there in front of me. I had no idea what to think or believe, honestly.

If he hadn't reminded me of the still-urgent need to find Jesse then I might have tried to get to the bottom of things right then and there. But as it was, I frowned and decided maybe it wasn't the best time to push the issue. Questions could wait, and if Hunter was really all right then I should probably be thankful for that and save my curiosity for later.

Nevertheless, I had no intention of forgetting about the incident.

We found Jesse buried under the heaviest part of the rock fall, but strangely enough I think that's exactly what saved him. He was trapped in a kind of pocket between two huge boulders, either of which would have crushed him like a bug if they'd landed on top of him. But one of them had landed right beside him, and the other had landed in such a way that it was leaning up against the edge of the first one, creating a cave of sorts about the size of the space underneath an office desk. Jesse was able to take shelter under that, and even though he was buried nearly ten feet deep in the rubble, he was actually hurt less than any of us.

Before long all five of us were gathered together again back at the rover, bloody and battered but all of us still alive, at least.

"So what do we do now?" Hunter asked, and again I couldn't get over the fact that he was actually still alive. His clothes looked hideous, torn and blood-soaked from neck to groin, but the boy himself seemed to have come through his death-defying ordeal with nothing worse than a few cuts and scratches.

"We wait right here," Captain Stone said decisively.

"Just wait? That's all?" Jesse asked.

"That's right. The folks inside the Redoubt will notice that one of their booby traps was sprung, and sooner or later they'll come to investigate. That's exactly what we want, and besides that it'll also keep us from running afoul of any more security measures like that landslide. The next time we might not be so lucky," Captain Stone said.

"What happened back there, anyway? I never saw a tripwire or anything like that," Jesse asked.

"I'm sure they used an invisible x-ray laser to cross the canyon at some point, and then when one of us crossed it and broke the connection, it sprung the trap. Very simple, very clever, and when it's done properly almost impossible to detect until it's too late. That's why we need to wait right where we are," Captain Stone said.

So wait we did, for what felt like hours even though my watch said it was really only about thirty minutes. But when a young soldier in rust-colored camo stepped out from behind a rock with his laser pistol drawn, none of us were much surprised.

We'd found the survivors after all.

Elysium
is available now from your favorite retailer!

Author's Note:

Freedom was something of a different book in this series. After writing *Nightfall* I was told by several readers that it was simply intolerable to leave them hanging like that, never knowing what happened to Mike and Annabelle or whether they ever met up with Tyke again or not. So, since I like to oblige the fans, here's the answer to all that.

My daughter asked me for a book about Venus this time, so that explains the choice of setting. But the book had to be about something more than just tying up loose ends, of course. There had to be a solid reason why Mike and Annabelle should reappear; some essential function which only they could have played and which contributed to the overall story. Helping Tycho reconnect with his past was a logical reason, and one which turned out to be crucially important considering the events related to Jesse's injury and everything which came about as a direct result of that.

Cadron Pool comes directly from *Many Waters,* of course, so it "already existed" in a certain sense, even though Tyke knew nothing about it until his father told him the story. It wasn't necessary to bring it in as a made-up solution to a problem. It was only necessary to pull it out of storage, so to speak.

The conditions and locations on Venus are fairly true to life, with some of the names changed to protect the innocent. Mount Maxwell is really an entire mile taller than Mount Everest, and the highland areas are exactly the size, shape, and location that I described. They are indeed separated by vast plains of lowland desert, and as always the other scientific facts are as close to reality as possible.

Tyke has continued to grow and mature in this book, both as an individual and as a believer. He's still got some issues to work out, but that's part of what makes him so much fun to write about.

Self-sacrifice has been an important theme in this book, particularly when Jesse loved Tyke enough to risk his life to try to save him from the stunner fire in Atlanta, and thus injured himself badly. But of course if he hadn't, then there would have been no miracle at Cadron Pool, and perhaps no promise from the grubs to build a Christian society to the extent that they were able.

The military of Tyke's time has sometimes been presented in a fairly unfavorable light in this series, and I hope that readers will not draw unwarranted conclusions from that fact. The armed forces are full of many good people, then and now, and several of the bravest and most heroic characters in this series have also been NADF officers. But it's quite possible for *any* organization to become corrupt and to start working against the very goals it was created to defend, sometimes without even realizing it. It happens all the time, sadly, which is exactly why we have to be eternally vigilant against those kinds of things.

The next book in this series, *Elysium,* will deal with Mars and the rescue of the fifty abandoned rebel soldiers who had to be left behind during the battle at Tharsis Tholus, not to mention several dangerous encounters with the infamous Colonel Burns and his henchmen. I won't say too much, but Tyke learns some things he never suspected before and has to make some major choices about what to do with his life from here on out.

William Woodall
December 8, 2013

Discussion Questions

1. Tyke says that it's possible for a person's heart to die long before his mind or his body, and when that happens then he's no longer fully human anymore. What do you think he meant by this? Explain your thoughts.

2. Tycho says that evil people have the idea that life is cheap, and individuals don't matter, and that it's worth inflicting terrible harm in the name of some greater good. Do you agree with this definition of evil? Give examples of times when people have used these kinds of reasons to justify doing horrible things.

3. Philip says that love is easy, for those who do it. Explain what you think he meant by this and how you could apply this idea in your own life.

4. Tyke says that the world is full of more wonders than he ever dreamed of, back in the days when he thought he knew it all. In what ways do you think being a know-it-all might blind someone to the real world or keep them from understanding something? Give examples.

5. Tyke says that even the brave and the good don't always find a happy ending in life. Discuss this idea, especially as it relates to your life as a Christian. Why do you think God sometimes allows bad things to happen to people?

6. Tyke says that treachery stings, even when you know full well that you should have seen it coming ahead of time. Discuss a time when you were betrayed by someone you trusted, and the feelings you experienced because of that.

7. After his parents arrive, Tyke finds himself forced to readjust many ideas he's believed for a long time. Discuss a time when you suddenly discovered something which made you see the world or some particular person in a whole new way.

8. During this story, Tyke learns many things about his grandparents and other family members which he didn't know before. In what ways do you think your ancestors have affected the person you are today? Are there any traits they possessed which you can see in yourself?

9. At one point, Tyke says that the Defense Forces have always liked to believe they were champions of liberty, even when they were anything but. Discuss this idea. In what ways do you think the NADF might have sincerely believed they were doing good, in spite of their actions?

10. The "theme" of a story is the underlying message or messages about life the author is trying to convey. It is the lesson or moral of the

story, such as "Love conquers all". What do you think the theme of *Freedom* is? (There can be more than one.)

11. One of the first things Tyke notices about the settlers on Venus is that all of them are young and good-looking. Suppose you were asked to select people to form a colony on another planet. What traits would you look for, and why? What traits would you want to avoid? Give reasons for your choices.

12. At one point, Jesse is almost killed while trying to save Tyke, and left with permanent injuries. How would you have felt about this, if you were Tyke? How would you have felt if you were Philip or Joan, or perhaps Leah? Consider this event from several viewpoints.

13. Tyke says that the cost of courage can be high sometimes. Explain what you think he meant by this.

14. Other than Tyke, discuss your favorite character from *Freedom* and explain why it is that you like (or dislike) this person so much. Give examples of things he/she said or did which you especially enjoyed.

15. Tycho and the other characters make several mistakes during the story, and they aren't always wise. What are some of the mistakes you think they made, and what should they have done differently?

16. Suppose you were one of the settlers on Venus. Would you have wanted to join Captain Stone's rebel group, or would you have preferred to wait things out and see if they improved on their own? Give reasons for your choice.

17. What reasons do you think Olivia might have had for remaining so loyal to Colonel Bartow? Do you think there might have been anything Tyke or the others could have said or done to change her mind? Explain why or why not.

The Curse-Breaker Books
By William Woodall

Long ago, there was a Godly woman named Marybeth Trewick, who for various reasons found herself married to a rich but wicked man named Daniel who practiced all kinds of evil. She could only watch helplessly as her five sons grew up to become just as wicked as their father, and as her only daughter was forced to flee for her life lest she be killed.

But in the midst of her despair, God sent Marybeth a dream that after seven generations had passed, there would be five boys born to replace and redeem the ones that she had lost. These five would be breakers of curses and fighters against all things wicked and evil, and each of them would have the same vividly blue eyes, the same color as Marybeth's.

And even though the Curse-Breakers are each called to very different tasks in the world, the basic goal of fighting evil and loving God is always the same. These are their names and stories.

Brian Stone: The oldest curse-breaker, Brian's task is to save his brother's life and to remind men of Heaven by showing them the beauty of what could have been if the world had never fallen.

Cody McGrath: Two years younger than Brian, Cody is called to break the power of a dangerous sorceress. He's a dreamer of true dreams and a healer of the lost and broken-hearted.

Zachary Trewick: Four years younger than Cody, Zach is called to destroy one of the worst remaining aspects of his ancestor's wickedness; the werewolf curse which most of his family still embrace wholeheartedly.

Cameron Parker: Cameron and Zach are the same age, not to mention third cousins and best friends. Cameron has a big role to play in the struggle against the wolves, and later becomes the leader of all the survivors of Earth.

Brandon Stone: Brian's little brother, Brandon is three years younger than Cameron and Zach. He has a gift to know the meaning of dreams, and he is called to defend the weak and to uphold all that is righteous and true.

The Curse-Breaker Books form a collection of related stories about these five boys and sometimes their children. Each series tells the tale of a different Curse-Breaker (or sometimes more than one), but they also fit together in ways you wouldn't expect, in order to form a single unified storyline. It's helpful to read the books in order if possible, but it's not strictly necessary. You can read more about each series on the following pages.

The Stones of Song Series
By William Woodall

"There's a thing called magnanimity, or greatness of heart, and to me it's the most beautiful thing that ever there was. It means courage, but it's more than that. It means to cast aside all thought of yourself for the sake of another, like Moses in Gilead or the martyrs who died with a smile on their face. In its own small way it's a reflection of the Lord Jesus at Calvary, and therefore of God, the Light so beautiful that no one who sees it can ever turn away."

So says Cody McGrath, and in many ways that statement is the central theme of this series; the casting away of self for love of another, the scorning of selfishness in all its forms.

These are the stories of the Stone family: Brian, Jenny, Lisa, and Brandon, and some of the people they know and love, most notably Cody. All of them were called for great and glorious things, though sometimes only after great suffering and many mistakes.

Unclouded Day: Brian Stone's life isn't easy. Abandoned by his father, abused by his alcoholic mother, and mocked by his classmates, his only treasures are his beloved little brother and his old guitar. This is the tale of his journey to find the Fountain of Youth, and perhaps to save the world.

Many Waters: Lisa Stone is a small-town waitress with heavy burdens to bear. Cody is a young cowboy with big dreams and some very dangerous enemies. But when the two of them must face down an evil witch who tries to destroy their very lives, it seems that only a miracle can save them.

Bran the Blessed: Brandon Stone hasn't always made the right choices in life, but he's never found himself in quite such deep trouble as this. With a baby on the way and a life that seems wrecked forever, he soon finds that the world can be a cruel place for a Christian who stumbles. But Bran still has a high calling to answer. . . if he can find the courage.

* * * * * *

"I would absolutely, without reservation, encourage you to read this wonderful novel, even if you aren't the fantasy genre type. It was a blessing."
-Sue, *Reflections and Reviews*

"There are so many nuggets of truth in this book. It's about Heaven. It's about bad things happening for a reason. It's about deciding for yourself what truly matters most in life. It's a really good book!"
-Tattie, *Christian Fiction Ebooks*

The Last Werewolf Hunter Series
By *William Woodall*

Zach Trewick always thought he'd become a writer someday, or maybe play baseball for the Texas Rangers. What he never imagined in his craziest dreams was that he'd find himself dodging bullets and crashing cars off mountainsides, let alone that he'd ever be expected to break the ancient werewolf curse which hangs over his family.

But Zach is the last of the werewolf hunters, the long-foretold Curse-Breaker who can wipe out the wolves forever, and he's not the type to give up just because of a few minor setbacks. . .

Cry for the Moon: What would you do, if your family wanted you to become a monster? What if they wouldn't take no for an answer? When 12 year old Zach faces questions like these, he seems to have only one choice; *run*. Thus begins a long search for refuge, and perhaps redemption also.

Behind Blue Eyes: When a stranger kidnaps him from his own back yard, Zach soon finds that the past isn't quite as dead as he might wish. For the time has come at last for him to break the werewolf curse forever; and his family has no intention of letting that happen.

More Golden Than Day: When his girlfriend and then his cousin fall into the hands of the wolves, Zach has no choice but to take on his enemies for a second round. Only this time the stakes are horribly high, and if he fails he may end up losing everything he's ever loved.

Truesilver: When a family of wicked ex-wolves is accidentally awakened, Zach soon finds himself locked in a desperate fight for survival that he never anticipated. And even though he's sworn an oath to fight evil to the utmost of his power, there are times when courage is awfully hard to come by.

* * * * * * *

"If you are looking for a story about a boy who learns valuable lessons about family, love, friendship and God this is the book for you. I recommend this book to a pre-teen or adult. I truly enjoyed this book."
-Rae, *My Book Addiction Reviews*

"I found myself captivated with the story and could not stop reading until I reached the final page. Everything about this story is thought-provoking. Readers of all ages will appreciate this wonderfully told story,"
-Jancy, Kansas

The Tyke McGrath Series
By William Woodall

In the year 2154, the world has become a dangerous place. Extremist groups would like nothing better than to wipe out humanity completely, and even the people sworn to defend civilization against such threats have become deeply corrupt and untrustworthy.

When a virulent plague destroys all warm-blooded life on Earth, a small band of survivors clings to life on the partially-terraformed Moon. But fresh dangers lie in wait for the unwary; nor have they left behind all the wickedness in the hearts of men.

Nightfall: When Micah McGrath suddenly finds himself thrust into a dangerous and ugly future after a lab accident, his only choice is to make the best life for himself that he can. But when the secret police get wind of his research into time travel, he soon finds himself in deep trouble indeed.

Tycho: Tycho McGrath is a high school honor student in Florida when he discovers a terrifying secret: a man-made bacterium is about to wipe out all warm-blooded life on Earth within days. The only hope for survival is to flee at once, a plan which carries its own set of unexpected dangers.

Avenger: After spotting an SOS coming from the abandoned Moon, the survivors must organize a rescue mission. But the expedition quickly becomes far more complicated, leading them to the icy world of Titan in search of a holy mountain that no human eye has ever seen.

Freedom: When a cruel and power-hungry military commander on Venus decides to reconquer Earth, the only thing he needs is the formula for Tyke's Orion vaccine. The survivors soon find themselves locked into a bitter battle over the future of mankind, and who will inherit the Earth after all.

Elysium: What began as a simple mission to recover lost comrades in the Martian desert quickly turns deadly when Tyke and the others find *themselves* stranded on the Red Planet, with only the slimmest of chances to make it home again, or to fulfill the destiny which God has in store for them.

* * * * * * *

"Reminiscent of Freedom's Landing, by Anne McCaffrey, Tycho combines the best of traditional space-exploration sci-fi with modern apocalyptic fiction. For any fans of hard science fiction, it doesn't get much better than this." **- Liz, OH2 Reviews**

"This story was awesome! A must-read book if you like sci-fi." **-Scott, Georgia**

Trewick Family Tree

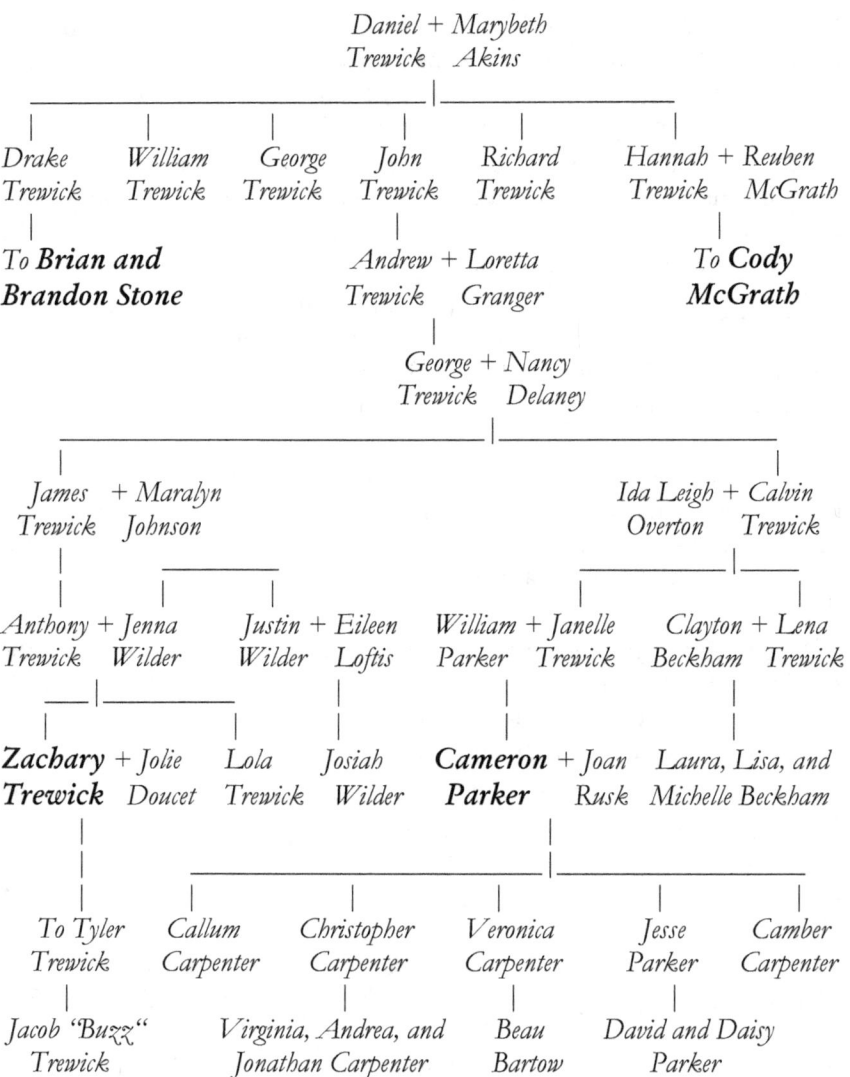

1. Curse-Breakers are in bold.
2. Cameron Parker later changed his name to Philip Carpenter.
3. Tyler Trewick is Zach's great-grandson.
4. Lisa Beckham's husband is Logan Tygart.
5. Laura Beckham's husband is Heath Coates, son of Albert Coates.

<u>Trewick Family Tree</u>

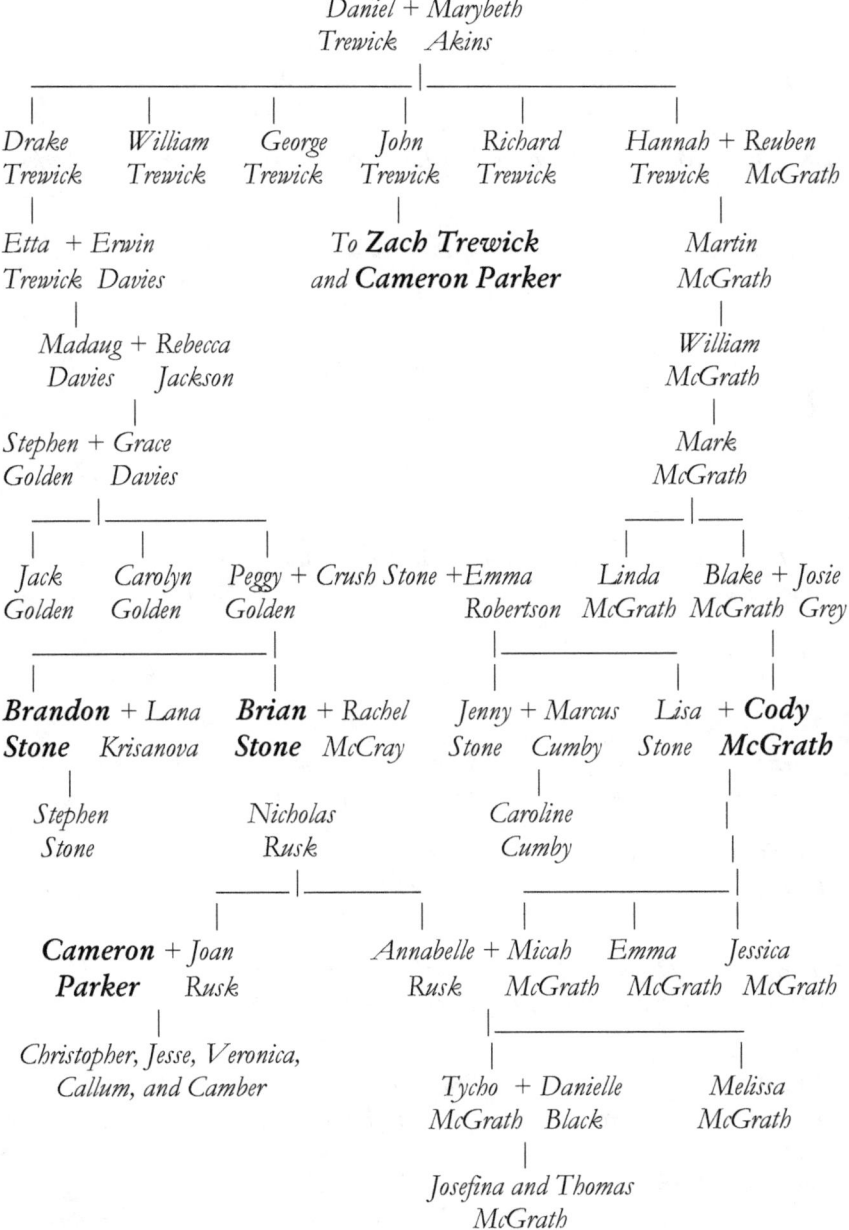

Daniel + Marybeth
Trewick   Akins

| Drake | William | George | John | Richard | Hannah + Reuben |
| Trewick | Trewick | Trewick | Trewick | Trewick | Trewick   McGrath |

Etta + Erwin
Trewick Davies

To **Zach Trewick**
and **Cameron Parker**

Martin
McGrath

Madaug + Rebecca
Davies   Jackson

William
McGrath

Stephen + Grace
Golden   Davies

Mark
McGrath

| Jack | Carolyn | Peggy + Crush Stone +Emma | | Linda | Blake + Josie |
| Golden | Golden | Golden | | Robertson | McGrath McGrath Grey |

Brandon + Lana   **Brian** + Rachel   Jenny + Marcus   Lisa + **Cody**
Stone Krisanova   **Stone** McCray   Stone   Cumby   Stone   **McGrath**

Stephen   Nicholas   Caroline
Stone   Rusk   Cumby

Cameron + Joan   Annabelle + Micah   Emma   Jessica
Parker   Rusk   Rusk   McGrath   McGrath   McGrath

Christopher, Jesse, Veronica,
Callum, and Camber

Tycho + Danielle   Melissa
McGrath Black   McGrath

Josefina and Thomas
McGrath

Doucet Family Tree

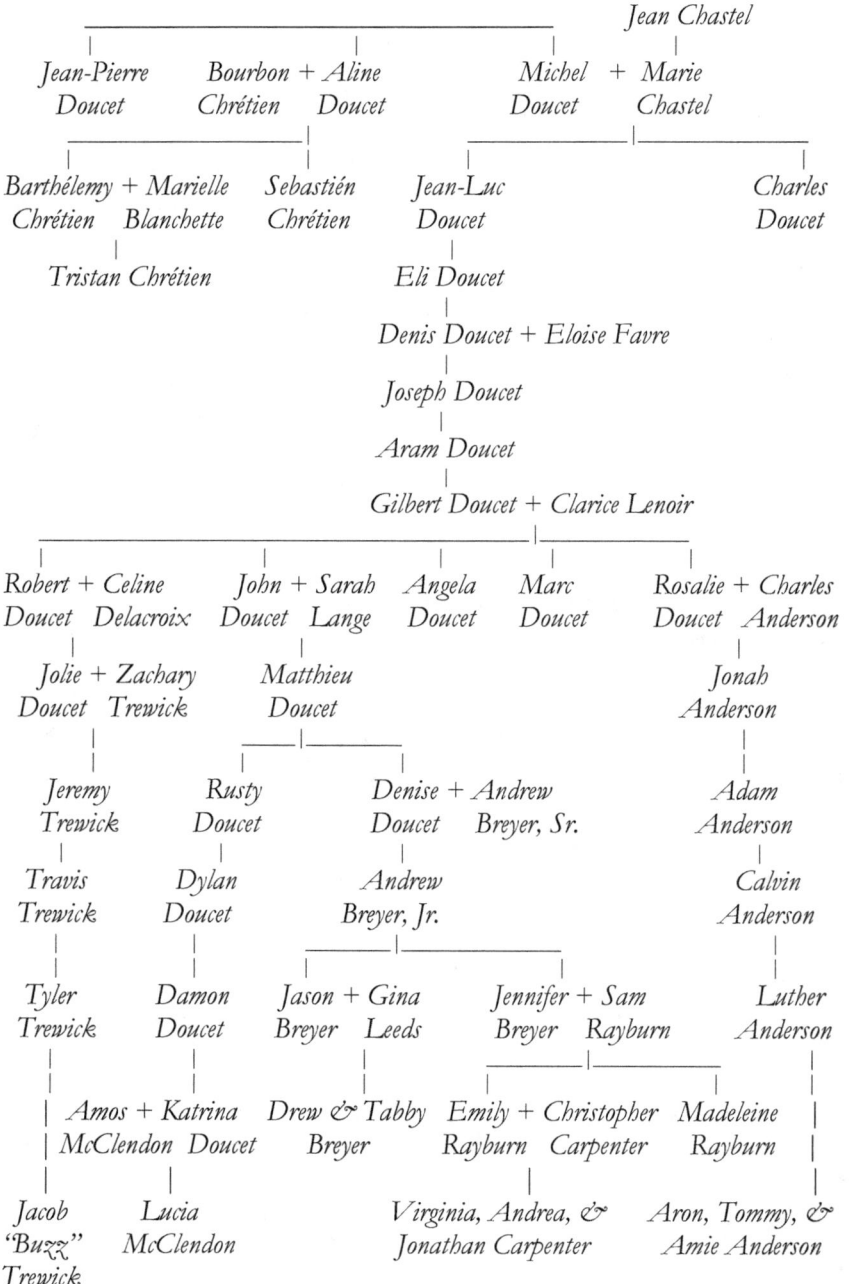

Bartow Family Tree

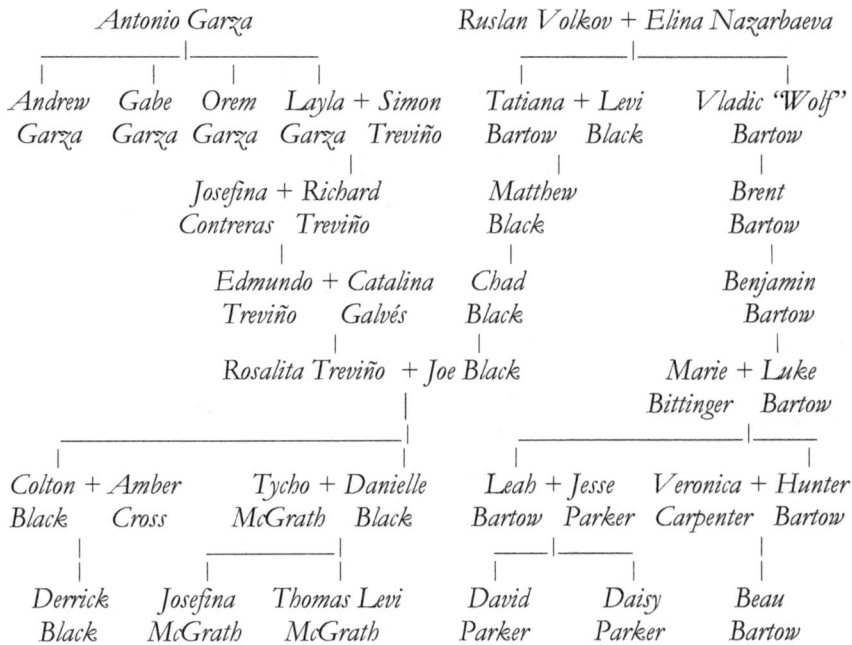

Jones and Golden Family Trees

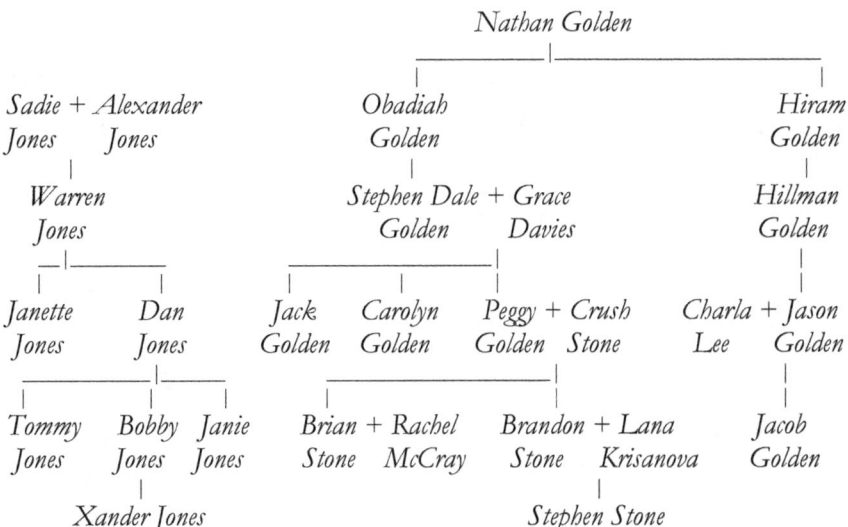

*If you'd like to find out more about
The Tyke McGrath Series and other books,
please visit:*

William Woodall's
Official Author Website

www.williamwoodall.org

Here you will find:

*Free short stories
Discussion questions for teachers and book clubs
Free sample chapters of all my books
Photos of characters and locations for each story
Articles
Interviews
Quotable Quotes
Contact Information
And much, much more!*

www.ingramcontent.com/pod-product-compliance
Lightning Source LLC
Chambersburg PA
CBHW050933120626
46552CB00001B/183